Rock Rebel

Rock Rebel

Nothing but Trouble
Book 3

TARA LEIGH

FOREVER
YOURS

New York   Boston

Copyright © 2018 by Tara Thompson
Excerpt from *Rock King* copyright © 2018 by Tara Thompson
Cover design by Brian Lemus. Cover images © Shutterstock. Cover copyright © 2018 by Hachette Book Group, Inc.

Forever Yours
Hachette Book Group
1290 Avenue of the Americas, New York, NY 10104
read-forever.com
twitter.com/readforeverpub

First published as an ebook and as a print on demand: December 2018

Forever Yours is an imprint of Grand Central Publishing. The Forever Yours name and logo are trademarks of Hachette Book Group, Inc.

The publisher is not responsible for websites (or their content) that are not owned by the publisher.

The Hachette Speakers Bureau provides a wide range of authors for speaking events. To find out more, go to www.hachettespeakersbureau.com or call (866) 376-6591.

ISBNs: 978-1-5387-1283-2 (ebook), 978-1-5387-1284-9 (print on demand)

#metoo
Enough said.

Acknowledgments

I always say that I'm going to write the acknowledgments as I'm writing the book. From plotting to drafting to first-round edits, second-round edits, then copyedits…the process is loooong. Spoiler alert: I never do. (Plus, by the time this book goes to print, there will be many more people I wish I could thank.) So, please forgive me if I miss anyone!!

A huge thank-you to my agent extraordinaire, Jessica Alvarez of BookEnds Literary Agency. Your critiques and career guidance are invaluable!

Lexi Smail—you have been an absolute dream to work with and have spoiled me for all future editors. Thank you for seeing the potential in this series and for inviting me to join the Forever family of authors. Many thanks also to the rest of the Forever team: the talented cover designers, the publicity team, Kallie Shimek, and everyone else who has played a role in bringing the Nothing but Trouble boys (and the women who love them) to life.

To my readers—you are EVERYTHING!!! I love reading your reviews and I value your honest feedback! And all those messages/posts/tweets/e-mails you send as you're reading—they make my day! **hugs** In so many cases you have become friends. Thank you for letting me into your lives!!

To all the amazing bloggers and author assistants who have championed this series—you are all rock stars! Melissa Teo (Booksmacked), I adore you for a million reasons. You are an incredible cheerleader for contemporary romance books and their authors—and the best ~~stalker~~ PA ever! Sarah (Musings of the Modern Belle), you are not just a belle; you are da bomb! Amy (Obsessive Book Whore), your enthusiasm is infectious, and your trailers are fabulous!! Maria (Steamy Reads), thank you for your encouragement and for coming up with a gorgeous Nothing but Trouble design for swag bags!! Tijuana (Book Twins), I love feeding your paperback addiction with my Nothing but Trouble boys…and I am (not-so-patiently) awaiting my nickname, lol! Candi Kane, you are an absolute powerhouse and beyond generous with your time and expertise. Serena McDonald, thank you for always having answers to my endless questions, for always pointing me in the right direction, and for your hilarious minions while reading! Sara Cunningham, thank you for pimping me all over! Sue Bee, from my very first book, you have been a valuable sounding board. Thank you for all of your advice and encouragement and especially for your unfiltered honesty. Tina, Karen, Sophie, Crystal, and Vicki (Bookalicious Babes Blog), you've created one of the most supportive places for newbie authors. Mary (*USA Today* HEA), your excerpts and features are my go-to source for finding new reads. My interview on your blog was definitely a career high—but meeting you in person was even better!

There are so many authors who have been beyond generous with their time and expertise—if I named them all, I might fill as many pages as this book! However, Alessandra Torre, your invaluable website www.alessandratorreink.com is a must for every new author, and you have built a virtual cheering section via Facebook. Al Jackson, thank you for setting the bar when it comes to rock-star romance. Sierra Simone, thank you for taking sexy to a whole other level. My In the Loop Group authors—love you ladies!

To RWA and everyone I've met through this incredible organization.

Shelly Bell, for loving Landon so much that you recommended him as your favorite "dirty talker"!

Lauren Layne and Anthony LeDonne of Last Word Designs, thank you for my gorgeous logo and website, www.taraleighbooks.com!

Jessica Estep of Inkslinger PR—you rock! Thank you for your insight and hard work.

Devyn Jenson, you know how to do *everything*!!!! I count my lucky stars for you!

Moments by Andrea, thank you for the fabulous head shot.

To my aunts Jill and Joan—I love seeing all your posts of support!!

I am lucky to have a great group of girlfriends surrounding me. You know who you are—and I'm sorry for ignoring your calls when I'm writing!

Nancy Valente, I cannot thank you enough for sharing your story about those hollow-stem wineglasses. They were the "awww" factor in Dax and Verity's romance!

My neighbor Cindy, you are a wonderful friend to me and an absolute blessing to my kids. Moving next door to you was one of the smartest decisions Stephen and I ever made! Thank you for being one of my first readers!!

Grandma, you left me nearly twenty years ago, and not a day goes by that I don't miss you. For any smokers reading this—put the cigarette down. Think of the people in your life who will one day watch you struggle to breathe and, when you lose that battle, will miss you desperately.

Thank you to my mom for never tearing all those "bodice rippers" out of my hands as a teen/tween and to my dad for showing me what it means to work hard. (Who needs weekends or vacations, anyway?)

Stephen, thank you for being a wonderful husband and for supporting my dreams. I love you. Logan, Chloe, and Pierce, thank you for being such great kids and genuinely considerate of my writing time. I am blessed to be your mother.

Our lives are enriched by our sweet rescue puppy, Pixie. The wonderful organization that brought Pixie into our lives is Goofy Foot Dog Rescue, and if you would like to welcome a dog into your family or donate to their organization, please visit their website: www.goofyfootrescue.org.

And if you would like to see more pictures of Pixie (and who wouldn't?), please sign up for my newsletter at www.taraleighbooks.com—she's my writing buddy!

Rock Rebel

Rock Rebel,

Prologue

Verity

Let's face it—in our lives, there are a lot of days that don't matter much. Days that go like this: wake up, eat some stuff, do some stuff, say some stuff, go back to bed. Lather, rinse, repeat. Years from now, will we remember any of it? Doubtful.

And then there are days—probably only a handful of them over an entire life—that we remember *everything*. What we ate, what we wore, what we said, what we did, who we were with. An entire day, down to the most minute detail.

Because those days are important. Because everything we do on those particular days matters. Because we know that every day to follow hinges on *that* day.

For me, *that* day was *today*.

I hardly slept, but I was up well before my alarm. I took my time with my hair and makeup, then dressed in the outfit

I'd painstakingly assembled last night—Versace blouse, Céline pants, Gucci belt, Jimmy Choo peep-toe heels.

No tight dress or towering heels or smudged mascara for me today. I wasn't going to a nightclub, standing among strangers with a cocktail in one hand and a cigarette in the other. The cigarette had only been a prop, of course. I knew better than to take chances with the only thing that couldn't be taken from me, signed over to someone else, or smothered into submission. My voice.

My voice was the reason Travis Taggert had agreed to see me. It sure as hell wasn't my reputation.

Shortly after returning to L.A., I'd sweet-talked my way into one of Travis Taggert's legendary parties and couldn't believe my luck when I saw the stage that had been set up in his Beverly Hills backyard. Seizing my chance, I'd grabbed the microphone in between acts and belted out an early Gwen Stefani hit, which had captured Travis's attention from the first note.

Had I sung one of my own, I might have been *boo*ed off the stage.

My name wasn't worth much in this town anymore.

Swallowing the bitterness gathering at the back of my throat, I turned a critical eye toward the mirror, studying the pull of designer fabrics across my body. Expensive armor made of silk and lace and leather.

A frown carved a shallow line across my forehead as I scrutinized every inch of my appearance. Was it obvious I was trying too hard—or was it just the look in my eyes that screamed of desperation? My nervous fingers fumbled with the slippery mother-of-pearl buttons. I shrugged out of the top, throwing my entire outfit across my bed.

And then I started over.

I had plenty of time—my meeting wasn't for several hours.

But after I finished trying on every item of clothing in the house, only to wind up in exactly the same outfit I'd started with, I saw that I'd used up nearly all of it. Thankfully Beverly Hills wasn't a big zip code, and I didn't live far from my future manager's office.

At least, I hoped Taggert would agree to take me on as a client.

I needed him.

If there was anyone who could restore my tarnished reputation and get my career back on track, it was Travis Taggert. Whether he could be convinced I was worth the effort...I wasn't so sure.

Sliding behind the wheel of my white Range Rover sport—not that it was in my name; nothing I'd ever earned was in my name—I checked my reflection one last time in the rearview mirror, smoothing down a few flyaways before shifting into gear. I wasn't sure what to do with my hair anymore. On *The Show*, I'd been contractually obligated to keep it long. And like the good girl I once was, I'd obeyed.

I wasn't such a good girl anymore.

I'd nearly hacked it all off at least a dozen times in the past month alone. I was so sick of being The Girl from *The Show*—a once-beloved child star my former fans now loved to hate. Or, if not hate, then at least dismiss as an overindulged, unremarkable Hollywood flame-out.

Could I really blame them?

My wake-up call had come last month. Even now, cocooned within a luxury SUV, thousands of miles away from the place where I'd finally hit rock bottom, my spine shuddered with revulsion.

Never again would I put myself in a position to be so vulnerable. It had been a hard lesson to learn, but I knew now that if I didn't clean up my act and take care of myself, no one else would bother.

Forcing a confidence I didn't feel, I parked the SUV and stepped into the agency's sumptuous office with my head held high and my shoulders back. Most talent managers lined their lobby with head shots of their clients. At Travis Taggert & Associates, they didn't have to. Taggert was the best in the industry, and everybody knew it. And I still had talent. I was sure of it.

A hunger that had nothing to do with not eating since yesterday churned in my belly. I wanted to be *someone* again.

Someone important.

Someone admired.

Someone safe.

I gave my name to the receptionist and took it as a good sign that she stood up from her desk and escorted me to Travis's office rather than have me cool my heels in the waiting room.

"Verity Moore." Travis's voice boomed as I was ushered into his personal sanctuary. Rather than the handshake I'd expected, he gripped me by my shoulders, kissing me on both cheeks before gesturing at the chairs facing his desk.

Sunlight poured in from the window at his back, making me squint uncomfortably as I adjusted to the glare. I'd sat across from desks like this often enough to know it was on purpose, a not-so-subtle show of power that would disappear only if I became his client.

"Thank you for agreeing to meet with me," I began, my tone steady, my smile bright. Betraying none of the nerves quivering beneath my skin.

"Of course, of course." Travis waved his hands expansively, as if he would take in anyone off the street. Hardly the case, and we both knew it. "So, you were previously managed by your mother, correct?"

He sighed at my nod, silently transmitting his disapproval. *Bad idea.*

So I've learned.

"I'll be honest, you've surprised me. And I'm not often surprised."

"Oh?" I braced myself for the worst. What did he know? What had he heard? What had he seen?

"It's been what—three years since *The Show* ended?"

"Two," I corrected.

"Same difference. I've seen your picture in plenty of magazines since then, and the paps still have a hard-on for you…but I haven't heard your name up for any shows. No pilots, no modeling contracts, no upcoming gigs. Why is that?"

I cleared my throat, relieved that the pictures he alluded to weren't the ones I'd been worried about. "I wanted to move away from TV to focus on my singing career. I took a bit of a break from the industry, but I'm ready to come back now. I really feel—"

"You're ready to come back?" Travis gave a throaty chuckle, his gold Rolex glinting as he rubbed the dome of his shaved head. "This business doesn't operate like that, and you know it. But"—Travis held my gaze, his dark eyes silently appraising my motives—"I can make it happen, if you're willing to put the work in."

"I am. More than willing, actually." My stomach gave a lurch at the words tripping from my mouth. Not *that* willing. There were things I wouldn't do for my career. *Not anymore.*

But Travis didn't leer at me from across his desk or give any indication that he expected me to crawl beneath it. Instead, he pointed a small remote at his window and lowered the shades to half-mast, then picked up a pen. "Okay, let's talk about what you want, and how we're going to get it."

I pressed my lips together, restraining my triumphant grin into a more professional Mona Lisa smile.

I was Travis Taggert's newest client.

Chapter One

Dax

Being back in New York City had me on edge.

These were my old stomping grounds. I'd been born and raised here, in the rarified air of the Upper East Side. I attended LaGuardia High School for the Performing Arts, then Juilliard.

I wasn't supposed to become a rock star.

Hell, until six years ago, I hadn't played anything but classical music.

Which was when wearing a suit became the exception rather than the norm.

Swearing at my reflection, I fumbled with the knot of my tie. I wasn't looking forward to the next few hours. Only within the snobby circles of classical musicians was a multi-platinum, Grammy Award–winning musician looked upon with disdain, as if playing sold-out arenas filled with thousands of adoring fans was some sort of rebellious phase.

With a last tug at my collar, I left my hotel room. As I headed down the hall, my phone buzzed in my hand.

> *Shane:* Dude, you're in NYC!
> *Me:* Yeah, just for a couple of days.
> *Shane:* You free tomorrow night?
> *Me:* Not sure yet.
> *Shane:* K. If you are, come over.
> *Me:* The new place, right?
> *Shane:* Yes. Bring whatever chick you're not telling me about.

I smirked. Now that Shane was head over fucking balls in love, he wanted everyone else to be, too.

Fat chance. I was definitely a lost cause.

> *Me:* I'll let you know.

The elevator doors slid open, and I darted aside just in time to avoid the kid who burst from the car and streaked down the hall, someone I assumed to be his harried nanny chasing him. With a sigh, I shoved my phone in my pocket and jabbed the button for the lobby. It didn't change color. I pushed it again. Nope, still bright yellow. Realizing that every button was lit up, I cursed again. No wonder the kid had run. He must have pushed every damn button before he took off.

"Hold the elevator!"

My arm shot out instinctively, my years in Manhattan training me to hold the elevator for any and all who asked, because you never knew when you would need the favor returned. Karma was a bitch best left unprovoked.

Something that kid had yet to learn.

"Thanks." At first glance the girl who burst breathlessly into the elevator car could have been anywhere from seventeen to twenty-seven. Her hair was piled into a messy bun on top of her head, her bright green gaze clear-eyed and direct, and she was wearing running sneakers and a thick sweatshirt that would have been too big on me. It was also unzipped, revealing a tight tank top and tiny bike shorts.

Goddamn. Just looking at her had my pulse stuttering for a few beats, then taking off at a gallop.

Her body didn't belong to a teenager, that was for sure.

She pulled one of her earbuds out, wisps of red hair framing a heart-shaped face. Haphazard and disheveled. "Can you press the one for the gym?"

Sexy as fuck.

I jerked my chin at the lit-up display on my side of the elevator. "Apparently we're on a local tonight."

Her full lips, a berry-pink shade that hadn't been painted on, twitched up at one corner, revealing a dimple etched into her left cheek. I felt a tug of desire deep in my stomach, and a ridiculous curiosity to know if it was part of a matched set. "Courtesy of the little boy who ran out of here like he'd just shotgunned a can of Coke?"

"That'd be my guess."

She broke into a full-fledged grin. I stared back, feeling like I'd won the lottery. Dimples, plural.

"Knew it," she said as the doors closed and the elevator trundled down a flight.

I should have kept my mouth closed when she looked back down at her phone, but I wanted to feel her eyes on me again. "Don't get too cocky. That was an easy guess."

She raised her head, a look of surprise on her face. Her *familiar* face.

Did I know this girl?

The elevator doors opened and closed. Again. And again. And again. With each floor, the energy in the confined space expanded, charged by something I didn't quite understand. The smile that had played on her lips disappeared, the bow of her mouth drawing tight. She crossed her arms, clearly piqued. "So any girl that dares to voice a correct assumption is cocky?"

The redhead was more spitfire than leprechaun.

A bolt of lust charged down my spine. "Only when it's too easy."

"Easy, huh? How about you give me a hard one, then?"

Jesus. Talk about a loaded question.

She arched a brow that was the same red as the hair on her head, which sent my mind down another direction.

A direction that was apparently all too obvious. "Whenever you get your mind out of my pants, of course."

I forced a gruff chuckle. What the fuck was wrong with me? Two hours in this city and I'd transformed into the horny kid I'd been when I left six years ago.

But before I could come up with a *hard* question, she changed the subject. "I'll bet I can guess your sign."

"My what?"

"Your zodiac sign." I must have still looked confused, because some of her irritation smoothed away as she leaned against the dark mirrored glass at her back. "You don't read your horoscope?"

"Ah, no."

"You're not exactly making this a challenge." There was something tenacious about her stance, the sharp set of her jaw. Like she had something to prove to me.

Or maybe just to herself.

"That what you're into?"

She stared at me with one finger pressed against her lips, those emerald eyes of hers narrowed at the corners. I ground my teeth, trying to tamp down the want flooding my veins with heat. Unsuccessfully.

"I was torn between Aries and Taurus, but you settled it for me. Aries, definitely." Holding her phone with both hands, she attacked it with her thumbs. "Born between March twenty-first and April nineteenth, no?"

I frowned. "How—"

"Oh please, you're a ram through and through." She flashed her screen at me. "Want to know your horoscope?"

"Not re—"

"Your love of the chase is your greatest weakness, but what you seek is already inside yourself. Today is a day to appreciate the road taken and go where your heart leads you."

I snorted, jabbing at the DOOR CLOSE button. "And that's supposed to mean something to me?"

She shrugged. "I don't know. Does it?"

I was silent for a minute, watching our descent on the screen above the doors. The redhead stepped forward as they opened on the third floor, the scent of vanilla and cloves rising off her fair skin. My mouth watered.

She was close enough to touch, and my fingers throbbed with the temptation of freeing her hair from the band holding it captive. She glanced up, meeting my eyes. "This is me." Her voice was soft, almost breathless, even though she'd long since recovered from her sprint down the hall.

The doors opened. "So, if I'm a ram, what are you?"

She crossed the elevator's threshold and turned back to face me, her elegantly sculpted features embellished by a mischievous half smile. "Wouldn't you like to know."

The elevator doors had closed before I could open my mouth and say anything else.

She was right though. I *would* like to know.

Verity

What's gotten into me?

Since when did I flirt? And with Dax Hughes…really? I'd seen him before, of course. A few times in person, hundreds more within the glossy pages of celebrity magazines. Flaunting bedroom eyes, shredded jeans, and an aloof expression, Hughes was every inch the cocky celebrity I made every effort to avoid.

Granted, in a dark suit, tugging at his collar, pulling at his sleeves, his normally tousled hair slicked back, Hughes had been more approachable than the rocker I'd seen before. More than approachable. Appealing.

With each one of Dax's heated glances, I'd felt the unwanted prick of desire sting my skin, as sharp and distinct as the snap of a rubber band. The damn man had made my head spin and my knees weak. My fingers twitching with the urge to tear off his tie, unbutton his shirt, and lay claim to everything beneath.

I had no idea if the feeling was mutual, and frankly, I didn't want to know.

I was taking a hiatus from men, from dating, from serving as a prop for someone else's overinflated ego. I was finally taking control of my life, my career. Putting myself first.

Thankfully, Hughes hadn't seemed to recognize me. Not that I should've expected him to. I mean, he didn't exactly fall within the targeted audience of *The Show*. And without so much as a swipe of lip gloss and dressed in workout gear, I wasn't exactly looking like the scandal-plagued party girl that was a favorite of all the gossip magazines.

Replaying the exchange my head, I groaned. *Wouldn't you like to know?*

So embarrassing. The man was Dax Hughes, for Christ's sake. The guitarist for Nothing but Trouble was exactly the kind of trouble I didn't need. And besides, he could have any girl he wanted—what would he want with me?

Verity Moore, disgraced pop princess.

The description followed my name so often, if I died tomorrow it would probably be carved into my headstone.

Why not? It was true enough.

Not for long, I reminded myself as I scanned my key card at the door. Travis never would have signed me if he didn't believe that I could overcome my bad reputation.

Meanwhile, at least the gym was empty and I could wallow in my mortification alone.

I pumped up the incline on the treadmill, setting the speed faster than I normally ran. I welcomed the sweat breaking out on my forehead, the shortness of my breaths, the strain in my muscles. Chasing an emptiness I craved, a zone where my body detached from my mind.

It took a couple of miles to get there, but when I did, I felt invincible, unstoppable. My self-defeating thoughts smothered, at least temporarily. Exactly the headspace I needed to be in to win over the cynical industry execs tomorrow.

Spending our entire meeting worrying about what they'd heard—or worse, what they'd seen—would hardly leave a favorable impression.

I ran and ran and ran.

And when finally the burn in my legs and my chest were too painful to ignore, I pumped up the speed and ran another mile.

Almost. MOM suddenly appeared on my phone, cutting off the music pulsing through my earbuds. "Damn it."

I slammed the emergency stop button and accepted her Face-Time call, wiping my sweaty skin with a towel. "Hi—"

"Where are you?"

"I'm working out. What's up?" I would have preferred to ignore her, but I'd learned that the only way to keep physical distance between us was to be reachable by phone.

"I can see that, but I asked where you were."

"I'm in New York."

The image wobbled, as if she'd grabbed her device, and then my screen was filled with a close-up of my mother's face, an age-progressed replica of my own. "What are you doing in New York?"

"Just a few meetings to see what's out here right now. I mentioned it last week." I hadn't, but I uncapped my Swell bottle and took a long drink, knowing she wouldn't bother arguing the point.

"You're going to see Jack, I hope."

Jack Lester. I nearly spit out my water. "No, I'm not."

"Well, I don't understand why you wouldn't. Millie called me the other day, and—"

"Millie called you?" I clutched my stomach, the water I'd barely managed to swallow transforming into curdled milk.

"Yes. Such a sweet girl. She said Jack is developing another show. I'll bet he'd put you in it if you—"

I wasn't doing *anything* with that man ever again. "Absolutely not."

Her features hardened. "Verity, I have been more than patient with you, but I am not only your mother. I am your manager. It's time for you to get back to work."

"That's exactly what I'm doing," I interjected, then immediately regretted it. I hadn't told my momager that I signed with Travis Taggert. And I wasn't going to—until I had a contract in my hands and money in a bank account without her name on it. My mother couldn't know that I was taking control of my own career, of my own life. Yet.

I had planned my escape as meticulously as a wife fleeing her abusive husband.

"That's it. I'm getting on the next plane. You can't make important decisions without me."

I already have. "I'm not making decisions. I just want to show my face around, let people know I'm ready to get back to work. I'll tell you how it goes, and we can strategize next steps." I'd already warned Travis that those next steps might involve sending my mother a cease-and-desist letter after she was fired.

She squinted at me. "Well, if you run into Jack and Millie, be nice. They've been so good to you, and I think Millie feels like you've taken them for granted."

"One day I'll be sure to let them know just how grateful I am. Don't worry." I nearly gagged on the words. "But I don't think I'll run into them here."

"Why not? They're in New York right now, too."

Blood rushed to my head, and I flung out a hand to grip the treadmill's sidebar. "What?"

"They're showing a new script to the networks, I think. Or maybe they're trying to lock down a record label first." My mother shook her head and sighed. "One or the other, I can't remember which."

The urge to reach through my phone and choke her neck was almost overwhelming. "I—I really have to take a shower now. I'll let you know how things go."

"You do that," she said.

Anxiety spiraled through my nerves as I sat down on the floor and leaned against the side of the treadmill. I launched the Internet browser, my trembling fingers managing to get Jack's name right after several tries. On the second page of my Google search, I found what I was looking for. An article about his new project—another music-driven, show-within-a-show concept. Just like his last—the one I'd starred in.

I would move into a homeless shelter before accepting a role in one of Jack's productions ever again.

Once I caught my breath, I hauled myself to my feet and left the gym, bypassing the elevators in favor of the stairs. My sneakers felt like they'd been made of lead and I was a sweaty mess, but the thought of a stranger's eyes scraping my skin was painful.

My mind was untethered, bouncing from Dax Hughes to Jack Lester to the ghosts of boyfriends past that still called Manhattan home, painful memories twisting my stomach into knots. With each step, I was pulled backward through time, felt the touch and press of unwanted hands, the harsh male cackle of intimidation assaulting my ears. My lungs tightened, each short, shallow breath echoing against the cement.

Needing a distraction, I pulled my phone back out of my pocket and opened the horoscope app I had used with Dax. I might as well admit that I hadn't actually guessed his sign. Honestly, I was a Nothing but Trouble fan. Who wasn't? A while back, they were on a late-night talk show, and I remember the host wheeling out an enormous cake for Dax's birthday. But instead of a beautiful woman, a man dressed in a bikini had popped out of it. Dax had been a good sport, joking that that's what he got for being born on April Fool's Day.

Of course, the man I just met was no fool, even if he didn't know anything about the zodiac.

You have a lot on your mind and the secrets you keep are preventing you from thinking clearly. To move forward, you must learn to let go of the past.

I read my own horoscope three times before shoving my phone back in my pocket. Maybe it really was nothing but a crock. True, I had a lot on my mind and plenty of secrets to keep, but I was definitely moving forward.

Because there was no way in hell I was going back.

Chapter Two

Dax

Shifting uncomfortably from foot to foot, I was thankful my suit jacket hid the raging hard-on trying to bust through my zipper. What the hell was wrong with me? Falling for some chick in an elevator. A redhead with the face of an angel, the eyes of a leprechaun, and a laugh that sounded like wind chimes.

For interminable seconds I remained trapped inside the five-by-five box, her scent all around me. Vanilla and cloves. My stomach grumbled, but it wasn't food I hungered for.

When the doors opened, I practically bolted through them, the people in the lobby scattering like pigeons. But this was New York—jumping aside for an asshole in a suit wasn't anything new.

A car was waiting for me outside. Although I generally preferred to walk or hail a cab when I needed to go farther than a mile or two in Manhattan, I wasn't in the mood to deal with crowded sidewalks or chatty cabdrivers today.

The thirty minutes I'd allotted to get from SoHo to the Upper West Side left plenty of time to dwell on the chance meeting that had me more keyed up than I'd been in my room—something I wouldn't have thought possible.

I'd probably never see that girl again.

Never hear the voice that had wrapped around me like spun sugar.

Discipline wasn't something I normally lacked, but I just couldn't get my mind off her.

And why had those few minutes felt like the beginning of a roller-coaster ride? That slow climb up to the first peak where you knew the ride had begun and there was no going back. Exhilaration laced with *this-is-a-bad-idea*.

The blocks slipped by, a few at a time between red lights. My trips back to New York were always filled with uncomfortable memories. This one hadn't been any different…until a few minutes ago. Until I shared an elevator ride with…Goddamn it—who was she?

When the car finally pulled to the curb, I shook my head, feeling disoriented. As my vision cleared, I realized we'd arrived. Lincoln Fucking Center. I used to know this place like the back of my hand.

The driver opened my door. "Should I wait for you?" he asked.

I stepped into the crisp air, breathing a deep lungful of New York's finest. Exhaust fumes and doughy street pretzels. "No. I'll find my way back myself."

Tonight, for the first time in years, I was doubting the path I'd taken.

Retrieving the ticket my parents had left for me at the box office, I made my way to my seat. I could well afford my own, but my parents insisted. Probably so that they'd know where to look to be sure I was in my seat when the curtain went up.

No one in my family had ever attended a Nothing but Trouble concert.

The lights dimmed, and I watched my thirteen-year-old brothers take to the stage, followed by my sister, who was four years older than the twins, and finally my parents.

Aria and I were eleven years apart, and there should have been another Hughes daughter between us. One day my parents had left me with a neighbor, saying they would be back soon with my new baby sister. But when they returned, their hands were empty, their faces filled with grief. I'd felt her absence, this sister I'd never met, all my life.

Long before Nothing but Trouble was even a glimmer on the *Billboard* charts, I'd been a member of Classic Hughes. An ensemble consisting of my parents, me, Aria, and our twin brothers. And Amelia. The neglected daughter of a neighbor who seemed to fill the dark void within our family.

I loved her like a sister.

Until I just *loved* her.

But now even her name twisted my stomach.

There was a moment of suspended silence, and then the haunting melodies my family was known for filled the air.

Six years and a lifetime ago I would have been up there with them.

My parents had instilled a love of music in all of us early on, and it was clear that our innate aptitude had been passed through their DNA. I was playing instruments before I could talk. Wood, string, percussion. Didn't matter, really. Music was a language I intrinsically understood. Still do.

At one time I thought Amelia was as much a part of me, a part of my family, as music.

Apparently that feeling wasn't mutual.

It didn't stop me from following her all the way to Los Angeles. Same country, same language, but the city itself felt foreign. Nothing made sense to me. Not my past, or my future. Everything was noise.

A sign promising live music had drawn me into a dark, gritty bar one night. Nursing a single beer as a rotating cast of mediocre bands took the stage, I'd been trying to decide how much longer I could bear to stay in L.A. How much longer until I'd be expelled from Juilliard. How much longer I wanted to spend looking for Amelia when it was clear she didn't want to be found. Not by me, anyway.

I'd just decided to call it quits for the night so I could get an early jump on my Amelia-hunting the following morning when the place went silent. I was used to silence at venues—classical-music audiences know how to keep their mouths shut and their phones muted. But this crowd…not the silent type.

Every eye in the place was trained on the guys that had taken to the stage, and an unmistakable thrill of anticipation shuddered in the air. I put my empty glass on the bar and gave them my full attention. It wasn't the lead singer's voice that drew me in—though it was a throaty growl like nothing I'd ever heard before—it was the musicians behind him that fascinated me. The drummer and bassist were in perfect sync, and though loud, their music could never be classified as noise. The guitarist was a different story though. I didn't know the song, but I could tell that he was three notes behind. Judging by the looks he was getting from his bandmates, they knew, too.

About halfway through their set, the front man stopped the show. "Tryin' something new tonight. T.J. here is gonna get off this stage before he falls off." He grabbed the guitar and half shoved the guy down the stairs. "Anyone here know their way around this thing and wanna join us?"

Music.

An instrument I'd never touched before.

An audience.

Fuck if I could resist the invitation.

Two hours later I was closing out the bar with three guys who already felt like family.

Meanwhile, my own family didn't seem all that disappointed that I never returned to New York, or to Classic Hughes. Without Amelia and me, they became the Hughes Quintet, traveling all over the world to perform in prestigious opera houses and musical halls.

And Nothing but Trouble was born.

Verity

The lights in the studio were dim. If I closed my eyes I could pretend I was alone in the room, that there was no one beyond the glass window lining the wall in front of me. That I wasn't being watched. Studied. Scrutinized.

I should be used to it by now. And I was. But there was always a part of me that felt worn down by the stares of strangers. Like beach glass abraded into insignificance by the bite of the ocean's spray, the scrape of sand.

I gripped the microphone in front of me like a lifeline. And in many ways, it was. It was going to give me my life back.

Correction—it was as going to give me a life. Period.

A life of my own. One where I didn't owe anyone anything.

Not a damn thing.

For an inanimate object made of aluminum and mesh, the mic pulsed comfortingly in my hands. But once the first strains of music came through my headphones, I let it go…and *I* let go.

My hair caressed my shoulder blades as I arched my neck and opened my mouth, my voice a balm that soothed the bitterness coating my tongue. With each word and lyric that escaped, I felt lighter. Like I could flap my arms and fly away at any minute. Free.

I was a singer. It was what I did, what I loved. How had I become an actress? A shell of a person playing a role. Mouthing words someone else wrote, pretending to be someone I wasn't.

The process had been gradual, I guessed. Especially since the role I played was a pop-star-in-the-making, singing saccharine-sweet songs every other episode.

I'd barely even noticed the bars going up around me until I was locked inside a cage. But here, now, in this small recording studio, alone and yet watched, singing a song *I* had chosen, it felt as if I'd finally come home. I felt heard.

For so long, my voice had been silenced.

But it had never disappeared.

It had been inside me, quietly biding its time. Well, that time was now. I was done waiting. Done letting anyone or anything, including my own fears and insecurities, silence me.

Too soon, with the last note still vibrating on my tongue, the music in my ears was cut off. I opened my eyes, and the world rushed back at me—a sea of faces turned my way. But rather than feel like a monkey in someone else's cage, I focused on Piper's huge grin, and the unobtrusive thumbs-up she gave me. Taking a deep breath, I gave a little curtsy, using the brief moment my head was turned to the ground to get my game face back on.

This time Verity Moore would not be played.

Two more auditions followed, and we were just leaving the last Sixth Avenue skyscraper when Travis pushed back his sleeve to squint at his watch. "I'm going to check in with Dax, and then I have a dinner tonight."

My nerves had quieted over the course of the afternoon, but at the mention of *his* name, they returned to high alert.

"Oh." Piper's face registered surprise as we stood on the sidewalk, a car idling at the curb. "I didn't realize Dax was in town, too."

Already scrolling through his phone, Travis responded without looking up. "Yeah, he got here before we did. Some family thing."

"So, I'll head back to the hotel with Verity for now and meet you—"

"No." Travis gestured to the car. "I want you to take Verity out for dinner, show her a nice night."

My cheeks flushed red. I didn't need a babysitter, and I didn't want Piper feeling obligated to entertain me. We'd spent a lot of time together over the past month or so, and not only did I respect her, but I liked her, too. But I wasn't sure whether she felt the same, and my track record with female friendships was horrible. "Travis, I'm perfectly capable of making my own arrangements. Piper doesn't need to—"

Piper put a hand on my shoulder. "Don't be silly. If you haven't already made plans, I'd love to spend tonight celebrating your success."

"Let's not go that far quite yet—bad luck to count chickens and all that."

Travis grunted as he looked at his phone. "Go ahead. Look like one of them has already hatched." He slipped it back in his pocket. "We'll see where we are after our meetings tomorrow. But in the meantime—keep it low-key. No nightclubs, no celebrity hot spots. The paparazzi don't know you're here, and I'd like to keep it that way."

Chapter Three

Dax

"Is this a setup?"

Shane hid his mouth with the neck of his beer, but I could still see the twist of his lips behind it. "Setup—what are you talking about?"

"I'm talking about you saying you were having a few friends over." I lifted a brow. "Your guest list is me and three chicks."

After meeting with Travis earlier, I'd been looking forward to kicking back with Shane for a bit before returning to the hotel, getting a few hours of sleep, and flying home tomorrow. This trip had kicked my ass, and I couldn't wait for it to be over.

I'd come to celebrate the twins' birthday a couple of days ago, and my parents had guilted me into staying for the Lincoln Center show last night. I would have already been on a plane, but then my sister had asked me to come to her in-school recital today.

Saying no to my only sister wasn't a skill I'd ever mastered.

I was hardly in the mood to play rock-star Romeo to someone I'd hopefully never see again.

"One is Piper and one is Travis's newest client, so according to you, they don't count. It's the other one I want you to meet. Dude, you should be thanking me. You're the one who refuses to date anyone in the music industry. Or, as you say, anyone who wants to fuck a musician for the sake of fucking a musician." He scoffed. "That's basically every woman we know. You're really culling the herd a little too thin, don't you think?"

I took a swig from my own bottle. "I do just fine, Shane. Don't need you playing pussy broker."

Shane shook his head. "From what I can see, you're not *doing* anyone."

I must have given Shane a blank stare, because he started going off about how much better life was with a girlfriend. And I was happy for him. I was. He'd really met his match in Delaney.

But I'd already met my match.

It hadn't ended well.

And I wasn't interested in a lecture either, although I didn't bother stopping him. I'd long ago mastered the art of looking straight at someone and not paying any attention to what was coming out of their mouth.

Unlike the majority of the past thirty-six hours, I was finally thinking about someone other than the redhead from the elevator. My sister.

Earlier today, Aria had shocked me by announcing that she wanted to leave the Hughes Quintet and move to L.A. There were a lot of things wrong with that scenario, not least of which that my lifestyle wasn't conducive to babysitting my seventeen-year-old sister. Of course, when I said as much to her, Aria had practically jumped down my throat, saying that if I didn't help her, she'd find someone who would.

What the fuck?

My sister was as sheltered as they came. Who could she "find" to help her leave her parents and move to Los Angeles? And what would they want in return?

I'd tried to get an answer out of her, asking those same questions a dozen different ways. Aria might be naïve, but she was no dummy. I got no information except that she wanted to leave the Hughes Quintet, move to L.A., get a job in Hollywood—as a musician or an actress—and become a famous celebrity.

What teenager didn't?

And if she'd been just another teenager, I wouldn't have worried so much. But Aria was beautiful and smart and insanely talented. Realistically, my sister had a damn good shot.

If her career was managed by someone who wouldn't take advantage of a vulnerable girl with stars in her eyes.

Which was why I'd met with Travis an hour ago. To ask if he would consider managing Aria—when she turned eighteen. He'd agreed. Now I just had to convince Aria not to rock the boat until she was of age.

Saying no outright might not be my strong suit. But stalling...

I was good at that.

Verity

Two hours later, after a pit stop at the hotel for a few minutes of downtime and a change of clothes, we pulled into the gated underground entrance of a Tribeca apartment building. I glanced at Piper in surprise once we were both out of the car. "Wow."

My nerves at meeting Shane Hawthorne, who had one of the most soulful voices I'd ever heard, and his gorgeous girlfriend were momentarily quieted as I gawked at the elaborate brick-work and thick marble columns surrounding us.

"I know," Piper murmured as we followed a uniformed atten-dant into the elevator. "This place is amazing. Shane bought it when Delaney decided to finish her degree at NYU."

"If the parking garage looks like some kind of ballroom, I can only imagine what their apartment looks like."

"Tell me about it. I stopped by last night and I kept expecting someone from *MTV Cribs* to appear around a corner, but I doubt they'd get in. The security measures in this building are over-the-top, which is exactly why Shane and Delaney picked it. The paparazzi have calmed down a bit, but things were pretty crazy for a while."

While I was on *The Show*, I'd felt the glare pretty hard, too. I'd expected it to fade once filming wrapped, but almost three years had passed and the spotlight had barely dimmed. "What about the band? Doesn't Shane have to be in California?"

"Sometimes. They bounce back and forth between here and Malibu, depending on her school schedule and his touring and recording schedule." She sighed. "If they didn't deserve their happily-ever-after more than any other couple I knew, I'd hate them both."

My lips twitched as I agreed. Everyone knew about the bumps that had littered the path of their relationship, and even I, a complete cynic when it came to love—especially celebrity couples—wanted to believe Shane and Delaney were as adorable as they appeared. "Are you sure they don't mind me tagging along?" I whispered, following Piper's long-legged stride down the hall.

"Of course not. Delaney and I had some girl time yesterday. As far as I know, tonight's just a low-key dinner. Us and a couple of others. Delaney said something about wanting to set up one of her friends from school with—"

The rest of Piper's sentence was cut off by a petite woman sporting dark, glossy hair and a huge smile bouncing into the hall. "I thought you guys would never get here."

She gave Piper a hug, pulling back to look closely at her face. "You okay?"

I couldn't see Piper's expression, but the concern on Delaney's face had me wondering if something was wrong. If there was, Piper hadn't so much as hinted at it. But her voice was strong when she answered with a brusque "Of course."

A momentary frown betrayed Delaney's skepticism, but it was gone by the time she turned to me. "Verity, so nice to meet you." I felt the genuine warmth in her gaze. "How are you enjoying being the latest project of Piper the drill sergeant?" There was an easy confidence to her and no hesitation when she reached out to hug me, too.

It felt nice. Really nice. And also foreign. When was the last time I'd been hugged without the weight of someone else's expectations pressing on me? Men with roving hands who wanted more than just a quick embrace. Fans who squealed in my ear as they held me tight, yanking at my waist while taking a selfie.

But tonight there was no apprehensive prickle at the back of my neck when Delaney touched me. No sense that there was any ulterior motive at play.

"Believe me, I've worked with worse." I squeezed a laugh through the tightness in my throat as I followed her inside the apartment.

She raised a sleek sable brow. "Sounds like you have a few stories behind that deflection."

"None worth telling, believe me," I said, ignoring the tremor that vibrated though my spine.

Delaney didn't push, instead leading us toward a kitchen on one side of the enormous open room. "Shane had drinks set up out on the terrace, but I nabbed a bottle of champagne so you can keep me company while I finish cooking. One of my friends from school was supposed to join us, too, but she had an incident with a bike messenger."

Piper and I looked at each other, then back at Delaney. "An incident?"

"Mmmm. I offered to sit with her at the hospital while they put her arm in a cast, but apparently the resident is a dead ringer for McDreamy and she's only too happy to play the damsel in distress." She opened a drawer and pulled out an enormous spoon. "They're going on a date next week."

"I love a good silver lining," I added.

Delaney grinned in acknowledgment, then turned away to stir something in the pot on the stove. "Piper, the champagne is in the fridge. Would you mind opening it?"

"Sure, but I'm not—"

"There's Vitamin Water in there, too."

I'd almost forgotten that Piper had been tasked to watch over me. "Piper, please. You don't have to pass up a glass on my account."

"It's not you. I promise." She looked uncomfortable for a moment. "I—I'm on a cleanse. No alcohol, gluten, that kind of thing."

Something about her answer was off, starting with the fact that I'd seen her eating crackers on the plane yesterday, but who was I to judge?

Piper uncorked the champagne and poured two glasses. By the time she'd filled hers with lemon Vitamin Water, Delaney and I were holding ours up. "What should we cheers to?"

"To Verity's career comeback," Piper proposed.

I cocked my head to the side. "You're off the clock, remember? And not everything has to revolve around me. I'd prefer it didn't, actually."

Delaney burst out laughing. "I like her," she said, talking to Piper as if I weren't there. "Okay, how about we cheers to fun nights with new friends and old?"

We clinked rims, and I felt my guard dropping a bit further. Celebrity had a way of insulating you from all but the most shallow relationships. Possibly because there were so few people in Hollywood whose depth went beyond their layers of makeup.

Piper and Delaney appeared to be an exception to the rule, in more ways than one.

My thoughts returned to Dax Hughes, and not merely because I was in his bandmate's apartment. I'd barely been able to take my mind off him since the elevator doors closed. The man was occupying space in my mind I didn't want to share. *What kind of man is he?* Yesterday, there had been a playful undertone to Dax's aloofness, almost an uncertainty. As if flirting wasn't something he did often.

This trip to New York was important to me, a stepping-stone vital to achieving my dreams. But I'd been dreading it. The last time I'd been here was a nightmare. The kind you awake screaming from, gulping breaths and soothing yourself that it wasn't real. That it was just your mind playing a horrible trick.

Well, the trick had been on me.

Which was why I was surprised that I'd been able to remain in the elevator with Dax, a man who could pin me to the wall without breaking a sweat. His eyes had made a leisurely, appraising sweep over my body, but there was no leer inside his smile, no malicious intent in his gaze.

Oddly, what had made me feel comfortable in that small box was that Dax looked so uncomfortable—and it wasn't just his pulling at the collar of his starched shirt, his fingers twisting at the knot of his tie. Beneath his gorgeous olive skin was a hesitant wariness, a man who wore his suspicion like a shield.

Wouldn't you like to know.

The truth was, *I* wanted to know everything about Dax Hughes. Not just what I could discover with a Google search or by poring through gossip sites. I wanted to break through that invisible barrier, chip away at it bit by bit. Reveal what he'd concealed.

Although the package he came wrapped in was a fantasy come true. The kind that sent butterflies swirling and soaring inside my belly, then migrating south.

Swallowing the disconcerting thought along with the champagne, I set my glass down on the immaculate kitchen counter and felt Piper's gaze settle on me once again. "I hope that didn't come across as rude. Career comeback, I mean."

Her eyes were kind, and determination made me straighten my spine. "Not at all. And believe me, I want that more than anything. I just don't need anyone else to want it for me, if that makes any sense."

Both Delaney and Piper gave me an appraising glance. "We get that," they said in unison, then laughed.

I joined in, too, and it felt like we'd done this before. Hanging out together, drinking and chatting.

"You should have seen her with the *Vanity Fair* reporter," Piper said. "She had the guy eating out of her hands. And today those stoic industry suits were in no rush to get back to their offices, believe me."

I blushed at the compliments. It was so much easier to accept criticism—or maybe I was just more used to it. "I think they were quite happy to be hanging out with you in the sound booth, Piper."

She hopped up onto a stool lining the oversized island. "Uh, no. Their eyes were definitely on you."

I took the one next to her. "Well, they can look all they want. As long as they go back to their offices and come up with a number to make this trip worthwhile."

Delaney came toward us with a spoon. "Hey, can one of you taste this?"

Piper leaned back. "Uh, my stomach's been a little sensitive lately."

Maybe that was why she'd been nibbling on crackers the other day. I accepted the spoon. "Sure, I'll try." As it got close enough to smell, I knew I'd made a mistake. Chasing the mouthful with a hearty gulp of champagne, I plastered a smile on my face. "It's great."

Piper busted out laughing. "Yeah, even you're not that good of an actress."

Delaney's features transformed into a scowl. "It's probably not done yet," she said, adjusting the dials on the stove and shaking various spices into the pot before coming back to the island, topping off my glass and then her own. "Anyway, I hope your trip has been worthwhile, whatever those stuffy executives say."

I instantly realized the way my words had come off and hurried to backtrack. "Shoot. I didn't mean it like that. This trip has been really wonderful."

She held up a hand. "No offense taken. I guess I've only known you from TV. You don't want to go back to that?"

I shook my head firmly. "God, no." Two pairs of eyebrows arched at my vehemence.

My horoscope came back to me. *You have a lot on your mind, and the secrets you keep are preventing you from thinking clearly. To move forward, you must learn to let go of the past.*

"Let's just say there's definitely a reason the #MeToo movement started with people on Hollywood sets. The land of make-believe wasn't a good fit for me."

Even as the admission skated through my lips, I was surprised by my willingness to let them in on the personal issues I'd dealt with.

It hadn't been a full confession, but I'd definitely gone beyond mere hinting at a few of my secrets. Maybe letting go of the past meant refusing to be bound by it anymore.

Sympathy softened Piper's features, though it was Delaney who spoke first. "That's horrible, Verity. I know it's way too common, but it shouldn't be."

"No one will even attempt to take advantage of you anymore. Travis is a vicious guard dog."

Delaney pulled a face. "That man is some kind of dog, I guess."

"I take it you're not a fan," I said.

She shrugged. "Sometimes I think he's a bit too involved in his clients' careers."

Piper rolled her eyes. "What she means is that sometimes Travis's clients expect Travis to run their lives, not just their careers."

I looked from Piper to Delaney, trying to read between the lines. Was Travis Taggert yet another man I should have known to avoid? "I take it you agree to disagree."

"Y—"

Piper interrupted, pointing at the overflowing pot. The contents had bubbled over and were running down the sides, directly onto the cooktop. The spilled sauce was already turning black, the unmistakable smell of burning food permeating the kitchen.

With any luck, Delaney would have to toss it.

Chapter Four

Dax

Shane had finally shut up about Delaney and we'd moved on to a subject we both felt strongly about—Landon. Our drummer was in a bad state these days, and it was hard to help someone who didn't want to be helped. But whether he wanted it or not, Landon needed us.

Travis wanted to do for Landon exactly what he'd done for Shane a few years ago—send a team of rehab specialists with us to some glorified log cabin in the woods. One with a recording studio, of course.

After Shane detoxed, we'd focused on our music and recorded a kick-ass album. But what worked for Shane back then might not work for Landon now, and I thought we should consider alternative options. "Maybe we should talk to Piper about it. Jett and I hung out with her and Landon about a month ago, and they looked pretty damn cozy. Maybe she can convince Landon to do a stint in rehab before our next tour."

Shane shook his head. "Yeah…Not sure that's going to work. Piper was over here hanging out with Delaney last night." He got up to fetch a fresh beer. "I made myself scarce when I saw the Kleenex come out."

"Shit." Piper had actually seemed like she might be able to calm the crazy in our drummer. "Maybe we'll be headed to that damn cabin in the woods, after all."

Shane gave a soft grunt, and we both fell silent, the sounds of Manhattan rising subtly around us. Twenty stories up, the car horns, bus engines, and occasional sirens were muted. Background noise rather than a soundtrack.

The piercing alarm that suddenly split the air, however, wasn't background noise. Beer forgotten, Shane bolted through the open patio doors, with me close on his heels. "Lainey!"

My gut seized at the panic in Shane's voice. Jesus. If anything happened to his girl—

"In the kitchen!"

"Babe, what happened?"

Delaney's face emerged through the wisps of vapor, the alarm still shrieking. "I ruined dinner," she cried.

The next few minutes were spent opening windows while Shane dealt with building maintenance and deactivated the alarm.

"Hey, Dax. I didn't know you were here." Piper's familiar face emerged through the clearing smoke.

"Yeah, Shane and I were on the terrace." I cleared my throat. "How have you been?"

She rubbed at her eyes, though whether it was a lingering effect from the smoke or from whatever she was talking about with Delaney last night, I didn't know. "Fine. I've started work-ing with a new client. A crossover artist, actually. I'll introduce you in a minute."

I swallowed the disparaging remark sitting heavily on my tongue. In our industry, a crossover artist was code for someone who'd burned too many bridges doing whatever they'd been do-ing and now were scrambling to salvage their career by working with people they hadn't fucked over yet. "No rush."

Verity

Shane Hawthorne needed no introduction, but he didn't notice me. He only had eyes for Delaney, his long stride swallowing up the distance between them. The moment the alarm was cut off, Shane crossed his hands at Delaney's back and pulled her in to his hips. Their kiss was the kind I'd never seen outside of a movie theater or Hollywood lot.

Envy streaked through my veins like a lightning bolt, the siz-zle echoing in my ears.

I didn't even notice Piper at my side until she bumped her hip against mine. "Sickening, isn't it?" Her voice was light, teas-ing. But I noticed her blinking away a wet sheen in her eyes. She caught me looking. "Must be the smoke," she said, before grab-bing my hand and pulling me into the living room. "I want you to meet—"

Dax Hughes.

I mouthed his name along with Piper.

At first glance Dax seemed caught somewhere between bored and aggravated, though both were quickly wiped away by a *don't-I-know-you-from-somewhere?* look.

I'll be the first to admit I look at least five years younger without my hair styled or mascara on my lashes. But in the half second it took for Dax to realize I was the girl wearing workout clothes and no makeup in the elevator, the expression on his face hardened. He scowled at me as if I'd tricked him on purpose.

Or maybe like I was a stalker.

Fighting the urge to squirm, I lifted my hand in an awkward half wave. "Hey. I'm Verity."

Shane and Delaney must have finally remembered they had company, because they suddenly appeared at my side. "Didn't I see you at one of Travis Taggert's parties?" Shane asked. "Covering an old Gwen Stefani track, right?"

Even with all my nerves on edge, I couldn't help but be flattered that Shane Hawthorne remembered me. "Great memory," I said.

"Great voice," he answered back without an ounce of snark or condescension before he spun around and glanced in the direction I've been avoiding. "Dax. You were there, right? Remember hearing Verity kill it that night?"

Dax looked away from me, back to Shane. "No. I must have missed it." His voice was deep and smooth, a rich baritone. I wondered if he could sing as well as he lied. Because I knew he was lying—I'd seen him at Travis's that night, leaning against a tree at the edge of the property. He was one of the few people not talking to anyone, not drinking anything. He'd stood alone, looking entirely comfortable in his own skin.

I remembered watching him, wishing I could borrow some of his ease, his assuredness. A confidence that came from belonging.

The awkward silence was broken by Delaney. "I'm really sorry I ruined dinner, guys."

Shane grinned. "No worries. I'll make a reservation."

"Oh. You don't just want to order in?"

"There's a pop princess in our midst. Can't have her breathing in smoke." Shane's sarcasm was delivered with a teasing grin.

"Shane, really?" Delaney turned back to me. "Don't mind him."

I offered a nonchalant shrug, pressing my lips together to hold back a matching grin. "That's *disgraced* pop princess' to you."

Chapter Five

Dax

Fucking hell.

I was looking at a runway-ready version of the girl from the elevator.

A bolt of jealousy cracked me over the head as her green eyes lit up like Christmas trees at Shane's teasing.

Verity Moore. Crossover artist and disgraced pop princess—one who apparently didn't take herself too seriously.

That red hair I'd been fantasizing about for the past day and a half was down around her shoulders, so silky smooth my fingers itched to run through it. Despite the cool temperature, she was wearing a shimmery gold tank top, her long legs encased in a pair of tight pants. Zippers slid down her thighs, looking like they served no purpose at all except to entice me to yank at them. And on her feet she was rocking sky-high heels.

My balls tightened inside my jeans, followed immediately by a fierce, deep tug in the pit of my belly. I shouldn't want this girl.

And now that I knew *who* she was—*what* she was—I couldn't have her.

But my dick—it was a goddamn traitor.

Standing there, dumfounded and furious, I didn't even notice Shane making his way over to me until his hand clamped down on my shoulder.

I flinched like a goddamn pussy.

Smooth. Real smooth.

This night just kept getting better.

"So, apparently Delaney's friend couldn't make it tonight. And it looks like we're going out to dinner." He glanced from me to the girls. "I'll make the arrangements. Why don't you all have another drink."

My mouth felt like I'd swallowed sand. One more beer and then I would get the hell out of here. I was about to walk away when Piper spoke up. "Someplace low-key, right? Verity's shopping around for a new label, and we can't have any bad press."

My eyes narrowed. I wasn't one to follow gossip, but I vaguely remembered Verity's name being batted around as the latest star to go off the rails.

Looking at her now, calm and sophisticated, her face perfectly painted, she didn't look like a Hollywood "It Girl" that had already flamed out.

"Did I hear that right—Piper Hastings is actually avoiding the paparazzi?" Delaney gaped at her friend.

"Ha ha. They have their uses, but not tonight."

"Low-key, private," Shane said, pulling out his phone and walking away. "Got it."

I headed in the other direction, stalking back outside to the patio to grab another beer from the bar. There was a distinct chill in the air, and with any luck the girls would decide to stay inside.

Didn't surprise me at all that I was shit out of luck tonight.

The scent of vanilla and cloves drifted beneath my nose as I leaned against the exterior ledge and popped the cap of a microbrew, pouring a healthy amount down my throat. Verity, Piper, and Delaney appeared, carrying champagne flutes and seating themselves around the sectional, making use of blankets that had been thrown over the back.

A chilly cross breeze picked up strands of Verity's hair and blew it across her face. Still wasn't enough oxygen for me to catch my breath.

Piper cleared her throat, drawing my attention. "Verity's meeting with your label tomorrow."

I lifted my beer. "Good luck."

Not that I meant it. I wanted her luck tomorrow to be as cruel as mine tonight.

My legs started moving before my head caught up with them, and I managed to mumble something about needing to hit the head before disappearing back inside and colliding with Shane around the first corner.

"Whoa, dude." His hand gripped my elbow. "What's up with you? You've been off all night."

I didn't even bother arguing with him. Shane and I had known each other for only the past six years, but when you practically live together on the road for six months out of every twelve and spend much of the rest laying down tracks in a recording studio, you get real close, real fast.

I was normally the laid-back one of our band of four, but tonight I was coiled tight, my energy agitated and restless.

Filled with want for a woman I couldn't have.

Because I knew better. Trying to make things work with someone in this industry wasn't worth it. Been there, done that. Had the scars to prove it. They were embossed in my brain, on my soul. Had left my heart a shredded mess.

Regret and surprise battled for control of my nerves, tying them in up in knots.

Shane rocked back on his heels, scratching his head. "Wait. Did you run into—"

"Amelia? No. Just family."

He gave a knowing glance. "No one can fuck with your head like family, right?"

I nodded, although my ex had done a pretty bang-up job all by herself. "My sister has a crazy idea about moving to L.A. Wants to live with me while she chases her big break."

Shane let out a hearty bellow. "Well, shit. Is that what's bothering you—anticipating an even longer dry spell while you pretend to be a good role model for your sis?"

I wiped the back of my hand over the beads of sweat suddenly shadowing my hairline. I had no business taking responsibility for anyone but myself. "You're really fixated on my sex life, huh? You and Delaney going through a dry spell yourselves?"

"Bite your tongue, man." He scowled at me. "Listen, I know that bitch really fucked you over, but that was a long time ago. When was the last time *you* got fucked?"

My hand squeezed the neck of my beer bottle, giving it a little shake in case there was anything left. "Christ, man. Worry about your own dick, okay? Lay off mine."

He raised his palms. "All I'm saying is, you should put yourself out there again."

I took a deep breath, knowing Shane was coming from a good

place. But my inhale was laced with just the faintest wisp of vanilla. Making me realize the truth. That there was only one place I wanted to put myself.

Inside Verity Moore.

I should probably chop off my own dick for even thinking about it.

Crossover artist.

Disgraced pop princess.

She wasn't going to be my kryptonite, too.

Chapter Six

Verity

Dax Hughes couldn't get away from me fast enough.

Not the *me* he'd met yesterday.

The *me* I was tonight.

Verity Moore.

Could I blame him? Not really. I wasn't exactly a fan of my alter ego either. It's why I'd hired Travis, to rehab my image and allow me to build a career and reputation I could be proud of. But that didn't change the fact that she was me and I was her.

I shouldn't care what Dax thought of me—I didn't even know him.

I didn't want to know him.

Well, I didn't *want* to want to know him.

But I did. And it hurt to be so coldly dismissed the second Dax realized who I was. A lot.

Finishing the last sip of my champagne, I wished it hadn't

been only my second glass in the past hour. Maybe if I had more alcohol in my system, I wouldn't feel like I'd been punched in the stomach when Dax rushed back inside as if he couldn't stand the sight of me.

I looked out at the buildings rising up around us, Piper and Delaney's casual chatter barely registering. The sky over our heads wasn't quite dark yet. Then again, in New York City, the sky never truly went dark. There must have been lights on the terrace, but no one had turned them on, and it felt like we were held captive by the night.

Uncertainty rippled through me as I grabbed at my drink, remembering too late that it was empty. And I wasn't about to go back inside to refresh it.

"All set. Let's go," Shane called, poking his head through the sliding glass door.

I wanted to say that I wasn't hungry, that I was tired. Any excuse to leave this ill-fated dinner party and return to my lonely hotel room, order room service, and change into pajamas.

But there was something about Dax's proximity that had a hold on me. A hold that only gripped harder once the five of us piled into the elevator together. It was spacious, as far as elevators went. I stood in front of Dax, his breath ghosting over my neck and shoulders, the heat radiating from him setting my entire back on fire.

I think I held my breath the entire ride, and by the time we arrived at the lobby I was dizzy. I must have swayed a bit, because Dax's steadying hand landed on the small of my back.

It was as if he'd prodded me with a hot poker.

I jumped, a hiss escaping through my teeth. Thankfully, the joking banter between Delaney, Piper, and Shane was an effective cover for my reaction. I scrambled after them, Dax following. In the underground garage, we were met by two men in dark suits and earpieces. Bodyguards. They directed us toward two black Navigators. Delaney and Shane got into one. Piper, Dax, and I, in the other.

I figured we were in for a long ride, but I was wrong. Five blocks later, we pulled to the curb. Piper got out first. "Let me go in and check on things first. Be right back."

Once the door had closed behind her, I glanced at Dax. "Is this how you guys always roll?"

His stoic expression cracked a bit. "No way. I'd lose my mind. But with four out of the five of us being paparazzi bait, it makes sense to take precautions."

I narrowed my eyes. "Travis got to you, didn't he?"

Dax grunted. "Called to reiterate what Piper said. Reminded us to keep your face off TMZ's radar."

My hired guard dog at work. Comforting and yet slightly oppressive.

There wasn't time to think about it though. The door was pulled open, and one of the suits motioned for us to get out.

Inside, the restaurant was dim and loud, and a woman in a skintight black dress was waiting for us. She brought us straight to a booth in the back, tucked into a corner where the lighting was even worse. Or maybe better, given that I was supposed to be flying under the radar. In my experience New York was more laid-back when it came to celebrity sightings than Los Angeles, but I wasn't in any position to test that theory.

Shane sat at one end of the U-shaped booth, with Delaney by his side, then Piper. Which left me between Piper and Dax. Of course. "Are you sure you wouldn't rather switch with me?" I whispered to her discreetly. "You know, in case you need to go to the ladies' room again."

She shrugged. "I think I'm good here for a little while."

I'm not! Digging my nails into my palms beneath the table, I managed to keep that comment to myself.

A waitress came over and took our drink order. Another bottle of champagne for Delaney and me, two more beers for Shane and Dax, a ginger ale for Piper, and a large bottle of Pellegrino for all of us. The menu was enormous, and I was content to let everyone else toss out choices we could share family style, participating just enough so that I wouldn't come off as aloof or standoffish.

Dax was quiet, too, but I was getting the sense that that was his default mode, since no one was really trying to lure him into conversation or seemed at all put off.

So when he leaned down to talk to me—just me—a ribbon of warmth began unspooling inside my stomach. "You knew who I was, didn't you?" The warm caress of his breath sent goose bumps racing along my skin.

I didn't bother trying to play coy. Swallowing heavily, my eyes flicked to his before rebounding back to my lap. "I'd have to be living under a rock not to."

"You also knew I didn't recognize you."

I gave a slight nod. "No one would ever put me on camera without my face on."

His brows pushed together. "What do you mean?"

I sighed, hearing my mother's voice in my head. *Thank god for makeup. Lord knows no one's going to pay to see that face of yours without it.* My eyes were too wide, my face too round, my freckles too prominent (until my mother took me to someone who lightened them when I was twelve), my dimples too childlike. I merely answered with, "Nothing," hoping Dax would get the hint and drop it.

Instead he made a slow, casual shrug, hiding the fact that he was dragging his thumb along my arm, from my wrist to the inside of my elbow and back again. Invisible to anyone else, but I felt it in my bones. "Tell me why you think I didn't recognize you?"

I caught Delaney's eye, pretending to laugh at whatever she just said. Then I angled my face just enough toward Dax so that only he could hear me. "It's no big deal, okay? I get it. Without makeup, I'm really plain. I wouldn't expect you to recognize me." It was why I wore cosmetics and blew out my hair only when I was in *Verity Moore* mode. Kind of like a reverse disguise.

"Plain? You think you're plain?"

This time Dax's voice was a little louder, but the waitress had arrived with half a dozen plates of food—even though we hadn't actually ordered yet. "From the chef," she said, making sure to bend low when putting them on the table, her ample cleavage practically spilling out of her shirt.

Dax barely flicked an eye at her.

For the next few minutes we all passed plates and helped ourselves. The restaurant was Pan-Asian, the scent of garlic and ginger heavy in the air. Champagne forgotten, I sampled salmon and shrimp and noodles and veggies, each bite more delicious than the next. We never did get around to ordering specific dishes, but more plates arrived, exchanged with whichever ones were empty.

And about halfway through our meal, I paused, my chopsticks hovering mid-air. I felt warm in a way that wasn't solely due to the champagne and spicy food, or my attraction to Dax—not that it was returned—but from being around people where the talk was easy and the expectations light.

I could breathe.

I remembered this feeling. When I was younger, when my mother still had hopes that her own career would take off, she would drop me with my grandparents every chance she got. Whenever I was having a tough time with my mother, or the kids at school, my grandmother would open a bottle of sparkling cider and pour it into champagne flutes. Then we'd sit at the little square table pressed into a corner of her kitchen and talk until I felt better. In their tiny, well-loved home, I'd known what it was like to feel comfortable in my own skin. To not be a pawn in someone else's game. To just *be*.

But the comfort had been fleeting.

When my grandparents died ten years ago, my world imploded. The walls around me had caved in, trapping me within the rubble.

"Excuse me," I mumbled to Dax, needing a few moments of privacy before I started bawling.

Scrambling across the seat, I headed in the likely direction of the ladies' room. Music pulsed through hidden speakers, the base heavy and sensual. All around me conversation rose and swirled, punctuated by staccato bursts of laughter. The atmosphere was sexy but fun, and I felt the sudden dip in my mood smoothing out.

Inside the restroom, I washed my hands and took a few calming breaths.

Pull yourself together, Verity.

Feeling calmer, I returned to the narrow hallway, heading back toward the main restaurant. I didn't notice the man walking toward me until we were about to pass each other. A shock of recognition slammed into me when our eyes met, the force knocking me against the wall.

Run.

But there was nowhere to go. An enormous potted plant was behind me, and he was blocking the way forward. I shrank back even further, a shiver of apprehension vibrating within my spine.

"Well, well. Tonight must be my lucky night." His Slavic features were arranged in a look of delight, the smirk I remembered all too well twisting his thin lips.

I forced a strength to my voice I didn't feel. "If you'll excuse me, I'm here with friends." I wanted to scream or kick him in the shins, but I couldn't afford to cause a scene or draw any attention to myself. Not tonight.

"I thought *we* were friends." He inched closer. "Special friends."

He may have been friends with my ex-boyfriend, but he certainly wasn't a friend of mine.

The contents of my stomach, the entire delicious meal, soured. "There is no definition of friendship that applies to us." He only leered, caging me in further and lifting his hand, slowly running the back of his knuckles along my cheekbone. Had it not been for the malevolence in his stare, the motion would have appeared sweet. Reverent even.

The reality was anything but.

And all that fear, that pure terror cooling my veins, turned hot. *How dare he?* The girl who'd surrendered to him, who had given up rather than fight—she didn't exist anymore. I smacked his hand away with the back of my forearm. "Don't touch me."

His smirk broadened. "Ah, so maybe you'll fight back this time."

"There's not going to be a—"

"Is there a problem?" Dax's gruff voice was the most beautiful sound I'd ever heard.

The man in front of me—I didn't even remember his name;

Alexei, Sergei, maybe—pivoted on his polished black wingtips, the angle of his body still preventing me from fleeing even though I could see Dax behind him. "There will be if you don't move on," he said, his accent even more pronounced.

Dax's jaw was clenched tight, the vein at his temple throbbing. "Not happening." Animosity heightened the air around us. "Verity, you want to come back to our table?"

"Yes." My throat was tight, the word little more than a squeak.

For a charged moment, the music and conversation and laughter that had seemed so buoyant only a few minutes ago turned ominous, like the sound track to a horror movie.

"You gonna let my girl out, or do we have a problem?"

My girl. The words echoed reassuringly inside my ears even though I knew Dax didn't mean them the way they'd sounded. The way I shouldn't wish he'd meant them.

Alexei/Sergei blinked, lifting his hands slightly, palms up. "Just catching up with an old friend." His thick head swung back toward me before he stepped away. "Until next time, Verity."

The second he left, I felt my knees tremble from relief. Determined not to show it, I folded my arms across my chest and balanced against the wall. "I was seconds away from kicking him in the balls, you know. I didn't need you."

Dax gave a slow blink, then coughed to cover his amused snicker. "I'm sure you were, Ronda Rousey. But Piper's looking exhausted. Pretty sure she wants to head back to the hotel."

"Oh, okay." I checked my watch. It was barely ten. "Um, thank you."

"For what? I just prevented a punk from a well-deserved ass-whooping." Dax stepped back so I could walk in front of him.

"Well, if that ass-whooping had been caught by someone with a camera, Travis would have my head."

A minute later I saw for myself why Dax had come to find me.

Piper's eyes were drooping, and she had an elbow on the table, her chin propped up on her palm. "Ready to go back?" I asked brightly.

"Yes," came her quick answer, and then she paused. "I mean, if you are. I could totally stay, if you wanted to."

Delaney rolled her eyes. "Please, take mercy on her before she face-plants in her ice cream."

Sure enough, there was bowl of pistachio ice cream barely an inch from Piper's chin. "I'm exhausted, too," I lied.

As Piper scooted out of the booth, Shane stood. "Great meeting you," he said. "Knock 'em dead tomorrow."

"Same here, and I'll try." I leaned down to lightly kiss Delaney's cheek. "Thank you so much for including me tonight. I had a really great time."

Her aquamarine eyes sparkled as she grinned. "We all did. Don't be a stranger, okay?"

"Okay," I agreed, and meant it. Delaney was under no obligation to hang out with me, like Piper was. But I sensed the tentative beginnings of a real friendship, and I didn't want to lose that.

Dax followed us out, and I was surprised when he got into the black Lincoln Navigator, too. "You're coming?"

"What, you think I want to be a third wheel while those two make moon eyes at each other and try to pretend they can't wait for me to leave?"

"I just meant that you didn't have to come back with us." Glancing at Piper, I saw that her head was back and her eyes were closed. If she wasn't sleeping, she would be in a second. "We're not hanging out. We're going straight up to our rooms."

Dax's only response was an irritated sigh as he turned his face toward the window. The hotel wasn't far, though it felt as if we hit every light on the way.

Finally we pulled up in front of the Soho Grand, and I nudged Piper awake. Inside the lobby, people were spilling out from the bar, clustered in small groups. I kept my head down, hoping no one would recognize me.

I could imagine the headline. VERITY MOORE AND DAX HUGHES ENGAGE IN THREESOME WITH UNNAMED WOMAN.

Out of the corner of my eye I noticed a man that seemed all too familiar. Alexei/Sergei? I glanced up. No, too short.

A few steps later, I spotted a pair of polished black wingtips and my heart stuttered again. Had he followed me? His face was turned away. But no, wrong color shirt.

I thought my nerves would ease once the elevator doors closed with just the three of us inside.

They didn't.

Staring straight at the panel marking our upward progress, I felt the altitude drop with each floor. By the time the doors opened again, it was everything I could do not to wheeze. Piper went right, waving an exhausted goodbye, her shoes dangling from one hand as she continued down the hall barefoot.

"You okay?" Dax asked, looking at me with concern.

I ignored the question, not trusting myself to speak as I fished in my clutch for the key card. My room was the last door on the left at the end of the hall, Dax keeping pace with me the entire time.

I wanted to believe that Dax was exactly what he appeared to be—a rock star whose sexy swagger and aloof attitude concealed an unexpectedly genuine kindness in his heart.

But my judgment couldn't be trusted. My instincts had been wrong before. More than once. Internal alarm bells rang until they were a painful roar inside my mind. What if Dax was just another devil in disguise?

Jack. Marko. I trusted them, too.

I had an abysmal track record when it came to men. Why would Dax be an exception? Key card in hand, I whirled around. "If you touch me, I'll scream my head off."

He took a quick step back, holding up his own and jerking his chin at the door across from mine. "Whoa there, Rousey. Wasn't planning on it. This is me."

My eyes bounced from his face to the card. "Prove it."

Without taking his eyes from mine, Dax pressed it against the sensor. An angry red light flashed, and I backed up, scrambling to get into my room before Dax could jump me.

He cursed, flipping his card over. I was halfway inside when I heard a *chirp* and then the inward swing of his door.

I slammed my own door closed, bolting it from the inside.

And then I ran to the bathroom and threw up my entire dinner.

Chapter Seven

Dax

What the fuck just happened?

One minute we were sharing a ride after what had been, with one glaring exception, a truly enjoyable dinner. No press flashing their cameras, no fans asking for selfies. Just an asshole in a hallway, who'd backed off without a fight, although I would have relished kicking his ass.

Growing up, my calluses had been earned by pounding the ivory keys of a Steinway or plucking the strings of a Stradivarius, but you didn't hang out with Shane, Landon, and Jett without learning how to win a bar fight real damn quick.

Verity had obviously been scared of the guy, but it was impressive—and enticing—to see her act like she was spoiling for a fight, too.

And ridiculous. The girl was a rabbit pretending to be a porcupine. All prickle with the softest middle.

She'd seemed fine in the car and then less so once we walked into the hotel. Inside the elevator, her anxiety had swirled around us, thick enough to choke on. I could hear the rapid rise and fall of her breaths, the grinding of her teeth. And despite the flush rising to Verity's clavicle, her face was pale.

I'd held my tongue as we continued toward our rooms, telling myself to leave it alone.

Not my girl, not my business, not my problem.

And I'd almost convinced myself of it, too. Planned on raiding the minibar inside my room and finding release though music. I never went anywhere without a guitar. My current favorite, a Rosso Corsa Les Paul, was the only girl I needed.

Until Verity had spun around, pointing her key card at me like it was a prison shank, every ounce of her body bristling with terror and suspicion.

Back at the restaurant, when I'd spotted Verity's red hair trembling on a branch because some asshole had backed her up against a potted plant—even before I saw her face, before I knew that she wasn't wearing a flirty smile or an interested expression, before I read the fear glazing her eyes or heard her false show of bravado—I wanted to grab the scruff of his neck and dispose of him like a rabid dog.

And then, when I actually did see the scared expression staining Verity's flawless features, I wanted to fucking kill him.

But right now—I didn't know what the fuck to do.

Because what I really wanted was to run my fingers through that flaming red silk that put every other color in the rainbow to shame, pull Verity into my arms, and prove that I would never do anything to hurt her. I wanted to see her look at me the way she had the other day, with an open expression on her face and a saucy grin topping that plump pink temptation of a mouth. I wanted to smooth my palms over her shoulders and down her back, wrap my arms around her waist, and hold her close.

God, I fucking *wanted*.

There was a wrench low in the pit of my belly, a deep pull and twist. Because as badly as I wanted to soothe her…I wanted more, too. I wanted to taste her, excite her, enflame her. Kiss her, touch her, fu—

Goddamn it.

I groaned, scratching at the back of my scalp.

Wouldn't you like to know.

Yeah. Yeah, I fucking would.

I just didn't know what I was going to do about it.

Nothing was what I should do. Of that I was one hundred percent certain.

But I *needed* to figure out why she'd shrunk from me in the hallway like she'd thought I would hurt her.

As my mind churned, I paced the hotel suite, my footfalls soft and quick on the tightly woven carpeting. Every second pass, I opened my door, glancing across the hall at the one Verity had slammed in my face. I'd heard the metal scrape of the bolt, too. The last thing I wanted to do was go pounding on it, acting like the kind of Neanderthal she'd been frightened of in the first place.

I'd give anything to erase that look on her face. Not just from my memory, but from her actual face. Because there was only one way you wound up with an expression like that—if someone had given you a reason to be that scared.

My breaths were coming sharp, scraping my throat with each exhale, the vise around my chest tightening with every step. *Who the fuck had terrorized Verity?* The guy from the restaurant? So help me god, I'd rip him limb from limb. My hands flexed and I began cracking each knuckle, one by one, imagining all the different bones I could break and the satisfying crunch they would make.

My phone buzzed in my back pocket, and I pulled it out with a muttered curse.

> *Aria:* So, have you given our conversation any thought?

In the last few hours—not at all.

> *Me:* Yes. Stay in NY for now. At 18, I'll get you a meeting with my agent.

There was a pause and then dancing dots.

> *Aria:* But I'm missing out on opportunities NOW.
> *Aria.* I don't want to be here anymore.
> *Aria:* I want to move to L.A.

Jesus. I wasn't in the right headspace to deal with my sister right now.

> *Me:* Leaving NYC isn't the answer to every problem.
> *Aria:* It was the answer to yours.
> *Me:* I wasn't running away. I was chasing someone.
> *Aria:* But you never came back. Not even once you found her.

I sighed. There was no arguing that one. I had eventually connected with Amelia, about six weeks after getting to L.A. But she'd made it clear she wasn't interested in reviving our relationship. I was devastated, but I was also wrapped up in my new band, playing music that was entirely new to me, and living in a new city. I'd been excited by the unexpected direction my life

had taken. New York and Classic Hughes—everything that reminded me of Amelia—had lost its appeal.

> *Me:*   I'll think about it some more. In the meantime, stay
> in NY.

There were no jumping dots after my last text, so I figured my
sister was sulking. But right now her desire to flee the nest was
the least of my concerns.

I opened my door again, staring at the one across the hall for
several minutes, willing it to open.

I wasn't a particularly patient man, and I had been spoiled for
too long by the immediate gratification that came at my level of
career success.

But I had an idea.

Verity

I was towel drying my hair after what might have been the
longest, hottest shower of my life when I heard the double ring
of the hotel phone.

Probably the hotel manager inquiring if my stay is satisfactory.

Swaddled in the plush robe I'd found hanging in the closet, I
plucked the chocolate off my pillow and lifted the receiver to my
ear as I slid beneath the cool, crisp sheets.

"Hello," I said, contemplating unwrapping the foil.

My stomach was completely empty, my nausea gone. I would
have to brush my teeth again, but the rich treat would probably
be worth it.

"I'm not comfortable with the way our night ended."

My hand was halfway to my mouth when the voice on the other end of the line made me freeze. "Dax? How did you get my number?"

His low chuckle did things to my body I didn't want to acknowledge, the sensual sound reaching places I thought I'd walled off. "I followed the directions on the phone. There's a pretty easy procedure for room-to-room calls."

I could have smacked myself on the forehead. *Duh*. I was still so rattled I couldn't think straight. "I can't remember the last time I used anything but my cell, I guess." Kind of like reading a paper book and tapping on the page, expecting it to turn itself.

"Thought I'd wait to call that until you gave me your number." The low timbre of Dax's voice was even more apparent now than it had been in person. I put the chocolate on my tongue, letting it melt against the roof of my mouth as the silence stretched out. "So, before, in the hallway…"

I swallowed the wrong way, coughing as I reached for a bottle of water from the nightstand. Sexy. After a minute, I wiped at my eyes and picked up the phone that had fallen onto the mattress. "Sorry about that."

"Are you always this skittish?"

"Skittish?" I repeated. "You might want to retire that word from your vocabulary. Kinda kills your whole bad-boy, rock-star vibe."

Another throaty chuckle had me pressing my thighs together. "So then I guess asking what happened in the hallway an hour ago would shred it entirely, huh?"

No, asking that would make Dax a nice guy.

I stiffened, pulling the receiver away from my ear. A kick-ass musician with a sexy smolder…who wasn't a selfish, arrogant bastard. The man was a damn unicorn.

Sporting a horn on his head that could gut me.

"Nothing happened in the hallway. We walked to our rooms and went our separate ways."

"So, I must have imagined you accusing me of being a rapist?"

"I did not. And I didn't realize you were such a delicate flower." I rolled my neck, feeling a pinch between my shoulder blades. The tension that had slipped away in the shower was back in full force. "We all good now?"

"Good? Actually, no. I want to kn—"

I set the phone back in its cradle, silencing Dax's voice. I couldn't handle this conversation right now. Did he expect some kind of explanation from me? How could I explain my behavior to him when I didn't understand it myself?

I didn't *want* to understand it. Didn't want to think about Jack Lester or Marko or Alexei/Sergei.

Some memories, just like some men, needed to stay firmly in the past.

There would be no men in my foreseeable future, either.

Chapter Eight

Verity

Glossy magazine spreads that looked so effortless and elegant…were anything but.

Cameras. Lights. Clothes that were too big or too small held together with pins and tape.

Too many people talking.

Too much touching.

Fake eyelashes.

Fake hair extensions.

Fake smiles.

A minute ago a stylist shoved her cold hands down my dress to push my boobs up, then stared at my chest with a frown on her face before yelling, "I need nipple shields over here!"

I'd rather have a pelvic exam. With a team of med students watching.

At least then the whole ordeal would be over and done in ten minutes.

This photo shoot was scheduled to last two days. It even had a theme. *Verity Embraces Her Truth.*

What did that even mean?

How could pictures of me wearing couture gowns possibly capture something that was essentially an internal struggle? And even if I did want to "embrace my truth," why on earth would I want to share it with anyone else?

I didn't bother voicing my opinion, of course. It wouldn't do any good. The only way to get through these things was to keep my mouth shut and do what I was told. It was how I'd survived three years of *The Show.* Pretending I wasn't a person, but a prop. Someone else's prop.

Being here reminded me why I'd been so desperate to get away from all this. Away from sets and sound stages. With a microphone in my hands, at least I had some semblance of control. If I wasn't feeling a lyric or a note, I could change it, make it mine.

We'd returned from New York a few weeks ago...and I'd spent much of that time thinking about Dax. Hoping I'd imagined the shiver that had run though my spine when his breath feathered across my ear in the restaurant, his thumb sweeping across my wrist.

Hoping I'd imagined the glint in Dax's eyes when he'd looked at me, the corners of his mouth reluctantly tugging upward. The feeling I got that he liked me, too...even though he wished he didn't.

Please, let it have been all in my mind—just like my sudden certainty that he'd followed me to my room with bad intentions.

The man was a song I didn't know the chorus to. A chord chart with missing notes. Frustrating. And so, so tempting.

Damn it. I didn't have time for temptation. I wasn't interested in intrigue.

Working with Travis was a second chance for me. If I screwed
it up, I wouldn't get another.

I hadn't signed a recording contract yet. There had been offers
though, thank god. Travis was doing what he did best, playing
one off the other to get me the best deal possible. It wasn't
easy for me to put my career in his hands, but what was the
alternative—let my mother keep handling it?

No. Just, no.

My mother was still in the dark about Travis. Since I had
never actually signed a contract with her, Travis said I was under
no legal obligation to end our business relationship—because
in the eyes of the law, we didn't have one. Ethically, of course,
I knew I would have to tell her she was no longer my
manager…soon. But for now she had a new boyfriend who was
keeping her happy and occupied. And I was perfectly content to
put off our inevitable confrontation until absolutely necessary.

There was a knock on the door to my trailer—we were shooting in the desert this morning, with plans to be at the beach later
this afternoon. Travis walked in, Piper close behind. I was seated
in front of an enormous vanity mirror, with three people hovering around me. Travis had a damn good poker face, but one look
at Piper and I knew I was about to get big news. Good news.

My spirits lifted. "I have a contract?"

"You do," he said with a nod. "And you have something else,
too."

Something else? Had Travis gotten me a gift? "Really?"

I half expected my manager to reach into his pocket and pull
out a small jewelry box with a charm bracelet or something. "A
world tour."

My stomach dropped, but in the very best way. Much better than a charm bracelet. "A tour? You're kidding!" One of the women shifted, blocking my view of Travis through the mirror. I nudged her to the side.

"You'll be on the same label as Nothing but Trouble, and the execs agreed you would both benefit from touring together."

"That's…amazing." An image of Dax flashed in my mind, immediately followed by a tug of longing deep in my belly. "How about the guys—are they okay with it? I mean, they're a rock band, and I'm…" Did I even know what I was anymore?

Travis's dark eyes blazed as he rubbed his hands together. "Who wouldn't want a front-row seat to the hottest rock band on the charts and the comeback of America's Pop Princess? It's a golden fucking ticket, Verity. It doesn't get better than this."

"Okay, then. That's great." I finally allowed the bubbles of excitement to fizz and shimmer inside my veins.

I was going on tour with Nothing but Trouble.

I was going on tour with Dax Hughes.

And then reality caught up with fantasy. "What—what did they actually say?"

Travis looked away from my reflection, cleared his throat. "They're getting used to the idea."

Was that code for they're-pissed-as-hell-but-I'll-convince-them-it's-in-their-best-interest?

I hadn't worked with Travis long enough to know for sure, but I had a feeling that's exactly what it was.

"Maybe I should meet up with them, get some feedback on what they want from their opening act?" The last thing I wanted was to be trapped on a six-month tour with four angry guys who didn't want me around. I wasn't worried about Shane. And Jett hit on me at Travis's party months ago. When I rebuffed him, he merely offered a charming smile and had two girls glued to his side within minutes. "I haven't even met Landon yet. I probably should, don't you think, before anything is set in stone?"

"Uh, Landon isn't available right now," Travis said evasively. "But I'll set something up when he gets back."

I glanced at Piper, but all her attention was trained on Travis. "Oh." My eyes ping-ponged from one to the other, the energy between them too charged for this small trailer. "When will that be?"

"Hard to say right now. A month, maybe more." He cleared his throat. "Or less."

I tried to read between the lines. Could be rehab. Landon was known for playing hard and partying harder. Or maybe the guys were having problems. Being in a band was like any relationship—there were good days and bad days. But after everything I'd been through, the last thing I needed was to be trapped in a difficult situation with four feuding rock stars. "Is there something I should know about?"

"No. Landon's fine. The band is fine. Absolutely nothing to worry about." Travis's reassurance was anything but reassuring. Especially with Piper looking like she wanted to claw his face for more information.

But there was no time. Three quick raps sounded on the door, and then a guy with a clipboard and a headphone mic poked his head inside. "We're ready for you."

No one looked happier about the interruption than Travis.

Chapter Nine

Verity

It wasn't difficult to find out where Dax lived.

It took much longer to decide whether I should actually show up on his doorstep.

The two-day photo shoot had morphed into three, and I hadn't stopped thinking about Travis's cryptic conversation for a minute of it.

Sure, going on tour with Nothing but Trouble would be the chance of a lifetime for me, but I'd spent three years—longer actually, if I counted my auditions before finally landing *The Show*—under the thumb of a man who treated me like a piece of meat. And after it was over, I'd rushed headlong into another bad situation. No matter how desperately I wanted the opportunity, I still wasn't desperate enough to put myself in such a vulnerable position again. I knew better now.

The interview that would accompany the photos wasn't until next week, and my calendar was looking pretty sparse. Piper had been glued to my side for the past three days of the photo shoot, and I knew she had better things to do than babysit me when I wasn't doing anything but hitting the gym and skulking around my house. I had a lot of dead time on my hands and no one to spend it with.

Maybe, if I were a different person, with a different past, I'd want to spend it with Dax.

Maybe, if I were a different person, with a different past, Dax would want to spend it with me.

But I wasn't.

And, clearly, he didn't.

It was for the best. I didn't need any distractions. Especially not distractions that looked like Dax. Distractions that played and performed like Dax. Distractions that made me drool like Dax.

Unfortunately, whether I wanted to or not, I needed to see him.

A six-month world tour with Nothing but Trouble—it was the chance of a lifetime.

There would be publicity and merchandise, interviews and photographs, venues booked and tickets sold. If I backed out, for any reason—it would be career suicide.

Before I committed, I wanted to be sure that those six months wouldn't be a living hell. Been there, done that, had the stamp on my passport to prove it.

They say that fish rots from the head. In the case of a concert tour, that meant the headliner—Nothing but Trouble. Shane had Delaney to keep him in line, Jett was an outrageous flirt with the attention span of a gnat, and Landon was unavailable, although Travis assured me I could at least have a phone call with him before signing on. But Dax…Dax might actually *be* trouble.

Setting aside my own reaction to his presence—hot, bothered, and embarrassingly tongue-tied—I had basically accused him of being a rapist…even though he'd come to my rescue like a white knight less than an hour before.

And how did he react? Not with anger at my accusation or the door I'd slammed in his face. Instead, Dax had called to check on me. Of course he had. I had to pick the one rocker on the planet who *might* actually be a nice guy.

But did I apologize? No. Of course not. I hung up on him.

Because I was Verity Moore. I didn't make smart choices. I didn't take the easy path. Ever.

Which was why I needed to see Dax this morning.

To apologize.

To prove that I wasn't skittish. Or unconscionably rude.

To figure out if going on tour with Nothing but Trouble wasn't just the right choice for my career, but the right choice for *me*.

And maybe, hopefully, I could leave without making a fool of myself. Again.

Looking for some guidance, or maybe just an excuse to procrastinate, I checked my horoscope.

Embrace those who make your heart beat faster and your days brighter, even when it makes you uncomfortable. Rise to the challenge—the view is always better.

I stared at my phone, the words blurring after I read them. Feeling like I'd been punched in the stomach.

Rise to the challenge—the view is always better. My grandmother had said that to me often, especially when I was having a hard time with the kids at school.

Dax was certainly a challenge.

He made me wonder what it would be like to *be* with someone *I* wanted to be with. Not to get a role. Not as part of an audition. Not because I was drunk or high or as some kind of rebound gone wrong.

And maybe that would be okay…if the man I wanted was anyone else.

But, of course, I wanted Dax Hughes.

A man who didn't want me back.

A man who could kill my so-called comeback with a single word to Travis. Insist Travis drop me as a client. Cut me from the tour. Or even just whisper into the wrong ear that I was "skittish."

Whatever sparks I felt around him had to be doused, the air cleared.

Today.

I decided against calling. This level of groveling required a face-to-face meeting.

* * *

In L.A., it was depressingly easy to get a celebrity's address.

With my stomach in knots, I gathered my courage and made the drive from Beverly Hills to Pacific Palisades, with a doughnut detour in between. It was yet another perfect California day. The sun was out, the day was warm, and there was barely a cloud in the sky. All around me people were walking or biking or driving their convertibles, but I kept my windows sealed shut, the air-conditioning at full force to cool my heated skin. My heart was beating a little too fast, and showing up sporting a ring of armpit sweat wasn't the look I was going for.

I gave my name and ID to the guard, who didn't bat an eyelash. He could probably put his daily sign-in sheets on eBay and net a small fortune. I bit my lip as he went back into the little house and picked up a phone. I watched his mouth move, then his small nod that could have meant *send her away* just as easily as *send her through*. The man's face was expressionless behind mirrored aviators as he returned my license. But then the bar rose and he stepped back, waving me through.

Was I making a mistake? What if I only made things worse? It was pretty presumptuous of me to just show up at Dax's home like this, uninvited.

What had made me think this was a good idea? It wasn't. It was a terrible idea.

I was working up to a pretty impressive panic attack when I pulled into Dax's driveway. He was leaning against his front door, wearing a low-slung pair of joggers and nothing else. His thumbs were hooked into the waistband, showing off impressive biceps and a long torso striated by muscles.

My mouth went dry, and I forgot to get out of the car.

I snapped out of my trance when Dax came down the steps, frowning into my window. Shutting off the ignition, I grabbed the white bag already showing grease stains on its thin paper and slid out of my seat. "I brought doughnuts," I said, holding it aloft like a white flag.

He didn't even glance at it. "You drove all the way here to bring me breakfast?"

I lowered my arm, the paper crinkling within my grip. "I was in the neighborhood."

Smooth, Verity. Real smooth.

Dax crossed his arms, his pectoral muscles rippling. "Why are you here, Verity?"

Wilting beneath his exasperated expression, I didn't even know anymore. "Do you want me to leave?" If I got back into my car and drove off, he wouldn't stop me.

When he didn't say anything, I started over. "I never actually thanked you for stepping up that night, in New York. I still think I could have handled it myself, of course. But I appreciate you looking out for me."

His lips twitched, fighting a smile. "No need to thank me. Like you said, you would have managed fine on your own."

"Of course." I took a step forward, pressing the bag into his hand. Our fingers brushed, and shock from the contact raced up my arms, the simple touch igniting a dozen different electrical explosions inside my body. *Jesus, what did this man do to me?*

It must have done something to Dax, too, because a muffled curse escaped his lips as he spun away from me and jogged up the steps to his front door.

It should have bothered me that he was walking away…but it was hard to feel anything other than grateful at the sight of his ass tensing and flexing with each step.

I stood, immobile except for my pounding pulse, waiting for Dax to hide behind a closed door, just as I'd done at the Soho Grand. But instead he paused in the open doorway and glanced back at me. "Want some coffee with your doughnut?" The question emerged strangled, as if his throat didn't want to set the words free.

"Sure," I said quickly, then hurried up the steps before either of us could change our minds.

Set high above the beach, Dax's house was an interesting mix of dark and light. The floors had been stained a deep, rich ebony. The interior walls were painted white, the molding and windowpanes a flat, matte black. A man cave fit for a sexy, brooding rock star. "Wow. Your place is—"

"Follow me." Dax was already at the other end of the entry-way, heading down a wide, circular staircase.

Noticing he was barefoot, I kicked off my shoes by the front door and followed, my head whipping left and right. Many of the walls were adorned with guitars, a framed photograph hanging beside each one. I recognized Slash and Eric Clapton, Jimi Hendrix and Keith Richards. Many more that I didn't. Dax was a collector, I realized. A serious one.

Downstairs was clearly the main living area of Dax's home, with an open kitchen on one side, a chestnut leather sectional facing an enormous flat-screen television on the other, and a rough-hewn farm table in the middle.

Dax opened the door to a deck that spanned the length of the house, and I gasped as I took in the view. The house had been built into a cliff, the Pacific Ocean spread as far as I could see.

I'd been in plenty of beautiful homes with gorgeous views, but this one was nothing short of spectacular. And a study in contrasts. Just like its owner.

Dax pulled out a chair for me, dropping the bag onto a table made of mosaic tiles, each stone gleaming in the sunlight. "How do you take your coffee?"

"Actually, I'm fine for now." I didn't want him to go back inside, and my racing heart might jump out of my chest if I had any caffeine.

I pulled an apple fritter from the bag and broke it in half. "Try this."

Dax accepted it carefully, without even the barest brush of our fingertips this time, and dropped into a chair. He ate his piece in two bites, then licked the sugary pads of his fingers, saving his thumb for last. A kaleidoscope of butterflies took flight inside my stomach, twisting and twirling. I swallowed heavily, second-guessing my decision to forgo a drink.

"Good, right? Blue Star Donuts. They're down in Manhattan Beach, but totally worth the trip. I got a couple of maple bacons, cinnamon sugars, and another apple fr—"

He interrupted my babbling. "You wanna tell me why you're really here?"

"Besides my belated thank-you and surprise doughnut delivery?"

He smirked, reaching into the bag and pulling out a maple bacon. *I knew he'd like those.* "Yeah, besides that."

I took a bite of the fritter to stall while I got my thoughts under control. "I wanted to make sure you were okay with me joining you on the road."

His eyes narrowed at me, a sudden wariness flashing as brightly as the mosaic tiles. "What are you talking about?"

Those butterflies ducked for cover. "I thought...Didn't Travis say anything to you?"

"About you opening for us? Yeah, he did." Dax's voice was low and deep, barely audible over the crash of the waves, fury and frustration etched into the shallow lines at the corners of his eyes and the deeper ones crossing his forehead. "But I thought it was a joke."

Joke. The word ricocheted like a bullet inside my brain, leaving a wake of pain and destruction behind. I should have expected it, prepared myself for Dax's disdain.

But I didn't, and I wasn't. At all.

Not wanting to give him the satisfaction of seeing me cry, I pushed my chair back from the table and lurched to my feet, practically running inside.

I'd been such a fool. My instincts in New York had been right.

Although his actions weren't physical, Dax was just like all the others. Just like the other men who had hurt me.

I made it as far as the stairs before Dax caught up with me, one hand closing over my wrist and the other curving around my waist. I stilled immediately, an instinctive fear rising up at being overpowered. The intensity exuding from the hard plane of his body, from the rough scrape of his stubble along my neck, from the warm gust of his breath through my hair, hit me like a rogue wave. Sudden. Unexpected. Overwhelming.

But…not in a bad way.

I closed my eyes, letting myself get caught up in the pure wildness of the emotions flooding my body with each beat of my heart. Knowing Dax was the reason for it.

A man who wore ripped jeans and leather bracelets and filled his home with valuable guitars that had belonged to the most famous musicians in the world. A former classical musician who was now one of the baddest boys on the rock scene.

Dax Hughes was a rebel, through and through.

I felt him take a quick inhale, the rise of his chest brushing against my back, as if he were breathing me in. The thought sent a shiver racing down my spine.

"You have no fucking idea, do you?" His words were shards of gravel, rough and sharp.

"What—what are you talking about?" Mine were a fine sand, almost weightless, easily carried away on the wind.

He gave a low grunt. "You're making me fucking crazy, Verity. Need to stay away from you. And I'm trying…But when you show up here, smelling as good as you do, looking as good as you do"—releasing my wrist, Dax dragged the calloused pads of his fingertips along my arm, goose bumps rising to the surface in response—"you make it damned impossible."

Confusion expanded within the marrow of my bones, making me ache. How could I be so attracted to a man who clearly didn't have any respect for me as a fellow musician? Had I learned nothing from the past few years? "Well, then, I'll make it easy for you," I said, gathering my resolve. I would not, could not, fall for a guy who used my body without regard for my heart and soul. I deserved more than that. "I didn't come here today for a booty call, Dax. And I'm not some Barbie doll, designed for your entertainment."

Breaking out of Dax's hold, I climbed the stairs, heading for the front door.

Dax didn't reach for me again, though he did follow. I grabbed my shoes, not bothering to put them on. He called my name before I opened the door.

I heard just enough remorse in Dax's tone to make me turn around. And in his eyes, in the pull of his lips, the tense set of his jaw as he gripped the banister, I saw shame. "I didn't think that. And I'm sorry for making you feel that way."

"Well, you wouldn't be the first." I sighed, trying to look away from Dax and failing miserably. "This was a bad idea. Forget I came. If you don't think I'm good enough to open for you, hash it out with Travis and your label."

A look of disbelief transformed his features. "That's what you think? That I don't respect your talent?"

"You don't have to lie or pretend. I'm a big girl. I can take it." Now *I* was lying. My fingers closed over the knob, desperate to get away from him before blinking away my tears wasn't enough.

His long strides ate up the distance between us, pushing the door closed before any light even came through the crack. "Verity." He paused to swear softly. "That's not what I think at all.

Different, yes. But no one who's heard your voice can doubt your talent."

My jaw sagged as I absorbed what he'd just said. "Then why don't you want me on your tour?"

"Because I don't get involved with women in the industry." He gave a reluctant smile. "And the more I see you, the more of you I want to see."

This man had the most aggravating ability to wind me up and then unravel me. To push me away and draw me so close that the sound of his heartbeat was louder and more reassuring than my own.

My tongue was incapable of forming words to give voice to my bewildered thoughts.

"You never answered my question, Verity." Dax's smile dropped. "Why did you come here? Because I have nothing to give a girl like you. Not anymore."

I tried to absorb what Dax was saying, but my mind was too muddled to decipher it. *The more I see you, the more of you I want to see.*

Dax moved closer, the air between us practically sizzling. His touch would burn me.

And I didn't care.

I wanted Dax's touch emblazoned on my skin, the taste of him seared into my lips.

If I was going to go up in flames, Dax could light the damn match.

"Back in New York," I sputtered, trying desperately to put some kind of order, some kind of sense, to the thoughts and impulses invading my brain. "I regret how I acted, in the hotel. You didn't deserve to be treated that way. I just—I just wanted to come here to say thanks. Say sorry. See if we could get past…"

Dax moved closer, reaching out to twist a lock of my hair. It was a movement I made all day long and thought nothing of. But when Dax's long, elegant finger was wrapped from knuckle to tip in red—*my* red—I could only stare, mesmerized. It was the sexiest, most intimate thing anyone had ever done to me.

And when Dax's knee nudged between my legs, his other hand gripping me by my waist, I was putty in his hands.

Yes, I was a cliché.

I'm not proud.

Whatever storm had whipped up between us, I was powerless to resist it.

Worse, I wanted to be caught up in the inevitability of…whatever *it* was. Feel the wind and rain on my face, let nature take over. Revel in the proof that something was at play here. Something much bigger than me.

A groan vibrated along my nerve endings, making them shake and shiver. The ribbon of red unspooled, and suddenly Dax's hand was along my face, his thumb lifting my chin.

God, we were so close. All that energy roiling in his eyes, directed straight at me. Hazel. Such a small word, just five letters. One for each element. The rich ochre and lush green of earth. The deep blue of the sea. The inky darkness of a night sky. Gold flecks of fire shining through. All whipped into a frenzy.

This man was waging a battle I didn't understand…and I was his enemy.

But if this was war, I wasn't reaching for the white flag of surrender.

Damn it, I wanted to fight, too.

Because what I was feeling—

Butterflies swirling in my stomach.

Breath catching in the back of my throat.

Exhilaration and excitement and an almost embarrassing level of attraction.

—felt so damn good.

Could I explain it? No. Not in words, anyway. But my body wanted to be near his body. The physical pull as invisible and irresistible as gravity.

Maybe these flames between us couldn't be extinguished. Maybe the only option was to fight hard. Fight passionately. Burn off this crazy energy between us.

Until he was mine and I was his.

Until victory was ours.

Or not.

"You like what you see, Verity?" Dax broke eye contact to look me over from head to toe. Slowly. Leisurely. Not missing an inch. And when he finally met my face again, his grin was bitter. "'Cause I sure the fuck do."

How could I respond to that?

He wanted me.

But he didn't want to want me.

"What are you going to do about it?" This time, my breathless tone was more than a little reckless, and I lifted both my hands up, placing them flat on Dax's naked chest. His heat scorched my palms, our energy exchange impossible to ignore or deny.

Maybe we were both crazy.

Dax clenched his jaw, discomfort written in hard lines and deep furrows all over his face. "I don't get involved with anyone in our fucked-up industry. Been there, done that. This career is all I have—I can't fuck it up."

My palms slid over his tense muscles until my thumbs rested in the hollow at the center of his collarbone. His pulse thumping against my skin. "You think I can afford to blow this chance? Dax, I have everything to lose here. And I don't have a backup plan."

What was I doing? Why was I touching Dax? Standing so close and wishing he would touch me back?

Nothing good could come of this.

Nothing good ever had.

Dax's Adam's apple bobbed once, twice. And then he captured my forearms and pushed me away.

He was walking away from the game.

Except that he didn't quite let go.

I seized on the sign of weakness, bending my elbows and stepping back to him. "What are you really afraid of, Dax?"

"I think you should go." His words were gruff, forced. Completely opposite of the plea that flickered in his eyes.

"Tell me," I whispered, aching with need.

The tension between us rose, then snapped in two as his lips landed on mine. The softest nibble, barely a breath.

And yet it was everything.

"I can't," he breathed, the words not hitting my brain until he'd already pulled away from me.

I sagged against the wall, staring dumbly at the mouth that had been on mine just a second ago. I should be thanking him—for being so much stronger than I was. But all I could think was, *Why not?* Which was exactly what came out of my mouth.

"This business brings out the worst in people, Verity. And from a business standpoint, a Nothing but Trouble/Verity Moore tour would be the hottest ticket around." Dax took a step back, then another. "You asked whether joining our tour would be a problem for us. It won't. Because there won't be an us."

Dax

It had been a few days since Verity showed up at my door, and somehow I'd managed to avoid hunting her down, fighting her pull the way I imagined an addict would—with white knuckles, a shit ton of denial, and keeping so busy I could barely see straight.

According to Travis, she was working on her album and plans for the Nothing but Trouble/Verity Moore tour were full steam ahead. I had a few more months before we'd be on the road together. Surely she would be out of my system by then.

Meanwhile, life in L.A. had been unusually calm. Shane was still glued to Delaney's side in New York, and Landon was now in rehab. I hung out with Jett occasionally, but I was too old and too rich to be anyone's babysitter, which was often what he needed by the end of the night.

I'd never needed to chase the high in my downtime the way my bandmates did. Shane was well past that now, and Landon was apparently trying.

Jett, not so much.

A few years ago, I bought a board and took up surfing. Not every day, but a few times a week. Incorporating it into my workout schedule. And it was a damn good workout.

These days I was on my board every fucking morning. Why? Because it was the only sport that not only got me out of the house, but out of my own head. On the open water, I couldn't fuck around on my phone or reach for my guitar. It was me, my board, and the ocean—and the second my thoughts drifted beyond whatever wave I was riding or chasing, the Pacific smacked me down.

At the asscrack of dawn, I dragged my board to the beach and gave myself over to the power of the tides. And in the afternoon I sat at my piano, or with my guitar, playing until my knuckles swelled and my fingers bled. Pouring my soul onto the page in the language I knew best—notes and symbols, harmonies and rhythms and lyrics.

I'd been writing songs for years, although not under my own name. Yeah, I lived a public life—it was hard not to when you were one-fourth of Nothing but Trouble. But what I put down on paper, that was all me. My thoughts, my hopes, my fears, my past.

Shane was good at putting it all out there and then singing about it, night after night.

Not me.

I kept my shit bottled up nice and tight until it exploded out of me in a fury of writing and riffing. Fugue states I eventually came out of to find my soul exposed on sheets of paper.

Today the song that ripped through me wasn't about me, not exactly. It was about Verity. About how I treated her. About her reaction to how I treated her. I was an ass. Worse, I was a predictable ass. The kind she'd dealt with before.

> *Long time ago,*
> *Someone picked me*
> *Painted me*
> *Dressed me up and shamed me*
> *Turned me into a bombshell*
>
> *But they didn't know*
> *Didn't wanna know*

I'm the bomb, baby
I'm the bomb, just me
Primed to explode
Broken bits,
But all you see is ass and tits

My mind's intact
No, you can't have that

Long time ago,
Someone picked me
Painted me
Dressed me up and shamed me
Turned me into a bombshell

But they didn't know
Didn't wanna know

My mind's intact
No, you can't have that

I'm a shell
Cracked and broken
The truth has spoken
My heart is beating, needing
I'm no bombshell
Look and listen
Watch me rebel

Oh yeah, that's what I'll be
Look and listen
Watch me, watch me
I'm a rebel

Not a single lyric was about me, and yet I knew that this was the most intensely personal song I'd ever written. I'd painted a picture of Verity Moore—how *I* saw her. Her rebellious spirit and soulful voice. A face so vibrant, so beautiful—but someone had convinced her it was flawed. And a fire that grew stronger with every beat of her heart, a flame not even cruelty could extinguish.

A powerful portrait made entirely of words and notes and chords.

Like I always did, I snapped an image of it, automatically adding it to the Google Drive where I kept all my songs.

And then I shoved the piece of paper in my piano bench and slammed the lid closed with a fierce growl.

I'd be damned if this one ever saw the light of day.

Chapter Ten

Verity

I finally slowed my pace when I was a block from J.J.'s, my favorite juice place. It was basically a hole in the wall tucked between a crystal meditation studio and a cell phone store. They made the best juices, coffees, and fresh muffins in L.A. Breathing heavily, I resisted the urge to stop completely and retch on the sidewalk. I'd really pushed myself this morning, going faster and farther than my usual easy three to five miles through Runyon Canyon Park. But after my visit with Dax, I needed it. I couldn't get him out of my head.

When I first came back to L.A. I had sworn off sex forever. Frankly, I didn't know what the fuss was all about. Sex was an expectation. An obligation. A transaction. It had never, not even once, been a pleasure.

But something told me sex with Dax would be different.

And something about Dax made me want to find out just how different it would be.

Thinking about Dax while still overheated from my run was sending my body into overdrive, and the air-conditioning was a welcome change from the heat outside. I got in line behind a woman with blue hair, self-consciously adjusting my baseball cap and sunglasses even though the odds of being recognized while my skin was the color of a peeled tomato were slim to none. It wasn't sunburn, just a side effect of being so pale that when I exercised, the combination of sweat and an all-over flush made me look like I'd been lying out in the sun, slathered in baby oil.

What I needed was to get out of here and take a cold shower.

And focus on something else, like my career. I should call up Piper and talk through the upcoming press events she'd put on my schedule. Tell her to add a few more.

And then call Travis, ask how soon I could get in a studio to start recording my new album.

I was lying low, just like Travis wanted. But I needed to keep busy, because spending my days—and nights—thinking about Dax's voice in my ear, his hands on my skin…

By the time it was my turn to order, I was so flustered I couldn't even decide between an iced coffee and a green goddess juice. So I bought both.

Still distracted, I didn't notice the gray-suited man taking up too much room in the small space until his elbow came out of nowhere. One minute I was double-fisting my morning beverages, and the next I was holding only one.

I saw my coffee fall from my hand in slow motion. It hit the ground once, bouncing up as the top came off and spewing coffee and ice cubes, splattering everyone in a five-foot radius, especially the man in the pale-gray suit.

"Goddamn it!" His outraged yell flipped a switch in my mind, cutting off my apology as we reached for the napkin dispenser at the same time. There was a flash of gold on his right hand. A man's signet ring. Flat top, initials carved into it. *J.L.*

His arm brushed my bare shoulder and the ground beneath my feet trembled, my composure dropping to the floor like my drink, exploding at my feet.

I knew that voice.

I knew that ring.

I knew that hand.

I knew that man.

I never again wanted to know his touch.

Breathe, Verity. Just breathe. Don't you dare pass out at his feet.

Staggering backward, I hid my head beneath the brim of my Lakers hat, unable to speak. Unable to do anything but flee.

Once I bumped into the door, I pivoted and pushed at it with both hands, forgetting that I was still holding my other drink. The plastic crumpled against the glass, the top popping off as a volcano of green goddess mulch erupted all over me. But I didn't stop moving. I sprinted toward the parking lot where I'd left my car, throwing myself behind the wheel like I was being pursued by the devil himself.

But the devil wasn't chasing me. He hadn't even come out of the shop.

Bile rose up my throat as I locked the doors and started the ignition, leaving green smudges on everything I touched. Throwing the car in reverse, I backed out of my spot with barely a glance. That was what motion sensors were for. A safety feature.

I could have used a safety feature in my interactions with Jack

Lester. Instead I had my mother—a woman who had been only too eager to push me into the arms of anyone who could get me in front of a camera.

Lester had put me in front of a camera, that was for sure. How many private "auditions" did I have with him? My mother would drop me off with his assistant, Millie—never asking why those auditions were taking place in hotels and not on studio lots. Drinking a martini and flirting with the bartender while she waited for me in the lobby lounge.

Afterward, Millie would bring me back downstairs. *Your daughter is such a natural performer. Jack just loves her. This role might not be quite right for her, but we'll bring her in for another audition in a week or two.*

And my mother would bow and scrape, acting like Millie was doing us all a big favor.

Until we got in the car and she laid into me for not getting the part. *Whatever Jack wants, you have to do. That's what acting is, Verity. Playing a role. Why can't you do that? Why can't you please him?*

I never answered. There was no point. Because I had pleased Jack Lester. I knew I had. His great big satisfied groan was all the proof I needed.

How many auditions had there been before I finally landed *The Show*? I couldn't remember.

Enough.

More than enough.

When I got home, I stripped off my clothes in the garage and threw them in the trash before walking inside the house. I was in the shower within minutes, scrubbing sweat and coffee and sticky green juice from my skin. It took three washings before I couldn't feel any pulp in my hair.

The tears didn't come until I was out though. Until I was wrapped in a fluffy white towel, my skin pink and glistening. Until I wiped the steam off the mirror and stared at my reflection. Until I realized I *wasn't* clean. I would never *be* clean.

The residue from Jack Lester's touch wasn't on my skin. It couldn't be seen in a mirror or examined with a microscope. It had collected in my mind. Tainted the lens through which I viewed everything and everyone, especially myself. Created a film of suspicion and self-recrimination no amount of soap or shampoo would ever wash away.

You asked whether joining our tour would be a problem for us. It won't. Because there won't be an us.

It wasn't my Verity Moore alter ego that Dax was put off by. It was *me*. The parts and pieces of me that had been corrupted. Corroded from the inside out.

Jack Lester's shameful smudges had turned me into the kind of woman who fell for a man like Marko. The kind of woman who didn't deserve a man like Dax.

I was dirty. So damn dirty.

Chapter Eleven

Dax

I noticed Travis's text when I got back from surfing. Well, trying to surf. The waves had been almost nonexistent. After a frustrating hour, I'd taken my board and gone home.

It was just as well. One of my songs was being recorded at a studio downtown. I took a quick shower and headed over.

There was a code among musicians, based on the language we all shared. No one batted an eye when I sat in on a session. The L.A. music scene was a small one, and there wasn't a studio in fifty miles I hadn't jammed in, whether for Nothing but Trouble, filling in for a friend, or working on my own stuff. It helped that I could play any instrument I'd ever picked up, too.

Slipping in through the back, I quietly entered the third door on my left. The sound engineer was talking, and a few people were crowded near the glass, preventing me from seeing the artist. Catching Travis's eye, I made my way to his side. "What's going on?"

"Thought you'd want to hear this." He lowered his voice further. "Also, I've been meaning to talk to you about Landon. I think we should visit him."

"In rehab? Not sure it's a place we can just show up at."

"We wouldn't just show up," he scoffed, frowning at me. "You guys are a family. He needs you."

I frowned right back. "Trav, if he wants us there, we're there. You know that."

He cleared his throat, lifting a hand to rub his shaved head. "Just checking."

The sound engineer called for quiet, and I reached into my pocket to make sure my phone was on silent. Then I nearly dropped the damn thing.

I knew that voice.

I knew that song.

What the fuck?

It only took a second to realize what had happened and less than a minute to confirm it. I'd put "Bombshell Rebel" into the iCloud folder I shared with Travis, not my work-in-progress folder that was set to private. Of course he'd found it and shopped it around. That was his job.

My gut twisted as I swung my head toward the tinted glass separating the sound room from the recording studio.

Verity Moore was singing *my* song. A song I'd written for *her*.

My instinct was to get up and leave, immediately. But I didn't. I couldn't.

From the sweetness of her teen hits, I already knew Verity had the voice of an angel.

From the old-school Stefani hit she'd killed at Travis's place a few months ago, I knew Verity had the voice of a devil.

Today Verity Moore had the voice of a siren. The mythical kind that could lure a man to his death, not realizing what was happening until his boat slammed into the jagged cliffs that would mark his grave.

One hour passed, then two. Verity must have sung each lyric a hundred times. Each take slightly different. Besides a couple of water breaks, she was the consummate professional. A sound engineer's dream.

Travis leaned toward me. "I want you to get in there with her."

I shook my head at the request, not bothering to look at him. No fucking way.

He dug an elbow into my side. "I'm serious. I think Verity should do an acoustic version of the song. Something to throw on the album to prove she's not an Auto-Tuned hack. An 'It Girl' who doesn't deserve to be in a sound booth."

Verity Moore was an It Girl, all right. And she sure as hell deserved to be here. Her vocals stole the show, and it would be a shame not to showcase them. I just didn't know if I could be in the same room with her and not want to *be* with her.

"Why don't you pair her with some boy bander looking to break out?"

Travis grunted. "Because I can barely name the ones with genuine talent on one hand—and I wouldn't trust any of them with Verity for five minutes."

I hated it when Travis was right. The man loved to gloat, and his arrogant smirk irritated the fuck out of me.

As if this had all been decided beforehand, the engineer waved me over. "I put your Les Paul in there. Need anything else?"

Most musicians were picky when it came to their instruments, and I was, too. But I'd given one of my favorite guitars to the producer of our last album as a gift. He happened to own this studio and must have kept it in his office.

I shook my head, stepping into the sound room. Verity's eyes lit into me, all bright bits of surprise glinting at me from a deep green sea. "What are you doing here?"

I opened my mouth to answer, but the intercom beeped. "Dax can play acoustic better than anyone I've ever heard. You good?"

Verity snapped back into professional mode, pasting an overbright smile on her glossed lips that had me wanting to reach out and wipe it off. I hadn't spent all that much time with Verity, but I'd seen a number of expressions on her face. Flirty, surly, happy, wistful, scared, angry.

But fake was the only one that made me want to look away.

Reaching for her wrist, I gritted my teeth through the jolt of electricity that bombed down my arm, pulling her just enough that she swiveled away from the two-way glass. "I don't have to do this. If you don't want me here, I'm gone. No hard feelings."

Verity stared at me for a beat, then at all the people assembled in the other room watching us. "Who am I to turn down Dax Hughes?" Tugging her hand free, she resumed her place in front of the mic. "Ready when you are, rock star."

Verity

Thank god. It was over.

When Travis sent me "Bombshell Rebel," I practically hyperventilated reading the lyrics. It was as if the person who wrote those lines lived inside me. Knew the pieces I shielded even from myself, or at least tried to. The shame and ambition. The frustration and disgust. And the yearning. The yearning to be heard, to be seen. To be something, someone. To just *be*.

I spent the past twenty-four hours preparing. No one needed to know that each word felt like a razor blade shredding wounds I so desperately wished would heal. Convincing myself that the song could have been written for anyone who had been chewed up and spit out by the Hollywood Star Factory.

And then Dax showed up.

Shattering my composure with one slow sweep of his onyx stare. *If you don't want me here, I'm gone. No hard feelings.*

I had a lot of feelings where Dax was concerned. But what I definitely didn't have was enough clout to turn away Dax Hughes.

Thankfully, the producer and sound engineer, and even Travis, appeared pleased behind the glass. My job was done. I breathed an exhausted sigh of relief. Somehow I'd managed to get through this morning and now all I wanted to do was collapse on my couch—

"I'm making a doughnut run. Wanna come?"

I'd been gulping from a bottle of water, and Dax's question nearly made me spit it out at his feet. Having spent the past couple of hours in the same small room with him, I should've felt more relaxed around Dax.

I wasn't.

Impressed, awed, starstruck, unworthy. All of the above.

It was one thing to listen to Dax Hughes playing guitar.

It was another to witness his mastery of the creative process.

And it was a whole other galaxy to be confronted by both simultaneously.

I was completely blown away. The man was a musical genius.

But did he have to come wrapped in a sinfully sexy package? It was like staring at the sun. My skin was flushed, my corneas burned, and there was a haze around my vision.

After ambushing Dax at his house, after running into Jack at J.J.'s—and even after reading over "Bombshell Rebel"—I'd been relieved to finally get back in the studio this morning. To focus on singing instead of flailing about in my own mind.

My relief lasted about two hours. One hundred and eighty blessed minutes alone inside my sound booth bubble. Until Dax Hughes opened the door and popped it.

"Nope. I don't like doughnuts."

He lifted a brow at the lie. "That's too bad. Because I heard about this place just east of here, where they make them right in front of you. And they have this apple cider slushie that would feel really good going down after you've been singing for a few hours."

My mouth watered just thinking about it. Doughnuts and a slushie. It was after noon and I hadn't eaten anything yet. And my throat was parched. "Where did you say it was again? You know, in case I know anyone who's interested."

Dax pressed his palm against the small of my back, his thumb pushing just beneath the hem of my shirt to swipe at the bare skin beneath. "I'm interested," he said in a gritty whisper, low and close to my ear, that didn't evoke any of the trepidation I'd felt with him in the past. The nerves that trembled from Dax's touch weren't because I still believed he would hurt me.

I let him propel me through the exit and toward his car. The back parking lot was gated, not a single photographer lying in wait.

Doughnuts and Dax…How was I supposed to resist an offer like that?

He opened his passenger door and I slid right in. "You were really good in there," he said, starting the engine.

I waved a hand in front of my face. "You mean, for a pop star."

He shifted into gear but didn't take his foot off the brake. "For anyone."

My lashes fluttered as I looked at Dax, trying to decide if he was being sincere. His attitude today had been a complete one-eighty from the last time we were together, at his house. Finally, I buckled my seatbelt and folded my hands in my lap. "Drive, rock star. I'm hungry."

Dax

I still wasn't sure what had possessed me to drag Verity out of the studio an hour ago. All I knew was that I wasn't ready to let her go.

Doughnut eaten, clutching a sweating plastic cup with her half-drunk slushie, she didn't seem in any rush to part company either. "How'd you find this place? I'm down here all the time and I've never heard of it."

"My sister visits during school breaks. Apparently she read about it in some top-ten list of things to do in L.A."

Verity bit down on her straw, dimples carving into her cheeks as she took a pull from it. "And did you do everything on the list?"

I grinned. "Of course. I'm a very accommodating host."

She lifted a skeptical brow, throwing shade. "Accommodating isn't the first word I'd use to describe you, Dax."

I feigned offense. "I'm accommodating. I'm accommodating as fuck, actually."

"Okay, then. If I told you one of my favorite shops was around the corner, would you go with me?"

The question Verity should really be asking was whether there was a chance in hell I could resist the teasing sound to her voice right now. Or the genuine grin that had replaced the saccharine-sweet one she'd worn in the studio. The answer was, No. Nada. Zilch.

But I had to at least make an attempt at playing it cool, so I offered a nonchalant shrug. "Sure."

A few minutes later, I was looking up at a painted sign that read ART DISTRICT CO-OP, which meant less than nothing to me. "What is this place?"

"It's a flea market," Verity responded, grabbing my hand and dragging me inside.

I could spend hours wandering through anyplace that carried vintage Les Pauls or rare vinyl albums, but the enormous warehouse Verity had brought me to looked like the contents of an entire shopping mall had been ripped up in a tornado and then blown into the building. Children's toys were strewn across an old surfboard, Christmas ornaments displayed beside a wedding dress. A vintage Harley was decorated with dozens of candles.

And a fat bulldog lay on the cement floor, furiously scratching himself. "Uh, I think that description might be entirely too appropriate."

Verity merely rolled her eyes and linked her arm though mine. "This place is so much better than anything you'd find on Madison Avenue or Rodeo Drive."

We passed a display of bug-eyed troll figurines carved from reclaimed wood. "If you say so."

After a few minutes the jumble started to make sense, the

pure enormity of all that was available under one roof becoming less overwhelming. "What are you looking for?"

"Champagne glasses."

"To toast your new album?"

"Maybe." She fingered a knitted afghan, then the beaded necklace lying beside it. "At this point I'll celebrate just finding the glasses I'm looking for."

Craning my neck, I spotted a display of crystal at the end of an aisle. "Let's go look over there."

Her steps outpaced mine, but after a quick glance inside the stuffed armoire, she backed away. "Not there."

"You barely looked."

She only shook her head, a disappointed frown trekking across her forehead. "I would know them in a heartbeat."

Now I was curious. "What do they look like?"

"They have hollow stems, kind of old-fashioned looking. And the crystal has an amber tint to it."

"You can't remember where you saw them originally?"

Pain streaked across her face, her smile faltering. "They were my grandmother's. She passed away about ten years ago, now. My mother didn't bother keeping anything. I've always hoped that one day I would find a set just like them."

"Ten years ago you would have been what, fourteen? And you were drinking with your family?"

She released a small giggle that made my blood feel as light and buoyant as the champagne we were talking about. "No. Sparkling cider only. But when I was having a bad day, she would pull out those special glasses. I swear, things always seemed better after we clinked rim—"

"Verity Moore!"

I spun around, instinctively bracing my arms to protect Verity from what turned out to be a trio of teenaged girls wearing identical awestruck expressions and openmouthed grins.

"Oh my god, can we get your autograph?"

"And a selfie?"

"Can you sing the theme song of *The Show* so I can save it as my ringtone?"

Backing away a few feet, I took a sudden interest in a towering display of hemp soaps and lotions, averting my face while still keeping one eye on Verity as she graciously handled the first two requests but gently declined the third.

For me, the worst part about being a member of Nothing but Trouble was the fame that came along with it. But fame was a necessary evil, and in this town, the most valuable of commodities. Fame had bought my home, my cars, my collection of guitars.

Talented musicians could be found working at restaurants all over town—waiting on the *famous* ones.

Verity was stepping back into the spotlight, not as part of a band, but as a solo artist. There was a big difference. She may have played a part on *The Show*. But onstage, she would *be* the show.

And right now she was soaking up the girls' adoration like a desert flower in a rainstorm.

Gorgeous and glowing.

Fucking breathtaking.

Even more so than she'd been in the studio. I had purposely hung around as everyone else was packing up and saying their goodbyes. Hunched over my guitar, pretending to adjust the strings, my ears strained for every sound that fell from Verity's lips. From the way she deflected every bit of praise aimed her way, to the respectful tone she used to address everyone in the room.

She had no entourage, no attitude. She was just herself. And goddamn it, I fucking *liked* her.

Verity Moore—disgraced pop princess—was a pretty cool girl.

I hadn't planned on spending the day with her. Just the opposite. At first I'd been counting the minutes until I could get the hell away. But only the first few minutes.

After that I didn't notice anything else but Verity herself.

Listening to her bringing my song—a song I'd written about her—to life. It was almost surreal.

Fuck. It was surreal. Like the best kind of dream.

Me and my guitar. A gorgeous girl with an even more beautiful voice. Making music together.

It didn't get much better.

Not with clothes on, anyway.

Too bad it wouldn't last.

Things that were too good to be true never did.

Chapter Twelve

Verity

I didn't understand Dax. And I *definitely* didn't understand myself when I was with Dax.

He had the strangest ability to make all the doors in my body, the doors in my mind—especially those I had closed, locked, and bolted shut—spring open as if he had a master key.

Dax made me feel like one of the teenagers who had come running up to me—excited and energized, their bright eyes looking at the world as if it was theirs for the taking. Their expressions radiating an eager confidence, a certainty that anything—everything—was possible.

Not at all like *me*. I wasn't a starry-eyed girl anymore…if I'd ever been. I knew exactly how ruthlessly this town could chew me up and spit me out. Because it had. I was a jaded Hollywood flame-out who had come crawling back, begging for a second chance.

As a fellow musician, Dax was both a mentor and a role model.

But as a man—he was a threat. To my motivation. My reputation. Turning this situation into a powder keg primed to explode.

I should be running from him right now. But instead, I was strolling at Dax's side, walking from the flea market back toward the doughnut shop. As if we'd been friends for ages. As if the occasional brush of his arm against mine wasn't sending electricity racing through my bones.

We could walk all the way to the ocean and I'd probably be wearing the same stupid grin when my feet hit the sand.

"So…your voice. Where'd you learn to sing like that?"

My grin faltered. "I don't really remember *learning* to sing. It was just something I used to do. Singing made everyone around me smile. So I kept doing it. At home, in church. Eventually, on auditions. It's always been a part of me."

His eyes crinkled at their corners when he gave me a sideways glance. "I get that."

"How about you? Where did you learn to play guitar like that?"

Dax's hearty laugh boomed off the gritty sidewalk. "Believe it or not, onstage. The first time I ever picked up a guitar was the night I met Shane, Dax, and Jett. But I practically grew up with a violin in my hands, so it wasn't a big deal."

I came to a stop in the middle of the block, looking at him incredulously. "No big deal? Are you kidding me? I don't have to know how to play a single instrument to know that's not normal."

Dax shrugged, shoving his hands in his pockets and rocking back on his heels. "You should meet my family."

I started walking again, Dax's long-legged stride matching my pace. "I have more than enough issues with my own, thank you very much."

"Lemme guess. You come from one of those big *Sound of Music*, sing-for-your-supper type families."

I had never known my father, and I was willing to bet my mother wasn't quite sure who he was, either. "Ha. Nope, although I did audition for a show like that once. It's just me and my momager. Picture Kris Jenner with only one Kardashian kid to manage." He laughed again. A seductive rumble that made the air inside my lungs feel lighter, buoyant. "You have a nice laugh, you know. You should consider letting it out more often."

"Then I guess we'll have to hang out more often." It was a casual response, almost a throwaway comment. Reverberating in the air like a bolt of lightning.

My neck swiveled his way so sharply, I lost my balance and tripped over a crack in the sidewalk. I pitched forward, my hands going up automatically to protect myself from the impending fall.

Dax's firm grip wrapped around my wrist, steadying me with barely any effort. My gaze dropped to his long, elegant fingers. The same ones that had stroked his guitar like a lover, pulling the most beautiful song from her strings. If he wanted to, I had no doubt he could play my body just as skillfully, just as masterfully.

My pulse was a frantic thing, erratically stuttering and then surging to tap out a beat beneath Dax's hand. Maybe an SOS.

With a determination I didn't know I possessed, I casually shrugged off his touch like it wasn't burning me. But it was. Another second and I'd be permanently branded. Property of Dax Hughes.

I cleared my throat to find my voice. "You know, we passed your car a few blocks ago."

His hand still hovered in the air, as if he hadn't realized I'd pulled mine away. "Yeah, I know. I thought we could grab a drink. Or some dinner." Dax gave me a sheepish look. "Unless…unless there's somewhere you need to be."

Dax

"I haven't met Landon yet. Have you spoken to him lately? Is he okay with me opening for you guys?"

We were in the corner booth of a Mexican restaurant, a margarita in front of each of us. The remainder of the pitcher sat on the table, along with guacamole and a few other plates to share. I pushed out a sigh and leaned forward. "I wouldn't worry about Landon. He's got his own shit to deal with right now."

A nervous frown pushed its way between Verity's brows. "That sounds kind of…ominous."

"Nothing I can say about it right now. He'll be fine. I know it." Landon had been through so much in his life, and his latest fuck-up was finally big enough to knock some sense into him. Took long enough. "How about you? A world tour isn't like showing up on the same studio set every day."

"I know. Or, rather, I don't know—but yeah, I imagine it's different." She took a shaky sip from her glass. "That's exactly what I'm hoping for."

The tentatively hopeful tone of her voice scraped away yet another of my preconceived notions. "Ah. A fellow runaway. You know what, Verity? I think you're going to fit right in."

She tilted her head to the side, her expression a mix of confused and curious. "Runaway? Is that what you call cabbing to the airport with a plane ticket in one hand and your Juilliard diploma in the other?"

I groaned a denial. "Not exactly."

"Okay, fine. You road-tripped cross-country, then."

"No. You were right about the plane ticket. But I never did get my diploma." The admission scraped the inside of my throat. It was something that still bothered me. All of that time studying, playing, practicing, and not even a year left before graduation. I gave it all up to chase after Amelia. In the grand scheme of things, that piece of paper didn't matter—but it was just one more thing I'd forfeited for a love that was nothing but a lie.

I shook my head to clear it, and when I looked at Verity again, she was brushing salt from the corner of her lips, sucking on the pad of her thumb. "What were you running from?"

"It's the reverse, actually. I was running toward something. Someone." I took a hearty gulp from my glass, the burn of tequila oddly soothing. "It didn't work out. How about you? What's in your rearview mirror?"

She closed her eyes for a moment, an involuntary shudder shaking her delicate shoulders. "Honestly, I'd rather not look behind me. Although I can tell you what isn't there—a diploma. I never even graduated from high school."

I would have liked to erase the bitterness clinging to Verity's voice, soothe the shame wrinkling her forehead. "You wish you hadn't left?"

"Left?" She dismissed the suggestion. "No. According to my mother, once school wasn't legally required, it became a luxury. One we couldn't afford. I needed to work." I stayed silent, watching Verity worry at her tantalizingly plump lower lip as she swirled her straw in her drink, ice cubes rattling. "I can't complain though. I missed too many days to make any real friends or to learn much of anything. I'm sure it was for the best."

"The best for who?" The question came out of nowhere and felt almost too personal. I probably should have taken it back. But I didn't.

Verity looked up from her drink. "Is everything in your life so cut-and-dried? Best or worst, black or white, wrong or right?"

Her penetrating stare launched an arrow of lust. It hit dead center, exploding on impact. "Pretty much."

"I envy you, then. So far I've only jumped from one bad situation into another. Each choice I make is connected to one I've made. And every time I try to draw a line in the sand, a wave sweeps it away."

"Hiring Travis. Coming on our tour. They seem like pretty good choices."

"They are. I think they are, anyway. But hiring Travis is going to wind up destroying my relationship with my mother. Not that it's a good one, but she's the only family I have. As for joining the tour... Well, it means we're going to be spending a lot more time together."

I refilled her glass, then my own. "Is that good or bad?"

"See, there you go again. Why does it have to be one or the other? What if it's a mix of both?"

I licked the salt from my mouth, wishing I was doing something much better with my tongue. *Jesus.* "Because mixing business with pleasure is just bad. That's a fact. I told you before. I did it once and it blew up in my face."

"That's not a fact," Verity shot back. "That's your opinion based on a tired cliché and a bad breakup."

Amelia and I didn't break up. She walked out on me. But I

popped a chip in my mouth instead of arguing a moot point. "Fine. Explain your mixed-bag theory to me."

"Performing with you, getting behind a microphone again, challenging myself musically—those are all good things. But if anyone sees us hanging out like this after the tour is announced, or while we're on the road, they're going to assume I screwed my way onto the tour. And then my reputation won't be any better than it is now." The smile she offered was sad, no trace of her dimples. "So, there. A mix of good and bad and sad. Because this has been really nice. I've never had a day I've enjoyed as much as this one...And it can't ever happen again."

Chapter Thirteen

Dax

We stayed at the restaurant a long time, talking about music and family and life in the industry. Verity had only two margaritas over three hours, so I offered to take her back to her car, but she said she'd rather just call a service tomorrow morning since she had to be back at the studio anyway.

It was just as well. I wasn't eager to say goodbye. Even so, the extra forty minutes driving to Beverly Hills went too fast. Sitting beside me, content and relaxed, her shoes kicked off, bare feet resting against the console, Verity looked like she was right where she belonged.

I turned off the ignition in her driveway, watching her pink toes slide back into her heeled sandals. "Today was really great, Dax. Thank you." I glanced back up to her face. My mouth watered, hungry to feast on those pretty, plump lips that had given shape to a song she didn't know had been written about her.

There was a moment when I thought Verity would lean over and kiss me, but she didn't.

And neither did I.

Feeling like we'd both lost an opportunity, I got out of the car.

How the fuck could I just let Verity go, let her walk away after the day we spent together? As she moved away from me, the gap between us growing ever wider, tension spread from my neck to the soles of my feet, every muscle screaming in protest.

Maybe Verity was doing the right thing. She had too much at stake and I had nothing left to give.

Not trust. Not kindness. Sure as fuck not love.

I watched her red hair swoosh against the skin of her shoulders. Skin that felt like silk and smelled like sugar.

My hands twitched at my sides, wanting nothing more than to plunge my fingers through that river of fire, brave the heat that would surely burn me up.

I shouldn't have stayed to watch Verity perform. I shouldn't have set foot in the studio with her. And I definitely shouldn't have left with her after our session was over.

Music was my passion, and Verity's voice—damned if she didn't make me burn with passion for *her*.

Verity Moore was a star. The kind of musician that burned so brightly she would become the sun in her own universe. And I knew what it was like to be drawn into someone else's orbit. To give up everything for something as elusive and ephemeral as love. For Amelia, I left my home, my family, my city, my school.

I should know better now.

I should let Verity go.

I should stay away.

But right this minute, I didn't give a flying fuck about any of those shoulds or shouldn'ts.

The way I once felt about Amelia paled in comparison to my feelings for Verity now.

I needed to know if she tasted as good like she smelled. If her kisses were as sweet as her voice.

I needed to know how that fine ass of hers, bouncing just the tiniest bit as she walked away, would feel in my hands. Christ—I wanted to bite it.

The other day, I'd been the one to walk away. In my own fucking house, no less. Not sure how I managed it then, and I sure as fuck didn't think I could repeat it today. Because as I stood there, every inch between us was a weight sitting on my chest. Heavier and heavier until it hurt just to take a breath.

If I let Verity go, let her disappear behind one more closed door, I was going to suffocate.

If I went after her, if she let me catch her, let me touch her, let me take her—there would be consequences. With my track record—bad consequences.

But right now I didn't want to think about them. Didn't care about anything beyond me and her and *us*. Here and now.

Consequences could fuck off.

"Verity." My boots thudded against the stone walkway that led to her house, each one of my strides swallowing up three of hers. She turned, her confused gaze latching on to mine as I grabbed her by her tiny little waist, hoisting her up. "I haven't said goodbye yet." I kept walking, stopping only when I got to her front door, pressing her back against it as my hands slipped to her ass.

Confusion gave way to understanding, the desire coursing

through my veins mirrored in Verity's expression. "Oh. Me nei-ther." She wrapped her legs around me, making a noise that was somewhere between a whimper and a purr before parting her lips and staring greedily at mine. Sexiest damned invitation I'd ever received.

I didn't need my hands to hold Verity up, so with a last squeeze of her delicious ass, I slid them along her spine and into the hair at the base of her scalp, gathering the silken strands into a fist and tugging, eliciting a moan that shot straight to my dick. Goddamn, this girl could make sounds like no other. If they came in a bottle, they'd outsell Viagra.

"So, this is goodbye, then?" Verity's skin shone alabaster beneath the light of the moon. Flawless as fresh cream. I dipped my chin, giving a long, slow lick from the base of her neck to the lobe of her ear, drawing it inside my mouth, biting at the tender flesh until I was rewarded with a breathy gasp. Following the line of her jaw, I planted light kisses as I made my way to Verity's sweet, sweet mouth.

"Yeah." She tasted like a blend of fresh cider and the spicy margarita we'd just shared. "Fuck, you taste good." I groaned.

The first tentative flicker of her tongue against mine brought a rush of urgency, a primal need for more. So much more.

I nipped at her lips, slanting my mouth over hers until our tongues were tangled, the kiss deepening with each lick and taste and tug. Christ, I was hungry. Hungry for everything Verity was willing to give. Hungrier still for all she was holding back.

Our breaths became ragged pants, punctuated by moans and groans and the wet slide of tongues.

An orchestra of lust.

Verity's hands wrapped around my shoulders, her fingers kneading the muscles that were bunched and knotted, so tight and tense. Her fingernails dug in through my shirt, and I felt a flare of hostility for the fabric that shielded me from the scrape of her nails, the heat of her palms.

My body was a linked chain of hard lines and rigid planes. Rough stubble and calloused fingertips.

Verity was all soft hollows and sweet curves. Miles of satiny skin. Mounds of silky hair.

Her soft yielding to my hard.

Her sweet surrendering to my rough.

As if we'd been made for each other.

Two souls with just enough wrongs to make everything right.

Verity's hips shifted forward, the friction sending a tsunami of lust that drowned any other emotion or introspection. It crashed over me, leaving me clinging to the only thing that was solid and true. Verity. I didn't need to use my years of Latin to know what her name meant. Truth. That name fucking suited her.

"Dax." My name was a whimper, a plea, a promise.

On Verity's lips, my name was *everything*.

My response was a growl against her mouth. I could taste the desperation on her tongue. A need that matched my own. Her hands slid along my shoulder blades, making the jump to my arms, gripping my biceps.

"Verity." It almost hurt to say her name. Because I wasn't giving her truth. I was using her radiance, stealing her light to ease the darkness in my soul. All I had to offer was this—the sharp prick of pleasure. Temporary. Fleeting. But fuck if it wasn't good while it lasted.

And for now it would have to be good enough.

Because I couldn't stop.

One kiss wasn't enough.

Not nearly enough.

I pulled back to take in the beauty of her face. Lips swollen, cheeks flushed, flaming hair a messy tangle. Eyes bottle green, dreamy and unfocused. Most gorgeous woman I'd ever seen. "What are you doin' to me, True?"

Before Verity could even attempt to answer the question I hadn't meant to ask, my mouth was on hers again, one hard press before I moved down her jaw. I was losing my damned mind, chasing each one of Verity's breaths, each beat of her heart that fluttered against my tongue as I made my way down her neck, sinking my teeth into the gentle rise of her shoulder.

Freeing my hands, I slid them along the outer curve of her ribs, the indent of her waist, the flare of her hips. The hem of Verity's shirt a barrier begging to be breached.

I didn't care that we were still outside. Verity lived in a gated community, and there was a line of hedges that protected us from street view, neither of which would prevent a dedicated paparazzo from taking a shot. But I hadn't seen any tonight, and the sight of Verity herself was my only concern. Without any hesitation, I lifted her shirt, drawing it up and over her head, the silken tendrils of her hair a waterfall cascading over my forearms. "Fuck," I rasped, feasting on the sight of Verity's breasts displayed in a barely there bra of see-through lace, the tight furl of her nipples pushing through the thin fabric.

Palming the gorgeous swells, I brushed my thumbs over the lacy peaks. Verity gasped, her back arching, breasts pressing into my hands.

My dick pulsed angrily, furious at its zippered confinement. If I'd had even the slightest intention of holding out long enough to actually get inside Verity's house, it was swallowed by that gasp, disappearing into her pretty pout of a mouth.

Slipping my fingers beneath the lace cups, I edged them

down, responding like one of Pavlov's dogs to the sight of her nipples peeking over the top. Dusky pink peaks, they called out for my mouth, my lips, my tongue, my teeth.

Christ, they were sweet.

Verity's raspy moans and groans seeped into my eardrums as I worshipped her breasts, moving from one to the other, wanting to devour this girl. Her hands moved up my arms, nails scraping my neck in their haste to dive for my scalp, pulling and tugging at my hair. "Dax…please. I want—I want—"

Her words were chased away by my ragged groan as I reluctantly pulled away just enough to check on her, needing to know that she wanted this as badly as I did. "What do you want, True?"

Her eyes were glazed over, struggling to latch on to mine. I loved seeing her like this. Not quite in control. Her sharp edges worn smooth by the blunt force of desire. I dragged the back of my hand over the line of her jaw, her flawless skin a satin caress against my knuckles. Verity closed her eyes, lashes like spiky crescent moons on the rise of her cheekbone, rubbing her face against my hand. "You, Dax. This." And then her eyes snapped open in a fierce blaze of certainty. "I want this."

In that moment, had she asked, I would have cut out my heart and served it to her on a silver platter.

A heart that was charred and ruined. Unpalatable.

If she could see what I had to offer, she wouldn't want it.

But *this*? This I could give her.

It was *all* I could give her.

"You've got it," I growled, sealing my promise with a kiss that was hard and demanding,

I might hate myself tomorrow, but I wasn't fighting that battle tonight.

I widened my stance, Verity settling deeper on the swollen bulge between my legs. A pressure that hurt so good. Her pants were made of a light, thin material that had been printed in a wild pattern. The kind best pulled off by women with long legs and lean muscles. They'd been driving me crazy all day. The slightest bit transparent, so that in the right lighting I could see the shape of her thighs through the fabric. Covered and exposed at the same time. Teasing me with every step.

My tongue plunged beyond her lips, tracing every inch of that hot, needy mouth as she rocked herself against my jeans, knees pressed tight along my sides, working the friction like I wanted her to work me, my cock cheering her on with every pass.

It had been too long since I'd given in to lust. Too long since I beat off, just me and my dick. No guilt necessary.

Through her thin pants, I swore Verity could have ridden all the way over the finish line, but I was too selfish for that. Desperate to touch her, taste her. To take her there myself. My hand slipped between our bodies, plunging below her waistband and down the flat plane of her belly to the apex of her thighs. She was slick with her own heat, slippery with need. And the cry she gave when my fingers rolled over that pulsing bundle of nerves at her core—almost a keening wail—had the hair at the back of my neck standing on end.

I gave a satisfied grunt. "So good it hurts," I rasped, setting up a determined rhythm as her head lolled back against the door, the fierce prick of her nails scoring the nape of my neck.

A deep exhale vibrated her lithe frame, her body so hot, so pliant. So fucking mine.

I wasn't at all tempted to rush this, to rush her. I'd wait forever if it meant I could watch the orgasm break over Verity's face, rolling in on a tide of garbled grunts and sweet sighs, panting breaths and muscle quakes. My pleasure just as potent watching Verity find hers.

I could feel my dick dripping, smearing its excitement all over my thigh. I might shoot off inside my jeans like a teenager stumbling onto his first porn site. The thought of sinking into Verity's heat, gliding all the way home, until we were joined together like a jigsaw, was almost too much to take.

Even though I was touching her, Verity's hips grew frenzied, the tempo picking up, her hold on me—her hold over me—tightening. I bit down on the smooth skin of her shoulder, deliberately hard enough to leave a mark she would see in the morning. Damn, how I wanted to leave my mark on this girl.

In this girl.

I felt the second Verity's muscles drew tight, as if there were a coil winding and winding. Waiting.

She inhaled a quick breath, holding the air in her lungs until the thread snapped, and then all those muscles went slack as she cried out her release, trembling wildly in my arms. Movements that were beyond her control.

Something inside me snapped, too. Broke off completely. I felt it, like a missed step. A dropped chord. A distinct wrongness when only a moment ago *everything*—Verity in my arms, my name on her lips, her pleasure at my hands—felt so right.

I pulled my hand from her pants, tracing her lips with the wetness clinging to my fingertips.

Kissing it right off her.

Fucking delicious.

Regret was already bubbling up inside my gut as I deepened our kiss, holding Verity by the waist as she slid down my body to stand on her own feet.

She ended it, pushing against my shoulders with the heels of her hands. "That was one hell of a goodbye...but it shouldn't have happened." Her beautifully melodic voice was barely a broken whisper. "And—and it can't happen again."

A half-assed excuse was on the tip of my tongue, but I cut it off before the lie could shame me further. Instead I gave a slow shake of my head and forced myself to meet her gaze. "I know."

"It's just...If I—if *we* become a thing, you know what people will think."

"Yeah." My shoulders sagged. "We wouldn't have worked out anyway."

Green-tipped daggers of hurt pointed their blades at me. "Thanks."

I took a step back, knowing she was reading my response in an entirely different way than I'd meant it. Meanwhile, my dick thumped my zipper in a rage. *You fucking fool. What are you doing?* The energy between us still blazed brighter than the full moon above, and I fought against gravity to take another step. "I'm sorry, Verity. You deserve better."

Chapter Fourteen

Dax

"No way." My answer was automatic, a hard fucking N-O.

Unfortunately Travis Taggert didn't know the meaning of the word. "Did you listen to the track?" he asked.

"I don't need to listen to it. I was there."

"Fine. You know who did?" No. And I didn't want to. But that didn't stop Travis from telling me. "Your label. They fucking loved it. I'm talking full-on *loved* it."

Pride welled up in my chest. I couldn't help it. Together, Verity and I had created an awesome fucking song. And it felt good to know others thought so, too.

Even though I wished it had never seen the light of day.

Travis was still talking. "The team working on Verity's album loved it so much they took it to the team that works on your albums. They loved it so much they took it up the chain, all the way to the head of the damn company. And he loved it, too. They don't want the acoustic version as just a fan extra. They want to release it as a single. And they're sending it out to Hollywood studios right now, looking to get a big-budget movie tie-in. Dax, this song's got legs. If it takes off—and it will—Verity's fans are going to want, and deserve, to hear it on the tour."

"They can have it. The song is hers. Verity can perform it with another guitarist though. It doesn't have to be me." I knew I was being unreasonable. Sitting onstage with Verity for one song wasn't a big ask. Especially since she was singing *my* song.

"It's the optics, Dax. A link between two acts that most people wouldn't think belong on the same stage—it's brilliant."

A harsh chuckle rumbled from my lungs. "We *don't* belong on the same stage." We didn't belong on the same tour, either. But that was a battle I'd lost, so I was dealing with it.

"There's only so many times I can tell you that you're being shortsighted." I heard the sound of friction and I imagined my manager smoothing his palm over his head as he paced the length of his office. "But it's your loss. I'll tell the label they'll have to go with plan B."

I didn't know what plan B was, but it sounded innocuous enough. I sighed, the tension in my shoulders easing. "Thanks. I appreciate—"

"Maybe it's for the best. You know how well Jett plays to the audience. The fans will eat it up."

I pulled up short, my fingertips turning white as I squeezed the phone. "Wait... What?"

"Just don't bitch at me when Jett makes your song his own. They're going to bring him into the studio to rerecord—"

"Are you fucking kidding me? We killed that song. And it's *my* song. *My* version is staying on Verity's album."

"It only stays if you're willing to commit. Plan B is Jett. You know he'll be perfectly willing to do a few events with Verity. I'll have Piper get a hashtag trending—"

I broke in as Travis started mumbling to himself, already coming up with a marketing plan for his next celebrity power couple. "Jesus. Fine. I'll do it. You're not dumping my track. I'll do it."

"Are you sure, because—"

I hated how Travis already seemed disappointed. As if he'd realized that Jett was a better fit for Verity and he'd rather make the switch. "Yeah, I'm sure. Verity and I made a great song together, and the music should come first. The track stays on her album. If that means I have to perform the song with her while we're on tour, so be it. But don't turn us into a couple, Travis. She doesn't want anyone thinking she slept her way onto our tour, and I agree with her."

"Sure. No hashtag. And I'll tell the label to keep your track."

I ended the call and groaned. The truth was, the thought of sharing a stage with Verity…Fuck. It got me nearly as hot and hard as the idea of sharing a bed with her.

What the fuck was I getting myself into?

Had my past come full circle? Was I doomed to repeat it again?

Because I sure as hell didn't want to.

The stage—any stage—was sacred space to a musician. Even more so when you grew up around Lincoln Center and Carnegie Hall and Juilliard. There's a give-and-take, a partnership, a kind of magic that happens beneath the lights, and it carries over to what happens after the encore, in real life. A little bit of that magic remains, and your expectations are different. Bigger somehow. Amplified.

When things don't work out, the betrayal is bigger, too. So loud it reverberates in your soul for years. A noise that won't be silenced.

Damn Travis for getting me involved.

And damn Verity for making me want to *be* involved.

This was show biz. Nothing lasted here. Nothing was real.

Verity Moore would open for Nothing but Trouble on this tour.

Six months. A hundred sound checks, a hundred shows, a thousand interviews.

Fucking hell.

I had no doubt she'd be headlining her own tour next year. We were a stepping-stone for her. A pit stop.

Then she would move on.

And I wanted that for her. I wanted to watch Verity blaze a path across the sky like the shooting star she was destined to be.

But I knew exactly what would happen if I got too close.

I'd be incinerated.

Verity

"He said *what*?"

"Yes. He said yes." Piper's voice was perfectly clear, and yet I still pulled the phone away from my ear, checking the screen to be sure I hadn't accidentally dropped the call.

"Verity, are you there? Is this a bad connection?"

I swallowed past the tightness in my throat. "Yeah, I'm here."

"Okay, good. Now that Dax is on board, the label is thinking of dropping 'Bombshell Rebel' before your album is finished, to get buzz going. So I've scheduled a…"

I tuned out as Piper continued talking. She would send me a detailed itinerary as soon as we hung up and add everything to our shared calendar anyway. This call was just a formality. Which was a good thing because I was still struggling to absorb her news.

I'd been surprised when Travis mentioned that the label wanted Dax and me to perform "Bombshell Rebel" during the tour. But I had been betting that Dax would turn them down flat. There was no way he would want to share the spotlight with me.

Which was why I'd agreed to it so easily. I'd assumed Dax would say no and that would be the end of it.

Apparently not.

Despite my nerves, the thought of performing with Dax again had my veins thrumming with excitement.

But it had me feeling uncomfortable, too. Like Dax was doing me a favor and now I'd be in his debt.

Judging from the other night, it was a debt I'd be only too happy to repay.

The pleasure definitely all mine.

I felt like a virginal freshman with a crush on the star quarterback. What would it take to pique his interest? And what would it take to maintain that interest?

But I was hardly a virgin. And I'd never had time for these silly, lovesick emotions when I was in high school. Not that I spent much time there.

My mother had finally stopped the charade of pretending my education actually mattered the day I turned sixteen. A fact no one besides Dax knew. High school dropout didn't fit the image of the girl I'd pretended to be on *The Show*.

Yet another reason to be intimidated around Dax. The best performing arts high school in the country. Then Juilliard. That he didn't actually graduate didn't matter at all. Just thinking about his skills being honed and developed for so many years made me feel inadequate. What did I know about music, really? I could sing, yes. But that was all. I knew nothing about chord changes or amplification effects or layering vocals with instrumentation.

Those two hours with Dax had shown me a side to music I'd never been exposed to—the technical aspect of creating art. Dax had been so confident, so professional. He wasn't passively following orders; he was throwing out suggestions and making adjustments as if he had a sound board in his head, a way of separating out all the individual components of a song and rearranging them in infinitely different ways.

It had been impressive.

And a reminder of how sorely lacking my own capabilities were.

Recording with Dax had been excruciating. And also, somehow, the most incredibly amazing musical experience ever. Dax had the kind of talent that was instinctive, innate. But he was also a Juilliard-trained musical savant. I learned more during our two-hour session than I had in my entire career.

How was I going to repeat that, night after night, in front of an audience of thousands?

Answer—I had no fucking clue.

How was I even going to look Dax in the face again after what happened at my front door the other night? I'd wanted him so badly I hadn't even asked him inside. And then I had shoved him away, proof of the orgasm he'd given me still on his fingers.

Same answer—I had no fucking clue.

"So, are you good with all that?"

"Um, sure. Of course."

"Great. I'll be at your house tomorrow morning with the stylist. It's never too early to lock down your red-carpet looks."

Chapter Fifteen

Dax

So, is it true? You're jumping ship?" Jett shook his head, a wide grin splitting his face in two. "Bros before hoes, or have you learned nothing from me after all these years?"

I rolled my eyes and punched his shoulder. "Shut the fuck up."

"I'm telling you, man. First you're recording with her, then you're on her album, and now I hear you're gonna share the stage with her. What the fuck—you looking to start singing duets or some shit?"

I hadn't told anyone about the song Verity and I had performed together, or the fact that it would be incorporated into her act—especially not my bandmates. Frankly, I'd been hoping that if I didn't say it out loud the situation would magically disappear. But no, our label's publicity machine had gone into overdrive, dropping the song early and hyping the shit out of it. It shot to number one on the charts immediately. "You're just pissed it's not you."

Jett grunted. "Fuck, yeah. That girl is fine. If Travis wouldn't cut off my dick, I'd be all over her ass already."

If any part of Jett touched Verity's ass, Travis would be too busy wrestling the knife out of my hands to inflict any damage on Jett himself.

"Not an option," I growled, shooting Jett a death glare.

He raised his hands, palms up. "Yeah, I was there when Travis laid down the law. Not that any of us are good at following rules, but I'll do my best to stick to the chicks I can have security block if they turn crazy." He waggled his eyebrows. "Not sure Verity could handle me once she had a taste, anyway."

"Jesus Christ, enough about Verity!" I didn't mean to explode, and I knew it was a mistake the second I yelled her name. I was the even-tempered one of our group. The one who'd rather nurse a beer alone in the corner of the room than be the center of attention, chicks hanging off me, promising anything I could want and nothing worth wanting. I didn't get all hot and defensive about a girl. Not since Amelia.

But Verity Moore had me hot all right. And the thought of Jett—or anyone—touching her, incited a rage within my chest I hadn't known I was capable of.

Jett slanted his eyes at me, arms crossed over his chest. "Holy shit."

I looked away, picking up my phone and pretending to do…something. "I don't know what you're talking about."

"You sneaky bastard," Jett murmured, not a trace of animosity in his voice as he clapped me on the shoulder. "Good for you. It's about time you did something worth getting shit for."

I shrugged him off, the unsettled feeling that had been dogging my steps for the past few weeks flaring back up. A sense that something—someone—was missing from my life. Or maybe I was just in need of a hard dose of common sense. "Not doin' anything."

Jett only gripped me harder, tugging at me to turn around. I did, and was instantly faced with his obvious concern. "Not sure that I believe you—but if you're not, you damn well should be. How long has it been, D? How long since you let loose? Got with a girl—any girl, for fuck's sake—and actually let yourself live in the moment? You're young and rich and almost as good-looking as me. You should be eating pussy with every meal."

I shifted on my feet, trying to find my center of gravity as I met Jett's defiant stare. I wasn't seeing his face though. The image of Verity the last time I saw her—the night we recorded "Bombshell Rebel"—was all too vivid. Her skin flushed from my touch, lips swollen from my kisses, hair a riot of red that had felt so damn good wrapped up in my fist.

Jett's eyes widened, and he poked me in the chest, grinning like a fool, the cleft in his chin that chicks drooled over on full display. "Aw, yeah. You took off your monk's robes for her, didn't you? Showed her some of what you've been keeping under wraps, huh?"

There had barely been any unwrapping, but the experience had been so damn memorable, it was permanently seared in my brain. I saw Verity's perfect breasts every time I closed my eyes. Tasted her on my tongue with every breath. Felt her body tremble in my arms with every movement. "Wasn't like that."

He choked back a laugh. "Uh-oh. Has it been so long that you forgot what to do? Need a few tips from an expert? I've got tricks that could really—"

I gave Jett a shove, although it was impossible to be mad at him. The guy was rude and crude and over-the-top audacious. But he was my brother in every way but blood. I shook my head, the glare I'd been going for softening. "I think I'll pass. Verity's on our tour. I'm on her album. We'll be sharing a stage together. It's like my ex all over again."

Jett frowned, thinking for a moment. Then he shrugged. "So kick her off the tour. Travis will get us another opening act."

Like it was that simple.

Like I would pull that kind of dick move.

I roughed agitated hands through my hair. "Not gonna do that." If I was willing to sink that low, I didn't deserve Verity at all. This tour was going to be huge for her career, and I couldn't—wouldn't—fuck her over like that. "Besides, I have unfinished business I need to wrap up before I can consider any-thing beyond a one-night stand—and you know I'm not into those. Maybe we'll get together after the tour. After I get my shit straightened out."

"I'll never understand you, D. Variety is the spice of life and all that. And…after the tour? That's what…a year from now? Scratch that—longer. You really wanna wait that long?" He gave me a serious, searching look. "Dude, you think she's not gonna get hit on left and right? That she'll take up knitting while you and your dick sulk in a corner?"

A deep, unsatisfied sigh shuddered through my lungs. "Jett, for my own sanity, I need to draw a line between what happens onstage and what happens off. Last time the two got confused, I moved three thousand miles away and pulled a one-eighty with my career. If I let those lines blur again and it gets all fucked up like I'm sure it will, what am I going to do? Take up bongos in Jamaica? Play the accordion in Austria? Right now Verity is too damn close to everything that matters to me. If things blow up, I can't have the fallout tainting my entire life."

He threw up his hands in a show of irritation. "I'd call you a pussy, but that would be an insult to the most beautiful thing on earth. When did you become such a wuss? The tour won't kick off for months. If you're so sure you and Verity will flame out, why not fuck her out of your system now? You'll have plenty of time to get back in the friend zone before our first show."

He grabbed his car keys and headed for the door. "Gotta go. Unlike you, I have someone waiting for me."

Verity

The number on my screen was unfamiliar, but I answered it because Piper said a journalist she trusted would be calling for my comment on the latest Verity Moore scandal du jour. I picked up the paper with the carefully crafted statement Piper had e-mailed me. This call was so that the reporter could tag their column as an EXCLUSIVE INTERVIEW.

Since "Bombshell Rebel" dropped, the Twitterverse had exploded with speculation that Jack Lester was the man who had "shamed me."

All the gossip sites and magazines were running with the story, and getting back and forth to the studio to finish my album had been an exercise in evading the paparazzi.

My label was thrilled. For them it was free publicity.

Travis and Piper didn't seem to mind, either.

For me it was a nightmare. The last thing I wanted was anyone asking about my *relationship* with Jack.

"Verity, can you hear me?"

Shit. Not the journalist. "Hey, Mom. Did you get a new number?"

"Bruce and I are on that cruise to Alaska. You remember I told you about it." I didn't, but she had mentioned having a new boyfriend. There was always a new boyfriend. "I dropped my phone and will have to do without it until I get back. What is this I hear about a song—'Bombshell something-or-other'?"

And just like that, my day went from bad to worse. "'Bombshell Rebel.'"

"What?" The connection was cutting out.

"'Bombshell Rebel.' With an *r.*"

"Please tell me you di—"

"Mom…Mom?"

"—en I get back."

The call cut off, and my head dropped forward on my shoulders. I took a shallow, shuddering breath. And then I stored Bruce's number in my contacts. If she called again, at least I'd know not to answer.

I had no idea how long the cruise would last, but I might as well take full advantage of it. No badgering phone calls or Face-Timing. No evasive answers or outright lies.

And once she returned, between the release of "Bombshell Rebel" and the announcement about my upcoming tour with Nothing but Trouble, there would be no denying that I'd taken control of my own career.

No denying that Travis Taggert was now my manager.

She was still my mother, though. A role that had never been enough for her.

We were definitely due for a long talk when she returned. Whenever that was.

* * *

Tonight was the party to celebrate the official announcement of the Nothing but Trouble/Verity Moore world tour, and even though it had been a week since my call with the journalist denying that "Bombshell Rebel" had anything to do with Jack, the rumor mill was still going strong.

And that wasn't the only rumor people were talking about. Despite Travis agreeing not to promote us as a couple, our fans had done it on their own. Speculation about Dax and me—now known as Daxity—had been going crazy since our song dropped. There were sightings of us everywhere, which was pretty surprising given that I hadn't seen him since he left me at my front door in a post-orgasmic haze.

It was exactly what I didn't want. People whispering that I'd gotten on Nothing but Trouble's tour, or their label, only because I was screwing the band's guitarist. I hadn't seen Dax in weeks, but according to the tabloids we were inseparable. I had pushed away the one man I could ever remember wanting precisely so the indictment couldn't be made.

But apparently it didn't matter. I was getting all of the heat but none of the benefits.

Between the accusations of sending a message through a song I hadn't written and pursuing a man I'd pushed away—I was fed up with Tinseltown and I'd been back only a few months.

I had tried to play by their rules, but I was being accused of cheating anyway.

And now, tonight, maybe I was finally realizing that there was nothing I could do about them. About the rumors, the gossip, the headlines. Those were things beyond my control.

I just wasn't quite sure what, if anything, I was going to do about it.

Piper had been buzzing around me all day, driving me nuts. Although, now that she'd shared the news of her pregnancy, I'd bitten my tongue.

It made perfect sense, of course. Piper's exhaustion, not drinking, and peeing all the freaking time. I had been so wrapped up in my own world that I hadn't put it all together.

But damn—Piper was the last person I'd expect to have any kind of craziness in her private life. I mean, she never really talked about her life outside of work. And she was always so perfect, so polished. Her blond hair straight and sleek, no fly-aways for her. Never merely on time, always early. And organized to a fault—color-coded calendar, lists for everything, her phone with scheduled alerts every other minute. Piper Hastings didn't miss a thing, and I was damn lucky to be working with her.

The woman planned for everything, including deviations from The Plan. Which was why, despite all the signs, I never imagined Piper would have an unplanned pregnancy.

And she refused to say who the father was.

What the what?

On one hand, Piper's situation made her seem human, at least. Like, no matter how many to-do lists we make, life was a tsunami none of us could control.

And on the other, I was trying to be on my best behavior. Piper didn't need me making her life any more difficult than it already was.

Of course, this only had me more on edge. I could vent with PR Piper, but now that she was Pregnant Piper, I needed to behave.

Nervous anxiety had festered in the pit of my stomach all day, and it needed to stay locked down for at least the next few hours.

For me this was a work event, not a party.

It wasn't long ago that I'd walked into Travis's office, unsure whether he would see any potential in my career. In the past few months "Verity Moore, disgraced pop princess" had been erased, replaced with: "Verity Moore, the pop princess currently taking the music scene by storm after linking up with rocker Dax Hughes." At least, when it wasn't "Verity Moore, former child star turned latest #metoo victim."

It was as if no one believed I could make it on my own. That I needed to ride on a man's coattails or a trendy cause to be relevant.

Maybe one day I would be brave enough to publicly acknowledge my experiences…but today wasn't that day.

"Pulling up now," I heard Piper say into her earpiece, jolting me from my own thoughts. "Verity, remember to walk slowly. Let them get shots of your dress from every angle. Dax is in the car right behind us. Just wait for him at the step and repeat."

The car came to a stop, and I edged forward in my seat. "Why do I have to wait—"

The door opened, and my question was cut off by the screams of awaiting fans and paparazzi. Plastering a smile on my face, I stood on my Swarovski-encrusted heels and took small steps along the red carpet, feeling like an idiot. This wasn't the Grammys, for god's sake.

I had said as much to Travis, but he'd only laughed, reminding me that this was as close as many of the people integral to my career would get to a star-studded Hollywood event. Corporate sponsors, venue owners, music journalists, advertising executives, and radio DJs. We were all just small pieces in a big machine, and every wheel and cog needed its share of oil.

Lights exploded around me, the world a bright blur.

Verity, show us your dress! Verity, over here! Who are you wearing? Verity, over here! Verity, can you give us a spin? Verity, over here! Verity, show us your shoes!

Look right. Look left. Spin. Step. Smile. Repeat.

Verity, are you throwing shade at Jack Lester with your new song? Verity, are you and Dax a couple? Is he the reason you're on the tour? Verity, are you angry Jack Lester didn't offer you a role in his new show?

I thought I was prepared for a return to the spotlight, but my fancy dress and flawless makeup were no shield against the onslaught of questions about Jack. I wasn't prepared for my former producer to intrude on this night, not at all. Suddenly, I was right back at J.J.s—coffee in one hand, juice in the other. The urge to run overwhelming.

I lost my sense of direction, my pupils burning from staring into the bright lights, cheeks already aching. I froze, my muscles tight and tense. Not even knowing which way to go.

A roar from the crowd drew my attention, and out of the blinding light came a dark silhouette, closer and closer until all I could see was Dax's crooked grin.

A surge of relief swept aside my embarrassment over my behavior the last time we were together. Maybe I didn't deserve Dax, but right now I *needed* him.

And when his arm wrapped around me, sliding over the bare skin of my back, I had to bite back a gasp at the spark of electricity that lit into me. A genuine current that moved from his body into mine. Adrenaline spiked, my pulse chasing after it. Joy following at a distance, its steps tentative and uneven.

We posed together for a long minute, and then Dax ushered me into the building. Once the shouts of the paparazzi had been muted by a closed door, I faced him, locking my knees so I wouldn't crumple at the sight of his face. Tanned skin and dark eyebrows set off those mysterious eyes of his, complicated colors that swirled inside his stare. Centered between a strong nose and jaw, his mouth was full and wide, the corners usually turning down slightly despite a seam that went straight across.

But right now those corners were pointing toward his cheekbones, showing a flash of white teeth. A smile entirely directed at me, filled with a warmth that penetrated to my bones, completely overshadowing my body's automatic response at the mention of Jack Lester. "You still with me?" Dax asked.

I pulled myself away from my thoughts and blinked up at Dax's concerned expression. "Yes, sorry. I forgot how obnoxious the paparazzi can be. There's no question they won't ask."

"You can't let them get under your skin."

"I know. But…"

"But what?"

"When it feels like everyone is saying you don't deserve to be here, it's almost impossible not to wonder if they're right." Not about Jack Lester, of course. I knew exactly where I stood on that front. But when it came to Dax…Was I really worthy of sharing the stage with him? How could I open for Nothing but Trouble when my only experience was singing on a TV show?

Dax's brows pushed together, making a vertical indent above his nose. "There's always going to be talk, but you have to tune it out. Because none of it matters. You have the most beautifully soulful voice I've ever heard, Verity. That's all the reason you need."

My breath caught in the back of my throat, and for a moment I couldn't breathe at all. "You didn't always think that. Admit it."

"I was wrong."

Again I found myself surprised by what had come from Dax's mouth. "A man who can admit when he's wrong. I'm impressed."

He gave a wry smile, sadness swirling inside his eyes. "I've made plenty of mistakes. Might as well own up to 'em."

I bobbed my neck in a shaky nod. "Yeah. Me too." Right then I wished we were someplace else, anywhere else. The charged air between us was vibrating with unspoken secrets. Secrets that might feel a little less burdensome if we dared to share them. A question I didn't intend to ask slipped past my lips. "How about the last time we saw each other...? Was that a mistake?"

"Shouldn't I be asking you that?"

I swallowed heavily. "What we did, or what we didn't do?"

"You tell me."

"I—"

The door behind us opened. Jett stepped inside, looking from Dax to me. "If this fool doesn't figure out how to seal the deal, you come find me, Verity."

Dax offered a good-natured "Fuck off" as Jett walked away. But the brief moment of introspection we had shared was over. He offered his elbow and we joined the party.

Within minutes we had drinks in our hands and were surrounded by industry influencers whose support was vital to both our careers. "There you are." Delaney suddenly materialized at my side, drawing me into a warm hug. "It's so good to see a friendly face at these things."

I returned her wide grin. "I feel the same way."

She gave Dax a squeeze, too. "Would you mind rescuing Shane? He's gotten drawn into a conversation with a radio station owner about the new FCC regulations, and I swear he might just fall asleep standing up."

Dax's lips twitched. "I can take a hint. I'll leave you two alone."

The second his back was turned, Delaney lowered her voice and leaned in close to me. "So…you and Dax?"

"No," I whispered. "We just walked in together."

She took a small sip from her wineglass, regarding me quizzically over the rim. "You were practically steaming up the window over here."

I was saved from answering when I spotted Travis across the room and he waved me over. Feeling relieved, I scurried away from Delaney and spent the next hour chatting with anyone Travis introduced me to. The man seemed to know the name and business interests of everyone in the room.

I was several minutes in to a conversation about copyright and royalty concerns in today's streaming-driven industry when I spotted Piper on the terrace. Something about her stance, both hands gripping the railing, shoulders hunched over, made me want to check on her. Extricating myself, I slipped outside. "Thought I'd join you out here for a bit. You okay?"

"Just taking in the view." Her voice sounded strangled, and she wiped at her eyes before looking at me.

"What's wrong?" Piper was always so put together, so polished, catching her with wet lashes felt like an intrusion.

She sniffed, tucking an errant blond strand behind her ear. "Nothing. Hormones."

"You sure?"

"Yes. And you shouldn't be out here worrying about me. This is your big night."

I glanced back at the room filled with strangers, spotting Dax talking to a stunning brunette in a bright red dress. I knew Dax wasn't mine, but my stomach clenched anyway. "Is it over yet?" I asked.

Piper choked out a laugh. "Has Travis made his speech?"

"No."

"Then it's not over." She looked back through the windows, squinting slightly. "But I think we're almost there. Come on."

I followed her back inside to find Travis standing in the corner of the room, on a raised platform where a DJ had been playing Nothing but Trouble songs interspersed with remixed versions of the ones I'd recorded for *The Show*, edited to be less "teen queen" and more "pop princess with a hint of rebellious rock chick." And, of course, the song I'd recorded with Dax.

"...we're thrilled to have everyone here, celebrating the upcoming tour with rock's hottest band and pop's most intriguing new talent. The Nothing but Trouble/Verity Moore tour is a once-in-a-generation opportunity. We're not going to have any live performances tonight, but I'd like us to recognize the men and woman who have made tonight possible. Verity Moore, Shane Hawthorne, Dax Hughes, Jett Evans, and of course, Landon Cox—who couldn't join us tonight but will be back from a long-planned vacation well before the tour kicks off."

After the applause and whispered speculation about Landon's whereabouts died down, I was swept up in more conversations with people I didn't know, moving through the crowd like dry seaweed pushed along the beach by a hot ocean breeze. At one point I caught Piper trying to hide an enormous yawn. It didn't take much for Delaney and me to convince her to go home.

No matter where I was or who I was talking to, I never lost sight of Dax. He'd managed to escape the brunette who had clung to his side for quite a while. One of the tallest men in the room, Dax pulled my gaze like a magnet with his dark, glossy mane. It was almost embarrassing, how many times he caught me staring at him. At least, it would have been—if I hadn't caught him doing the same thing to me.

The man was charming and charismatic, whether he was speaking to the wife of an industry executive who'd had a few too many cocktails or a journalist trying to convince him to give an exclusive interview.

All the while, everything I'd been feeling—relief, desire, joy—had been building and blending. By the time Dax had maneuvered us into a quiet corner, I was near to bursting.

"Who knew you could be such a charmer?" I said softly.

A low chuckle rumbled from Dax's throat, those green-gold eyes sweeping over my body. I flushed beneath his appreciative perusal, my nipples furling in pleasure and pushing against the beaded fabric of my dress. The designer creation was fun and flirty, and I'd be lying if I said I hadn't had Dax in mind when I'd agreed to wear it tonight.

Starting at my bare shoulders, he took in the low V of my white dress, which didn't allow for a bra, then the rows of tiny pleats that ended at midthigh, before continuing to my strappy silver heels. He repeated the process in reverse, his eyes finally coming back to my face, lips wearing a sexy grin. "You haven't made it easy. In fact, you've made it damned near impossible to look at anyone but you."

"You clean up pretty well yourself." I wasn't going to get any points for originality, but as least I managed to speak at all. The way Dax was looking at me, as if he wanted to pull me into the nearest closet and tear my dress right off me, had me feeling tongue-tied and practically paralyzed with lust.

Dax was wearing a suit with no tie, his crisp white shirt open at the neck, dark hair just the right amount of shaggy, chiseled jawline shadowed from stubble. Looking much more comfortable in his skin than he had the night we first met in New York.

I wanted to borrow some of his confidence. A part of me was

expecting someone to tap me on the shoulder and escort me out the door. Tell me that I didn't deserve to be here.

"Did you come to rescue me again?" I asked, only half kidding. There was no jerk cornering me, but I'd run out of small talk an hour ago and the evening had become tedious.

"Maybe it's your turn for that." His voice was a gritted rasp, like the admission took effort.

I titled my head to the side, staring into Dax's eyes. "I didn't know bad-boy rockers needed rescuing."

He sighed, closing his eyes for a moment before lifting his lashes once again and staring at me with a renewed sense of urgency. "That makes two of us."

A tremble shook my spine, goose bumps breaking out on my skin. There was a beat of silence, and the song changed, Dax's soulful guitar riffs pooling in my ears like the sweetest honey. Our song. He lifted his hands. "May I have this dance?"

I stepped into Dax's arms, feeling like I was floating on air as my palms slid up his shirt to wrap around his neck, his hands gently riding my hips. "Sing to me," he whispered in my ear.

I pulled back just enough to look him in the face. "I am singing."

He shook his head. "No, not through the speakers. Now."

A wave of something—infatuation, desire, happiness—smashed into me. I wobbled on my feet, Dax steadying me with a smile.

And even though my recorded voice was perfectly audible in the small vestibule between the coatroom and restrooms, I raised my chin and opened my mouth. Singing along to my own track.

> *Long time ago,*
> *Someone picked me*
> *Painted me*

Dressed me up and shamed me
Turned me into a bombshell

Every time I sang the words, I was amazed that someone had written a song so perfectly tailored to me. I'd been so absorbed by my own reaction, it hadn't occurred to me that anyone would read into the lyrics and assume that "someone" was Jack Lester.

But it should have.

I'd asked Travis to put me in touch with the songwriter. He said he'd "look into it and get back to me." Code for at-the-bottom-of-my-priority-list, don't-hold-your-breath.

I'm a shell
Cracked and broken
The truth has spoken
My heart is beating, needing
I'm no bombshell
Look and listen
Watch me rebel

The powerful lyrics fortified me as the music wrapped around us, lifting us up, pushing us together. A world made up of his guitar and my voice coming through an overhead speaker, his voice and mine mingling in real time. Our two hearts pulsing to the same beat.

"Bombshell Rebel" wasn't about my mother. And it wasn't about Jack. The song was about *me*. And I was done letting anyone else ruin another minute of *my* life.

Dax joined in, crooning the words as he stared straight into my eyes.

I wanted the song to last forever.

It didn't though. Three minutes and twenty-three seconds was exactly what we got.

And when the last note trailed off, in the suspended moment when there was only silence, Dax dipped his head and took a quick breath, inhaled oxygen whispering along my cheek as it entered his mouth.

Breathing me in.

This man could swallow me whole. Consume me. Own me.

And I might just let him.

All the parts of me that had tried so hard to resist the man in front of me finally gave up the fight. I was a rose at dawn, preening beneath the sun's rays.

"Will you take me home?"

Chapter Sixteen

Dax

There was a chaotic storm churning between Verity and me. A wildness that had grown bigger and more inevitable over the course of tonight's elegant event. Even though I knew we would only end in disaster, I wanted to bask in the warmth of Verity's smile, savor her sweet scent, rejoice at the desire shining from her eyes.

"Fuck yeah."

We didn't bother with goodbyes. I caught the eye of a man with a jawbone microphone at his ear, and he muttered something into it. By the time we got to the door, my driver had pulled up out front. There were still a few paparazzi outside, their cameras flashing like crazy. They knew the gossip rags would be shitting all over themselves for pictures of Verity and me leaving together.

Well, they were in luck because I wasn't forfeiting a single minute with her tonight.

Sliding in after Verity, I was engulfed in the scent that was so intrinsic to her. Vanilla and cloves. The girl was practically edible.

The car pulled away from the curb. I shrugged out of my jacket and shifted on the bench seat, drinking her in like a glass of water after a day in the desert.

So goddamn tempting. Every part of her. Her face with its symmetrical features and creamy skin. Her long legs, tiny waist, and lush cleavage. Her voice that didn't need any accompaniment at all. Verity's looks were a lure on their own, but I was most attracted to the little glimpses of a woman who had seen the worst of too many people but was still willing to take chances. To take a chance on me.

She blinked up at me now, fidgeting self-consciously beneath my steady gaze. "What?"

"Nothing."

"Do I have something on my face?" She opened her purse, pulled out a compact. "Something in my teeth?"

I slid my hand over hers. "No. You're beautiful."

She brushed off the compliment with a disparaging roll of her eyes. "No, really. What is it?"

I thought about how to answer her for a moment, deciding between an easy lie or a brush-off. What came out instead was the truth. "I haven't wanted anything but music in a long time." A deep groan wrenched from me as I roughed fingers through my hair. "Never planned on wanting another woman—not any one in particular. But I want you, Verity. So fucking badly."

Verity didn't stare at me like I'd lost my mind. Instead she looked away, down at the fingers twisting together in her lap.

When her voice finally emerged, it was quiet but firm. "You're the first person I've ever wanted to sleep with."

My heart stuttered to a stop, then jumped back into action, frantically trying to catch up with itself. "Wh—"

"That came out wrong. I've had sex before—I've just never had moments where it was something I genuinely wanted. It just kind of…" Verity paused, streetlights illuminating her face in quick streaks of light interspersed with moments of darkness. I read her expression in pulses. Brief impressions of sadness and confusion. Rawness. Vulnerability. An openness that ate at my defenses like acid. "Sex is something I've done, something that's happened to me. It's never been something I've craved, something I've initiated."

I tried to read between the lines, to understand exactly what she was saying. Were the rumors about Verity and Jack Lester true? There were too many shades of gray in her words. Was Verity talking about bad sex? Or sex she regretted the morning after? Had she been *forced*?

The first two possibilities made my hands curl into fists at my sides, my muscles itching from anger. The last one, though, sent fury streaking through my veins, a desire to grab whatever man had hurt her by the throat and not let go.

"Verity." Her name was a groan. And a plea for truth.

She slid her hand over mine, squeezing my fingers. "You make me want to know what it's like to want, just as much as I'm wanted. To take, just as much as I'm giving."

Her unease filled the car, burning the back of my throat with each breath. How had this gorgeous girl, who could command a stage with nothing more than a microphone in her hands, never owned her sexuality? "You haven't been with a man, then. Not one worth a damn."

She glanced at me, her tongue darting across full lips, want etched into her finely drawn features. "Show me how it can be, Dax. How it should be."

My dick swelled, eager to fulfill Verity's every wish. But there was a sliver of my soul that held back, not wanting to be just another asshole who took advantage of someone who deserved a hell of a lot more respect than she'd been given.

"You would still be settling, Verity. I need you to know that. I'll fuck you so good, no one else will live up to my standards." In my head, the words were sarcastic and playful. But as soon as I said them, I realized I was dead serious. My eyes skimmed luminous skin I was dying to touch. "And then where would that leave you?"

Verity dragged in a breath, her emerald eyes holding mine. "I guess if you're as good as you say you are, it would leave me pretty damn satisfied."

I barked out a laugh. *Jesus.* "Our tour starts in a few months—whatever we are to each other has to end by then."

"So you're already thinking about more than just one night?" She arched an eyebrow, a teasing pout on her mouth.

I slipped my hands beneath Verity's thighs, gathering her peach of an ass in my hands and sweeping her onto my lap. "One night wouldn't be enough."

She wrapped her arms around my neck, touching her forehead to mine. "The one who broke your heart—she was a musician, wasn't she? Someone you performed with?"

I gave a brusque nod. "She was. Until some schmuck filled her head with all kinds of crap about moving to Hollywood and becoming a star. Then the life we had wasn't good enough for her anymore. I followed her to L.A., wanting to win her back. Instead I found Shane, Landon, and Jett. Never returned to New York, or to the kind of music I'd grown up playing,"

"So when you lost her, you lost your love of classical music?"

"For me they were intertwined."

Verity's bright eyes dimmed with sadness, and I could see she was struggling for a response. When it came, her words were soft, tentative. "And you're worried that if we blow up while we're on the road together, it will sour the band, or at least the entire tour, for you."

I winced at the truth, reluctant to stare it in the face right now. "We've got better things to do with our mouths than talk."

Verity

The air-conditioning in the car was on full blast, but that wasn't what was making my skin feel paper thin and hypersensitive. Every word, every breath Dax and I had shared was pressing on me, sharp and heavy.

I wanted to wrap myself in his embrace, lose myself in his kisses. Let the heat of our lust incinerate our doubts and resistance until there was nothing left but charred embers. Unrecognizable. Inconsequential.

Was it possible?

I had no idea, but damn it, I wanted to try.

And in the second before our mouths met, before I felt the slide of his tongue along mine, I almost pulled back.

I barely knew Dax. He barely knew me. But this invisible thread between us—I knew it deep in my soul. It was universal, primal, powerful.

There was a chance, a slim chance, that thread would make us stronger. Better together than apart. But was it worth the risk?

Dax growled, a gritty, possessive sound that traveled straight to the pulsing heat between my thighs, the flare completely destroying my capacity for rational thought. I didn't even realize the car had stopped until the driver pulled the door open.

Dax gently helped me off his lap and out of the car, his hand holding mine. And before I could ask the question, he lowered his mouth to my ear. "This time I'm coming inside."

My stomach executed an elaborate triple flip before plummeting entirely. Summoning the last of my willpower, I glanced up at Dax's strong profile, his five-o'clock shadow making his chiseled jaw look as if it had been dusted with black sand. "Good. Because I'd rather not give the driver a show."

His lips parted in an amused grin, exposing a straight line of white teeth that had nibbled on my earlobe just a minute ago. "I'm only interested in my audience of one."

I was silent as we continued up the walkway to my front door, both of us looking at it and remembering exactly what had happened last time. I took a quick breath, feeling both vulnerable and strong. "If we were standing at *your* front door, would you invite me inside?"

Tension thrummed between us, as conspicuous as the chirping of the cicadas. Neither of our stares wavered as we sized each other up like opponents on a field. What were we battling for?

Beneath the glow of the lantern hanging above our heads, Dax's expression was inscrutable, his bone structure carved by a deft hand, all strong lines and aggressive angles, offset by the full curve of his lips and high arc of his cheekbones. Masculinity tempered by passion and empathy.

My eyes dropped to follow the heavy bob of Dax's throat as he swallowed, then darted back to his face. "Tonight? Yes."

"And tomorrow?" I asked, hating that my breathless voice sounded so hopeful.

"I can't promise there will be a tomorrow, Verity. I can't promise anything."

I wanted to reach out and smooth away the frown crawling across Dax's forehead, lay my hand along his clenched jaw, sweep my thumb over the throbbing vein at his temple. To reassure him. To comfort him. I was a big girl. He didn't need to worry about me. I could take care of myself. "I don't need promises, Dax. I need proof. Proof that I'm not the only one of us who wants more than a make-out session at my front door."

The gold specks in his eyes lit up, overshadowing the darkness within. "Open the door. I'll prove it to you all goddamn night long."

My breath hitched as I punched a code into the security panel. The sound of the lock disengaging shattered the suburban silence. Chills feathered down my spine as I stepped over the threshold and turned around, nearly eye to eye with Dax as he slipped a hand along the curve of my waist, the heat from his palm burning me through the thin fabric of my dress. "I need you to be sure, Verity. Right now I can still leave, pretend we just shared a ride. No harm, no foul." His voice was gritty and rough, almost a plea. The look on his face making it clear that my answer would determine whether he followed me inside or walked back to his car. Letting me know the choice was entirely mine.

A breeze gusted through the door, my hair sliding across my neck in a caress I wanted to come from Dax. "I don't want to pretend." I reached for his elbow and gave a tug. "I just want you."

It was like throwing a brick through a window. There was no going back.

In one movement, Dax stepped inside and hoisted me into his arms, kicking the door closed with the back of his heel. A light from the upstairs hall illuminated the wide curving staircase, and Dax carried me as if I were Vivien Leigh in *Gone with the Wind*, my favorite movie of all time.

I didn't have a chance to revel in the moment though. His mouth was on mine, stealing my breath, biting my lips, his tongue slipping through the gate of my teeth. God, he was good.

At the upstairs landing, Dax entered the first open door. A guest room I'd rarely set foot in. But it had a bed, and that was all that mattered. He set me down, his knees pressing into the mattress on either side of my thighs as he cupped my face in his hands, our mouths barely a breath apart. His stare awakening parts of me I thought long since destroyed. "You weren't supposed to be so fucking irresistible," he rasped.

And then we were kissing again. This time harder, deeper. Licking, sucking, biting. My moans. His groans. Our panting breaths as if we couldn't get enough air, couldn't get enough of each other. And yet I wanted more. So much more.

Dax's hands were everywhere. Mine were wrapped around his neck, my fingers threading into his scalp and holding on for dear life as he took my body on the ride of its life.

The sound of my designer dress tearing, ripping in two, should have broken the spell, should have horrified me—it was thousands of dollars and on loan only for the night—but it didn't. The sound of shredding fabric was an appropriate accompaniment to the angry act of passion we were engaged in. I didn't care about anything but Dax's hands on my skin, his kisses that were trailing sparks down my throat, then lower. Dax's lips closed over my breast, his teeth grazing my nipple, his tongue flicking the needy peak. My head lolled back as I arched my hips, rocking against him, my nails digging into shoulders still covered by his shirt. "Off," I muttered, frustrated by the barrier between us.

A low chuckle rumbled from Dax's lungs as he pulled away

from me, the cold air making my wet skin tingle in protest. "Your wish is my command."

I pushed up on my elbows, a rapt audience as Dax unbuttoned his shirt, muscles bulking and flexing as he shrugged his shoulders and pulled out of the sleeves, the white cotton whispering to the floor. Then the metallic *ping* of his belt buckle, the whisper of it sliding through the loops, falling soundlessly on top of his discarded shirt. Dax's thumbs disappeared behind the band of his pants, long fingers working the button, then the zipper. All the while the corded muscles of his abdomen tensed and rippled.

Every part of this man was perfectly defined strength. He was skill and discipline and ambition and restraint.

That restraint had been kicked aside just for me. Just for tonight.

If tonight was all I'd get, I would take it. Eagerly.

Which was why I slipped off the bed and onto my knees, falling at Dax's feet like a sinner before a priest.

Would this man be my salvation?

No. Never.

But for tonight I would worship at the altar of Dax Hughes.

And I was going to enjoy every damned moment.

Encased in black boxer briefs, the bulge between Dax's thighs was enormous. I rubbed the side of my cheek against it, my hands gripping his quads as I breathed him in, a smile stealing onto my lips at his ragged groan. When I glanced up, my chin sliding along the cotton covering his hardened length, the raw desire radiating from his expression made my head spin. Holding his gaze, I pulled at his waistband, edging the fabric down until he finally sprang free. Thick and heavy, Dax's cock bobbed in front of my face, a creamy bead already gracing the crown.

I couldn't help it—I leaned forward, my tongue outstretched, desperate for a taste. Salty and tart. I moaned, wanting more.

Dax's fingers plunged into my hair, curving around my scalp. "Christ, Verity. You don't know what you're doing to me."

Anther milky drop leaked out, and this time I spread it across my lips like gloss, licking it off with a swipe of my tongue as Dax watched, rapt. He cursed, his voice straining with need, a tremor running down his arms and through his fingertips.

Before Dax could lift me up and throw me back on the bed, I leaned forward and took him into my mouth, the silky head pushing beyond my teeth as I ran my tongue over the crown.

God, I could make a meal out of this man.

Lust spiked, threading its way between my thighs, expanding and swelling. I slid forward, inch by inch, filling my mouth as I pressed my legs together, craving friction. Craving fullness. Craving Dax.

I fluttered my tongue along the underside of Dax's cock, the crown sliding along the roof of my mouth, going deeper, my mouth stretched wide around his shaft. Dax was muttering to himself, guttural sounds and incomprehensible words. Trying to hang on to the last bit of control that kept him from thrusting down my throat. But that last bit was getting thinner and weaker by the second. I reveled in it, taunting and teasing, moaning my pleasure.

Finally Dax snapped with a hiss, rocking forward as he buried his fingers in my hair, cradling my scalp with his hands. "Fuck, Verity, I can't—I can't hold back anymore."

His words had been stripped bare of any pretense at consideration or restraint, but his hold was loose enough that I could escape if I needed to. If he was too much for me.

Dax was definitely too much. But the last thing I wanted was escape.

Unable to take him all in, I gripped his shaft at the base. Dax's hands slid forward, his palms against my cheeks, tilting my face up to meet his gaze. His groan was raw, tortured, as he took in the sight of me with my mouth still wrapped around him, lashes wet and spiky from that brief moment when he'd slipped past my gag reflex.

"You're the most beautiful thing I've ever seen." There was a tenderness to his expression that hadn't been there a moment ago. A softening, just slightly, of all those hard edges and rough words.

I moaned again, the vibrations traveling through my tongue as he jerked inside my mouth. His eyes flashed, tenderness giving way to the purest lust. So deep and dark and bold I had to close my eyes from the intensity of it.

Dax's hips rocked forward, his shaft plunging down my throat, stopping just shy of my limit and setting up a rhythm that was forceful but not brutish. Needy and reverent. So fucking hot.

My hand wanted to creep between my thighs, but I stopped myself, wanting to keep my focus entirely on Dax. He was making all sorts of sounds, as close to out of control as I'd ever seen him.

And yet entirely in control—of me. Of my mouth, of my body, and—as much as it terrified me—he'd staked a claim on my heart, too. Just a small piece, but his territory kept expanding. As many times as Dax had warned me off, I'd ignored him. The man was too enticing. Too tempting.

And now, taking him in my mouth, reveling in the taste and feel and even the implied submission of being on my knees before him, it was like nothing I'd ever experienced. Oral sex was an act I'd performed with other men in the past—begrudgingly and without any enjoyment. An act that had made me feel used and degraded. Violated.

But not now. Not with Dax. This act wasn't an *act* at all. And it wasn't one-sided, either. I welcomed every thrust and groan, grateful for the chance to prove to Dax that we were worth more than just one night. Wanting to give him a memory he couldn't resist coming back to.

Maybe it was ridiculous—tonight wasn't even over—but I already knew I wanted more.

Dax's pace quickened, his thrusts turning frantic. Desperate for relief. My name fell from his mouth, grunts of one syllable at a time. My jaw was aching, but I opened my mouth further, took him in deeper, welcoming that moment at the end of each thrust when I couldn't breathe, couldn't swallow, when I was speared by Dax, held captive by his hands and his thighs and his pulsing, leaking cock, which seemed to grow thicker and longer and harder with each passing second.

The energy picked up, Dax's muscles trembling with strain. With one last bellowed curse, his hands clamped down on my skull. His back arched, his body a rigid, powerful statue, still except for the part of him that was jerking and spurting against my tongue, emptying itself deep inside my throat.

I watched it all in awe, my eyes open, my mouth too full for the smile beating within my heart.

Dax Hughes, succumbing to an orgasm I'd given him, was the most beautiful creature on earth.

But if I thought it would weaken him, even for a moment, I was wrong. As the last pulse echoed against my tongue, he was already pulling out, his thumb sweeping over my swollen lips as he stared at me, a riotous world I was sorely incapable of deciphering visible behind his eyes. Before a single word could be exchanged, Dax picked me up and lay me back on the bed, tossing my legs over his shoulders, my feet still strapped into glittering sandals, his head diving between my thighs.

Stars blazed at his first lick, explosions of light that obliterated everything in my field of vision. There was only the sweep of Dax's tongue, the pull of his lips, the press of his fingers.

My body was ruled by the cavern deep inside of me. Everything else was blank, a bright white void.

Was this how Dax felt? How I made him feel?

Weak and powerful. Desperate and determined. Breathless and bursting with life.

I gathered the duvet into my fists, needing to hold on to something, anything, before I was lost entirely. Because there was darkness, too. A place Dax was taking me to, pushing me to.

Mercilessly.

My heart was pounding, terrified of making the jump, not knowing if I would soar or sink, destroyed by the fall. "Dax, Dax, Dax." His name was a whimper, a whine, a wail. Just the one syllable, over and over and over.

Darkness came for me anyway, rolling over me so suddenly I couldn't breathe, couldn't scream, couldn't see. But it was accompanied by an explosion of pleasure that burned me up from the inside out, hot and bright, leaving nothing but charred remains behind after it devoured all the oxygen in my veins.

Never more alive.

Dax's head shifted, the weight of it pressing on my stomach. I reached for him, my fingers running through the mess I'd already made of his hair. Feeling empty and full at the same time. Limbless and exultant. I hadn't crashed.

I'd soared.

And it was fucking amazing.

So when Dax bit down on my hip, unleashing a string of guttural curses, I thought he was in the same headspace, on the same mental plane. As overwhelmed and awed as I was.

He wasn't.

Dax pushed off me, not meeting my eyes, although the look of fury on his face was easy to read from his profile. Only a minute ago I'd luxuriated in my nakedness, but now I pulled the end of the duvet over me, wanting to hide my body as he yanked his pants on, gathering everything else in his hands—shirt, shoes, belt. "Dax…?" The tone of my voice was entirely different than it had been a minute ago, too. High and thready. Hesitant.

"This was a mistake. A huge mistake." His eyes flashed, all darkness, like polished onyx. "Fuck!"

I shivered from the coldness in his voice, in his face. "I don't—I don't understand. Please, talk to me." I hated the way I sounded. Weak. Desperate.

He scrubbed a hand over his face, shaking his head. "I did talk. I told you *this* was wrong. That *we* were wrong."

"There was nothing wrong with what we just did, Dax. Nothing."

Was I saying it for his benefit, or mine?

Dax stilled, the faintest bit of sadness stealing over his features. "It was all kinds of wrong. I'm sorry, Verity."

What did he need from me? How could I convince Dax that he was wrong? That we were nothing but right. Or at least, more right than wrong. A lot more. Words bubbled up in the back of my throat, but I swallowed them down. I would do just about anything for this man.

But I was no one's beggar.

Not for him. Not for anyone.

And just knowing that—that there was a line I wouldn't

cross, that I was strong enough to hang on to the tattered remnants of my pride rather than let Dax take it with him—assured me I would be fine. With or without Dax.

I had my voice. I had a kick-ass agent. I had an upcoming album and a tour.

It was a hell of a lot more than I had a few months ago.

I didn't need a man just for the sake of having one. If Dax didn't want me, then he didn't deserve me.

But I couldn't resist one last parting shot. "For a tough guy, you sure are afraid of taking a risk."

He walked to the door, pausing at the molding. "You're right. I am." After a moment he turned back to face me again. "Verity, you're just hitting your stride, with everything ahead of you. I'm at the top of my game, with everything to lose. We share an agent, a label, and soon we'll be sharing a stage. If things go south, who do you think will get cut loose?" His stare turned sad, his words a warning. "Don't waste your second chance on me. I'm not worth it."

With a parting rap on the door, he walked through it, his softly plodding footfalls on the stairs a mournful salute.

The quiet close of the front door was a *boom* that ricocheted inside my chest. I rubbed at the ache, knowing there would be no bruise, no broken bones. The kind of wound Dax inflicted, it didn't leave a scar.

Because it wasn't the kind that healed.

Chapter Seventeen

Dax

Guilt ran over me with the subtlety of an oil slick. Clogging my pores, blinding my eyes. I felt it in my ears and mouth. Tasted it on my lips.

Vandalizing the entire fucking night.

Everything I'd just done with Verity. *Everything*.

I tore at my clothes the second I got back to my house, leaving a trail of them on my way to the shower. Setting the temperature as hot as it would go, I sucked in steam like it could break up the thick knot of desperation trapped inside my throat. Wet heat pounded my tense muscles as I coughed and yelled, lathering soap and shampoo until I was covered in a thick white film, tugging and twisting at my hair.

But as the suds ran down the drain, I didn't feel any less dirty. Not one goddamn bit.

I turned off the water and wrapped a towel around my waist,

staring at the fogged-up mirror. Seeing only Verity's face when I called what we'd done a *mistake*.

I never wanted to hurt her.

But I had. I had.

And Verity's hurt... It was fucking *killing* me.

Earlier, with her thighs trembling against my neck, her satin skin pressing tight against my ears, tasting the potent sweetness of her on my tongue, I'd reveled in the moment. She was with me and I was with her and everything was fucking perfect. And then—

The pure joy of it had flipped.

Right became wrong.

Until all I could feel was *loss*.

The soul-shattering pain of losing a woman who was threaded into every atom of my existence.

So I made it happen. Before I could lose Verity, I made myself give her up.

And now... sitting here, alone in my house, the arrogance of it was astounding. Appalling.

I was a coward flaunting my fears like a crown, tripping over a pretend throne.

I grabbed my phone from my discarded pants, swiping a thumb over the screen. Shane answered on the third ring, his tone alarmed. "What's goin' on?"

"Everything's fine. I just have a question," I said quickly.

He exhaled a relieved sigh. Late-night phone calls were hard for Shane. "Sure."

"You and Delaney, you had your ups and downs, right?"

I heard him mumble something that sounded like "be right back," then, "Fuck yeah. We were a goddamn mess."

"What made you decide to go for it? To clean up your shit and go for it?"

There was a pause, and I could tell Shane had moved outside, as I had. His Malibu beach house was just north of here, but we were staring out at the same ocean. "Well, I have my brother to thank for that. After I let Delaney go, too lost in my own head to see straight, Gavin called me, completely disgusted with me. And he said two words that changed my life. 'Choose happy.'"

"Choose happy," I repeated, feeling disappointed. It sounded like a cheesy bumper sticker.

"Yeah." Shane laughed. "I would have expected more from my brother's brilliant legal mind, too. Turns out, it's so simple it is brilliant. You make a million choices every day, right? What to eat, when to sleep, what to say, when and where and who to fuck. Why not make the choice to be fucking happy?"

My mind was trying to process the concept. "Because happiness isn't a choice; it's a state of mind."

"Ah, but that's where you're wrong. Once the basics are covered—food, clothing, shelter, blah, blah, blah—the rest is pretty cut-and-dried. Just choose happy, man."

Verity

"Verity? What on earth are you doing in here?"

I squeezed my eyes tightly at the explosion of bright light, quickly slapping a hand over my face and ducking beneath the covers. "Mom?" My voice was hoarse from all the tears I hadn't let myself shed, although judging from the dampness of my pillow, I'd cried buckets in my sleep.

"Don't sound so surprised. What did you think would happen when I heard all about your new song, your new project? Did you think I would just let you humiliate me? That I would roll over and play dead, while you and your hotshot Hollywood agent destroyed everything I built?"

I'd expected a confrontation with my mother, but I thought it would be preceded by a phone call or some sort of warning before she returned to L.A.

I should have known better.

Her heels stabbed at the carpet as she walked across the room, and I braced myself as she yanked at the duvet. "You are going to call that man right now and tell him you made a terrible mistake. I am your manager and agent. Me. I am your mother. You can't just throw me away like yesterday's news."

Blinking rapidly, I tried to get my pupils to retract. When they did, and I could finally see, I took in my mother's flushed skin, the furious pink patches on her cheeks obvious even through her fake tan, the scowl no amount of Botox could mask. "I'm not throwing you away. But I'm not making that phone call."

"You most certainly are. Because you are not going on some tour with a rock band. Honestly, Verity. I just don't understand what you're thinking."

I yanked the duvet from her hands and tucked it beneath my arms. "No, I'm not. And I'll tell you what I'm thinking. I'm thinking that I'm almost twenty-five years old and it's about time I took control of my own career. If you want to discuss this, we can. Preferably after I get dressed." What I really wanted was a few minutes to clear the cobwebs from my mind and wash the streaks of makeup from my face so she wasn't speaking to a sluggish raccoon.

My mother's jaw sagged for a moment before she snapped it shut and stalked from the room.

I had just sat up when she reappeared in the doorway, looking at me as if I'd suddenly grown horns. "I really can't believe this is up for discussion at all. Do you know how much I sacrificed to make you a star? And this is the way you repay me?"

I knew exactly what my mother had sacrificed—because it had been *my* sacrifice.

My childhood.

My innocence.

My trust.

"Repay you? What more do you want from me? This house is in *your* name. The car I drive is in *your* name. Every one of my bank accounts has *your* name on it."

"You were a child actor, Verity. Of course everything is in my name."

"Were. Past tense. I haven't been a child in a long time. Travis Taggert takes a percentage of my income; the rest is mine. When did you ever do that?"

"So this is about money? You've kicked your own mother to the curb for a few more dollars?"

"No. I wanted to shift from acting to music. To make albums that reflect who I am as an artist—"

"Pfft. Artist." She spat the word like an insult. "Is that what Taylor promised you? That you could be an artist?"

"Travis. Travis Taggert. And yes, that's exactly what he promised me. He's delivered on it, too."

She crossed her arms. "Really? You are the opening act on someone else's tour, Verity. Have you forgotten that *I* got you the starring role in a nationally syndicated television show? I'm hardly impressed, and you shouldn't be either."

I didn't need to be reminded what it took to earn my role on *The Show*. I would have given anything to forget it. "Well, that's too bad. But you're entitled to your opinion, and I'm entitled to mine."

Her stare turned cold. "If that's the way you feel, I want you out of my house."

I laughed at the absurdity of her demand, but her frown only deepened. The laugh died in my throat, disintegrating into a bitter coating of ash. "You can't be serious."

"Like you said, this house is in my name."

"Bought with money *I* earned."

She shrugged. "Who's to say it wasn't bought from my cut as your manager?"

"You know what, fine." I leapt from the bed—naked—my shoulder brushing hers as I passed by on the way to my bedroom. Well, not mine anymore. Apparently it never was. "If this is how you want it, I'm out."

I closed the door, using all the restraint I had not to slam it behind me. Although I'd intended to get dressed and leave, one look in the mirror was all the proof I needed to take a shower first. I turned my face into the water, the stream pelting my swollen eyes and mascara-streaked cheeks, erasing the last taste of Dax from my lips. Before I could sink too deeply in my mess of a mind, I opened bottle after bottle. Soap, body wash, shampoo, conditioner. Rubbing the contents into my hair and skin, rinsing them down the drain.

All the while expecting a knock on the door. Not an outright apology. I'd never get one of those. But maybe just an "It's late. Go to bed. We'll discuss everything in the morning."

There was no knock while I was in the shower.

There was no knock while I dressed and packed a small bag.

There was no knock when I decided to blow-dry my hair.

I would have put on makeup, just to kill time, but my skin was tender to the touch and I didn't want to look in the mirror and see Verity Moore—Hollywood creation. Not when I felt like a little girl inside, dangerously close to severing the last fragile tie I had to my mother. We weren't close, true, and Janet Moore would never be a candidate for Mother of the Year.

But she was all the family I had.

Err on the side of forgiveness.

It was one of my grandmother's favorite expressions. Easy to say, difficult to practice. When dealing with my mother, it had become something of a mantra. With a heavy sigh, I dropped my bag in the hallway and knocked once on the door to the bedroom my mother used when she was in L.A. before opening it. She was sitting on the edge of the bed, her gaze expectant.

"Mom, I don't want to fight with you. I really don't. I'm excited about the direction I'm headed in, and I wish you were, too."

"What direction? You're an actress, not a singer."

"No, I'm not. You're the one who wanted to be an actress. And when it didn't work out for you, you decided I would be. I love singing. I've always wanted—"

"Oh please." She shot me down with a disparaging shake of her head. "You have no idea what you want."

"Stop. Just stop. I do know what I want…but you've never cared." I paused for a moment. "I think this will be good for us. I do. Maybe we can actually figure out how to have a mother-daughter relationship, rather than a working one. I'm sure you've heard what people are saying about Jack, what they think I'm saying about him in 'Bombshell Rebel…'"

"It's sick, Verity. Absolutely disgusting. And I'm embarrassed that you're not jumping to his d—"

"I wish I could defend him. I really do. But it's true. He and Millie—"

Her eyes narrowed. "They did no such thing, Verity. I was there. I would know."

"You weren't there, not in the room with us." My voice was a choked whisper.

But my mother's lips were set in a hard line. "How dare you, Verity? If you do this, make these accusations, move forward with another manager, we won't have a relationship at all."

My throat tightened. I couldn't have said another word if I wanted to. But apparently, I didn't need to. There was nothing left to say. I stepped back into the hall and picked up my bag.

I wasn't quiet on the stairs, the zipper of my bag *ping, ping, ping*ing on each rail of the banister. And I wasn't quiet when I went into the kitchen and grabbed a bottle of water from the refrigerator, purposely bumping into a barstool, the legs dragging across the tile floor.

But the silence from my mother was deafening.

With one last glance upstairs, I walked out the front door and down the driveway. The keys to the Range Rover were in the car, but if my mother was kicking me out of the house, it wasn't a stretch to assume that she would claim the car as hers, too. I wasn't about to give her the satisfaction of calling me a thief.

Travis had assured me he would get control of the assets my mother had claimed as her own…as soon as I decided how badly I wanted to fight for them. Legal battles weren't only pricey—they were public.

In the cul-de-sac of my gated community, there was a landscaped clearing with a gazebo. I headed there, considering my options. I could call an Uber and check into a hotel, but the chances of the driver or front-desk attendant phoning in a tip to a gossip site was high. I could call Piper, but she was pregnant and I didn't want to wake her. And if I called Travis, he would just call Piper.

I had made a few friends on *The Show*, but I hadn't spoken

to any of them since the series ended. And none of the people I used to party with had been worth keeping in touch with.

Laughter bubbled up from deep in my throat, a bitter gurgle that reverberated within the small enclosure. Not long ago I'd felt like the luckiest girl in the world. Like my life was finally falling into place and I had everything I'd ever wanted.

Wrong.

I had nothing.

It was a trick of light, a sleight of hand.

I didn't have a home or a car. Or a mother to whom I meant more than a paycheck.

Pulling out my phone, I saw I hadn't slept nearly as long as I thought. Dax had left only an hour ago, maybe two. It felt like a different decade.

Don't think about him. Not now. You can't afford to fall apart.

Scrolling through my contacts with trembling fingers, I realized that I didn't have a single friend in this town who wasn't on my payroll. Not one.

When it vibrated in my hands, the screen flashing with Dax's name, I was so surprised I automatically accepted the call.

Damn it. I had nothing to say to him. Nothing.

"Verity, I—fuck—I'm sorry for—" There was a clatter on the line, as if he'd dropped the phone. "I don't even know what to say. My head is a fucking mess and…God, I have a lot to explain—"

His flustered apology was a pin, popping the indignant bubble that was the only thing keeping me afloat. "Dax," I interrupted, a salty tear slipping into the corner of my mouth as my shoulders sagged.

"Yeah?"

"Shut up and come back."

Chapter Eighteen

Dax

I'm not sure what I expected when I arrived at Verity's home, but it definitely wasn't to find her standing in the middle of the road before I even turned into her driveway. Illuminated by my headlights, Verity's pale skin looked almost ghostly in the mist, her red hair a mane of fire. I slammed on the brakes, and she ran around to the side of my car, flinging a duffel bag into the back and fumbling with her seatbelt, the metal clanking as she locked it in place with visibly shaking hands. "What's going on?"

She lifted wet, red-rimmed eyes to mine, the tip of her nose pink. "Just drive." Her voice was a throaty rasp. "Please."

Verity appeared to be a breath away from a breakdown. Despite the questions crowding my skull, I took my foot off the brake and pulled out of her street, making the trip back to the Pacific Palisades in silence.

I eased into my garage, resisting the urge to tug Verity against me as I held open the door to my home. She looked like a fragile doll in her ratty jeans and oversized sweatshirt, her tear-streaked face evidence of real pain.

"Do you want to go right to bed, or would you rather a mug of something warm first?"

There was the barest twitch at the corners of her mouth. "I don't think I could sleep yet. Something warm sounds perfect."

I grabbed a blanket from a basket by the sliding glass door to the deck. "Take this and go sit. I'll be right out."

I watched Verity arrange herself in one of the lounge chairs and then returned to the kitchen. I'd picked up a container of apple cider on a whim earlier in the week, and now I was glad I had. Heating it on the stove, I added a few spices and a liberal pour of whiskey.

"Is this what I think it is?" Verity asked as I held out a steaming mug to her.

"Mulled cider was the pick-me-up drink of choice in my house growing up. I made us the spiked version."

Verity gave an audible sigh as she took a sip. "Thank you. I could definitely use a pick-me-up right about now."

"Care to talk about it?"

Her strangled laugh rippled through the quiet night air. "You sure you're ready for a ride on the Verity Moore crazy train?"

"I think I can handle it." I settled myself in the chair beside her. "Tell me something true."

A long moment passed, and as Verity alternated between sipping her cider and worrying at her lower lip, I wasn't sure whether she would decide to open up to me. Eventually, she said, "The CliffsNotes version is that my mother is having a temper tantrum because I signed with Travis and am no longer her docile little daughter, playing by her rules. Everything I've ever earned is in her name, so she's trying to bully me into submission." Verity glanced over at me, her eyes blazing with defiance. "But it's not going to work."

Right now, Verity was a study in contrasts. Clean-faced and dwarfed by her oversized sweatshirt, she looked like a stubborn child. But an inner strength was shining through, glimmers of hard-won wisdom earned by being forced to grow up too fast.

"I tried to talk to her again before I left, hoping we could somehow salvage whatever was left of our relationship. I even told her something true," her voice broke on the word and she paused, swallowing heavily. "But she didn't believe me. So, I think I finally have to face facts. We've never *had* anything."

Verity pressed the heels of her hands to her eyes. "I'm sorry. I'm such a mess. God, no wonder why you ran away from me tonight."

I got up out of my chair, taking Verity's mug from her hands and placing it beside mine on the table. Then I lifted her and took her place, settling her in my lap. "You've had a really shitty night, and I'm sorry for playing a part in it. A bad part."

Verity made some sort of sniffling laugh. "Not all bad. Some of it was good."

I ran my fingers through her hair, kissing her forehead. "And how is this? Is this good?"

A long sigh trembled from her chest. "Yeah. This is really good."

* * *

I got out of bed as the first strains of light crept over the horizon. Normally I would be wrestling into my wetsuit by now, but the surf wasn't calling to me this morning.

There was no way in hell I was leaving the sleeping girl I'd carried to bed just a few hours ago. It had been painful enough to slip her beneath the covers of a bed that wasn't mine, to go to sleep—or try, anyway—knowing there was a closed door and a plaster wall between us.

I was on my second cup of coffee when I spotted her coming down the stairs. "Good morning."

Verity gave me a wary glance, as if she wasn't sure who she would get this morning. The asshole who ran out on her, or the man who had let her fall asleep on his chest as they looked for constellations in the night sky. "If you say so." She put her cell phone on the island and folded herself into a barstool opposite me.

"No cider this morning," I said. "Coffee?"

She nodded. "That would be great, thanks."

I filled a mug and put it in front of her. "There's milk and—"

She cut me off with a shake of her head. "Black is perfect."

A ribbon of pleasure swooshed across the back of my neck. Such a small, irrelevant thing, but I liked that Verity didn't make a fuss over her coffee. The few times a woman had spent the night, I was met with disbelief that I didn't have almond milk or coconut creamer, stevia or agave. Verity took her coffee black, like me.

Cupping the porcelain with both hands, she took a few sips, her gaze bouncing around my messy kitchen. "Please tell me you're expecting to feed half the neighborhood, too."

I surveyed the tower of pancakes, the skillet full of eggs, the bowl of berries, the bread on the counter waiting to be sliced. "They're coming by later. For now it's just us." My words hung on the air, sounding almost too intimate for the early hour.

Verity was the first to break eye contact, tucking an errant lock of hair behind her ear and staring down into her coffee.

She made a cute, throat-clearing noise as I set about plating our breakfast.

I could have carried them outside, or over to the table, but instead I pushed her plate across the island and ate mine from where I was standing. There was so much we weren't saying, keeping five feet of stone and wood between us seemed appropriate.

"I called Travis this morning. Filled him in on what's happening with my mom. I should be out of your hair soon."

My chest squeezed, my heart giving a reluctant thud. Despite the veins of tension running between us, I was in no hurry for Verity to leave. "I'll bet Travis is frothing at the mouth. He lives for shit like this."

Verity grinned. "Yeah, he seemed pretty pumped when I filled him in. He said he would send Piper over this morning to take me car shopping. I might stay in one of his places until my house situation is sorted out."

I sympathized with Verity's family drama. My own parents had basically washed their hands of me once I left New York. But they had never tried to claim my fame as their own. They lived their lives, and I lived mine. Thinking about my parents, I realized I should probably check in with my sister. Make sure she was behaving herself in New York.

Verity's phone chirped. She picked it up, frowning at the screen. "Scratch that. Piper has a sonogram today and won't be available."

"I am." The words were out before I'd even considered them.

"What?" She put her phone down and picked up her fork, glancing at me again.

Choose happy. "I'm free today. I can take you." *I want to take you.*

Verity blinked a few times, her fork hovering in the air. "Don't worry about it, Dax. I'm sure you have much better things to do with your time."

What I really wanted was spend the entire day with Verity—in bed—making up for the dick move I pulled last night. But because of that dick move, I hardly expected her to feel the same. I'd settle for car shopping. "Nope. I'm all yours."

Might have been the most honest sentence I'd ever spoken.

Verity

I helped Dax clean the kitchen, then returned to his guest room. It had been a shock to wake up in a strange bed this morning. More than shocking, actually. Terrifying.

Laying there, barely able to breathe, I struggled to piece together my memories. The last thing I recalled was falling asleep in the lounge chair. No—not the lounge chair. In Dax's lap.

My mind had raced, heedless of logic. *Oh my god—was the mulled cider laced? Had Dax…?*

The weight of my past pressed heavily on my chest, my rib cage feeling like it would crack from the strain. Had another man I trusted taken advantage of a situation I—

Until I realized that, except for my shoes, I was still fully dressed. And I was alone, the other side of the queen-sized bed still perfectly made. Talking to Dax about my mom last night, fresh from our most recent confrontation…I must have crashed hard and he'd carried me to bed.

I had exhaled a choked breath, blinking back yet another onslaught of tears, forcing my tense muscles to relax one by one. I was safe. Dax hadn't hurt me.

I was safe.

Now, with a fresh dose of caffeine running through my veins, I turned my attention to pulling together an outfit from the paltry selection of clothes I'd brought with me. Travis had offered to loan me one of his cars, or send a driver to take me wherever I wanted to go. But that was the thing—there was no place I needed to be. Because of the party last night, I didn't have any public appearances scheduled for today, no meetings to take or interviews to give.

But I did need a car. In all the years I'd had my license, I'd never once picked out my own ride. Poor little rich girl problems, I know. My mother could keep the Range Rover she bought for me…with my money.

I wanted to go car shopping.

I wanted to go house—no, apartment—shopping. A rental was fine for now.

I wanted to build my own damn life, filled with things I'd chosen myself. A life filled with more than *things*. Friends. People that weren't paid to pretend they cared about me.

I was swiping gloss over my lips when my phone pinged with an incoming e-mail. I didn't recognize the sender, but the subject was a line from "Bombshell Rebel." *Long time ago, someone picked me…*

It was the text contained in the message that had my stomach plummeting. *Make it clear that "someone" isn't the man who gave you your big break, or I'll be forced to show the world how you earned it.*

I sat down on the floor, scooting myself into a corner of the room. The attached video took a few seconds to load, just long enough for my breakfast to become a gnarled lump, twisting and churning in the pit of my stomach.

Drawing my feet inward, I balanced my phone on my knees as my face filled the screen. I was holding a piece of paper with my name, age, and date, wearing a simple white dress, my hair long and straight. I looked so young. So nervous. Desperation shined from my overly bright smile, from the flutter of the paper in my trembling hands, from every rapid nod I directed at the camera, from my rehearsed answers that didn't quite match up with the questions being asked.

I remembered that day so clearly. I remembered not eating breakfast because my mom had only enough money for a pack of cigarettes. I remembered going to the Peninsula Hotel in Beverly Hills and being embarrassed because my stomach was growling so loudly I worried Jack Lester would notice. And I remembered my mother telling me that if I didn't get this role, she was washing her hands of me entirely. *You're eighteen now. You can take care of yourself.*

Upstairs, Lester told me there would be a scene in *The Show* where the lead role wore a bikini, and that I should take off my dress…if I wanted the part.

So I did.

He said there would be scenes in *The Show* where the lead role would kiss boys, and that I should kiss him…if I wanted the part.

So I did.

Neither of those requests were anything new. I'd undressed for him before. I'd kissed him before. I'd done things to him with my hands and mouth before.

Things I still wished I could forget.

But then he said there was a scene in *The Show* where the lead role lost her virginity, and that I should have sex with him…if I wanted the part.

So I did.

And I got the part. The lead.

My mother was thrilled.

I wasn't anything, really. I was numb.

As we entered production, everything Jack Lester told me was true. I wore a bikini for at least one scene practically every episode. My character kissed a boy by the end of the first season. And in the third season, my character lost her virginity.

What happened next was a surprise to everyone.

Parents were so incensed that they organized a boycott of the advertisers and petitioned the network to cancel the show.

My character was labeled a whore.

The Show was canceled.

Overnight I went from *Hot* to *Not*.

I couldn't get an audition, let alone a featured role on a popular show.

I was the girl who had brought down *The Show*. A ratings juggernaut. An advertiser's dream. The number one show for teens in the country.

No one would touch me. At least, not in Hollywood. Vegas, with its soft-core porn industry, was definitely interested.

I flew to New York, hoping to get swept up in the crowded city. To let the uproar die down while I enjoyed a well-earned break from five a.m. on-set calls and the endless publicity machine required to feed *The Show*'s fans just enough of me to ensure they'd be hungry for more.

And now, my back against the wall of Dax's guest bedroom, I watched myself swallow a scream of pain as Lester tore into me, saw the sparkle of tears turn my lashes into wet spikes, even as I tried to pretend the overweight man more than twice my age was my teenaged boyfriend.

I heard the guttural grunts of my...What exactly was he? Was he a rapist? I never said *no*.

Never said the word.

Never even thought it.

I saw him whisper into my ear, remembering what he'd said accompanied by a wave of nausea. *Be a good girl, Verity. Show me what a good actress you are.*

I had forced the muscles in my face and neck to relax, twisted my lips into a wondrous smile. Let my eyes drift shut as my mouth opened on a sigh. It looked like I was thoroughly enjoying myself.

There's my girl. You want this.

Inside I'd been screaming.

The knock on the door had me scrambling to stop the video, darken the screen. Dax poked his head through the door, his eyes sweeping the room until they fell on me. "Hey, you okay?"

"No." Saying the word felt so good, I wanted to yell it.

It didn't matter that it was to a different question, to a different man. I wiped my eyes and stood. "But I will be."

Chapter Nineteen

Dax

"You think you're a real badass now, don't you?"

Verity plucked the sunglasses perched on her head and slid them over her eyes, her mouth wearing a saucy grin. "Hell, yeah."

After making the rounds of half a dozen dealerships, we were waiting for a salesman to complete the paperwork on Verity's new Audi. It had been surprisingly fun watching Verity shopping for a car. She was like a kid, bouncing up and down in the leather seats, pressing every button, asking a million questions, honking the horn of cars on display.

But once she made up her mind, she was done. No doubts, no hesitation.

A far cry from the defeated woman who appeared outside my car with a canvas bag and a tear-stained face last night. Or the determined one from this morning who seemed to think that if she acted like nothing was wrong, I would actually believe her.

Twenty minutes and a few signatures later, Verity was waving the key to her new silver R8 in front of my face. "My ass might even be as bad as yours, Dax."

It was impossible not to laugh at her. She joined in, and the salesman backed away, looking at us strangely. Verity's phone, sitting on the hood of her new car, chirped. She broke off to look down at the message on the lock screen. "Piper wants to know what I decided on."

I outstretched my hand. "Lemme take a picture of you and your new ride."

Her face, if it was possible, got even brighter. "Great idea." She handed it to me...a split second before my ears were assaulted by the unmistakable sound of sex—harsh grunting and skin slapping skin.

The screen, already facing me, came to life, and the sight will forever be burned in my corneas. A much younger Verity, cinnamon eyelashes resting on her cheekbones, pink lips parted, red hair strewn across a white pillow. The rest of her was obscured by a wide hairy back. The kind of back that belonged in a retirement community in Boca, not on top of Verity.

She snatched her phone from my grip, but there was no denying what I'd seen. What I'd heard. But my brain wasn't able to process it. "What the fuck was that?" I growled, keeping my tone low.

She silenced her phone, tossing it into her bag. "Nothing."

I grabbed her arm as she was turning away to get into the front seat. "That wasn't nothing. I don't know what that—" I cut myself off. "Wrong. So fucking wrong." There were probably other words for it, too. But they were for Verity to say.

She pulled away, surprising me with her vehemence. Without thinking, I rounded the hood and slid in the passenger seat.

"Verity." For someone whose name meant truth, she had a hell of a time telling it.

"I have a meeting with Travis. Get out."

Leaving her right now wasn't a possibility. Instead I pulled the sunglasses off her face and laid my palm along her cheek, shifting her toward me. Her eyes were a riot of pain and shame, the emotions so toxic they glowed almost neon. "Tell me something true," I said softly.

She hesitated, her chin quivering. "It's ugly, Dax. The truth—*my* truth—is so, so ugly."

I spoke slowly, softly. "That was what you were talking about—when we were in the car the other day. Sex before you were ready. Something that's happened to you, not something you wanted."

Her thick lashes were the most elegant of fans, fluttering over twin vaults bursting with secrets. "That was an audition."

Fury prodded me, as harsh and hot as a scalding poker. I winced, shifted uncomfortably in my seat as I stared at Verity through the fog of rage clouding my vision. "An audition? Some fat fuck was…" This time, my voice trailed off not because I couldn't finish my thought, but because Verity's expression confirmed it.

"Why?" I confined my question to just the one word, feeling like I was treading on unsteady ground and that at any minute it would collapse beneath us.

Verity looked out the window for a moment, and when she turned back to face me, a bitter laugh gurgled from her throat. "I've done a lot of things I'm not proud of, Dax. That tape…" She shook her head. "That tape is just a log on the pyre."

I'd never attempted to be an actor in Hollywood. Never been dragged through the gauntlet of Manhattan talent offices that mainly casted for commercials and print work. Sure, I'd heard about the casting couch. But had I ever given it a second's thought? No. Not once.

Not to wonder if it existed or to decry the practice at all.

The anger expanding in every atom of my body was painful, like I was being flayed apart from the inside. "Is that Jack Lester?" The bastard would wish he were dead once I got through with him.

She glanced away from my outraged expression. A sweep of red hair fell over her cheek, shielding her profile from me. I went to tuck it behind her ear, and Verity jerked away from my hand. "Shit. Sorry," she said, her face pinched, the burst of fear already fading as she made eye contact again.

I exhaled, leaning back against the car door. "Not a damn thing in the world you have to be sorry for."

She gave me a tentative half smile, wistful and sweet. "I'm carrying around a lot of baggage for someone who's currently homeless. You sure you don't want to get out of the car?"

I shook my head slowly. "Not a chance."

It was the truth. The more I knew about Verity, the less willing I was to keep her at arm's length. Her baggage hadn't dragged me down. If anything, it made me feel like the shit I carried around was nothing to complain about. And it had me wanting to ease her burden, as much as I could. "So, I've gotta ask. Is there a reason you were watching that?"

"The video was e-mailed to me this morning. I guess I didn't actually shut it down earlier."

"Who…? Who the hell e-mailed it to you?"

"Someone who thinks 'Bombshell Rebel' is a little too revealing."

My jaw sagged. "You're being blackmailed because of m—our song?"

"Yes." The word trembled on a sigh. "Whoever wrote it didn't realize how accurate those lyrics were. The press is trying to make it into an accusation against my former producer."

"So that's who sent the video?"

"Not exactly." Verity reached around the back of her neck and squeezed, like her muscles were protesting our conversation. "His assistant, more likely."

I replaced her hands with my own, massaging the strained tendons on either side of her spine, the rounded hunch of her shoulders, the tender skin behind her ears. She exhaled a long groan, relaxing under my touch.

I felt like an ass for not appreciating the gift Verity had given me, not just access to her gorgeous body, but her trust. Her pleasure. Her honesty.

And until now I'd taken it all for granted.

"Millie coordinated his auditions—the ones he oversaw personally." With her head tipped forward, her words came out haltingly, punctuated by sweet little sighs that belied the ugliness of what she was saying. "She and my mother have kept in touch over the years, and apparently they're shopping around a new show. If I had to guess, 'Bombshell Rebel' is just enough of a nuisance to make getting a commitment from a network a little trickier. Millie sent this video as a warning."

"But if that video gets out—wouldn't it kill *his* career, not *yours*?"

"Doubtful. It looks like a consensual sex tape with an eighteen-year-old actress. Trust me. Jack is powerful, and he won't go down without a fight. He'll say I *lured* him into a sexual relationship. That I'm a woman scorned, releasing it now because I wasn't cast in his new project. Powerful producers like Jack Lester control the narrative, Dax. My career, my second chance in this industry, would be destroyed. Exactly what Millie is threatening…" She exhaled a heavy sigh. "It's going to take a lot more than sex with a disgraced former actress to bring him down."

Even now, faced with a deck that was stacked against her, I could see that something inside Verity wasn't willing to fold. "Is that what you want to do, bring him down?"

She lifted her head and leaned back, rolling her shoulders as she glanced my way. I let my hand drop to the back of her seat. "I kind of do, yeah."

"Kind of?"

Her lips twitched, then pulled outward, exposing the glint of sharp, shiny teeth. "I want to bury him."

Verity

My stomach dropped when a photo popped up on my screen. *Oh god. What now?* I nearly fell over with relief when I saw it was just an overstuffed grocery bag…followed by a text.

Dax: Perfect night for hot dogs and s'mores…?

Having spent most of my afternoon with Travis, recounting my experiences in Hollywood, particularly my interactions with Jack Lester and Millie, and then sitting across from him while he watched the video on my phone—in its entirety—I wasn't sure that I was fit company for anyone.

But knowing the alternative was spending my night all alone, reliving my fucked-up past in intimate detail…

Hot dogs and s'mores with Dax sounded pretty damn good.

Dax had left my name with the guard at the gatehouse, so this time I was just waved through. I knocked, but when I realized the front door was unlocked, I poked my head in and called Dax's name.

"Down here," came his reply. As soon as I shut the door behind me, I heard the rich strains of his piano pulsing through the air. Toeing off my shoes, I left them haphazardly by the door.

As always, the first sight of Dax Hughes was a jolt to my heart. Peering over the railing, I took a moment to drink in the sight of him at his piano, fingers flying over the keyboard, the sounds he was making caressing my eardrums like the richest velvet. Luxurious yet delicate. Each stroke of the keys a resonant note Dax had tamed, crafting into an elegant, complicated web that wrapped around me like a shroud. I was caught, entranced, completely mesmerized.

Despite my unfamiliarity with classical music, it was impossible not to hear the emotions that had been woven into the song. Impossible not to be moved by them. Joy and sorrow, hope and pain, love and hate, desire and discipline. Words were unnecessary.

Music was a universal language.

Without realizing it, I found myself on the stairs, drawn to Dax by the inescapable, undeniable gravity that existed between us.

Walking to the piano, I stood by the curve of the wooden case, spreading my hands flat on the lid. The pulse of the music was a heartbeat against my palms. The rhythm vibrated through my bones, changing the consistency of the marrow inside. Making my limbs feel looser, my body lighter.

Dax didn't look up. He was in the zone. That place where music took over and you were just a conduit, a means of expressing something bigger and more powerful than you could fathom unless you'd experienced it yourself.

All bristling intensity, Dax was so beautiful in this moment. His passion pure and potent.

He took my breath away.

His hands sped up, then slowed, sped up again only to lift off the keys entirely, a final explosion of sound resonating in the stillness of the room.

I couldn't help it—I clapped as if I were the new president of Dax Hughes's fan club. Maybe I was. "That was amazing," I gushed, my cheeks straining from the wide grin splitting my face apart.

An embarrassed flush crept up Dax's neck. "You hungry?"

"For more of that?" I jerked a chin at the piano. "Definitely."

He stood, a chuckle rumbling from his chest. "Well, I'm hungry for actual food." Gently setting down the cover, he stepped away from the bench and threw his arm over my shoulders, leading me toward the kitchen. "Indulge me?"

The two words were wrapped up in sexual innuendo, tied with promise. I swallowed down the heavy knot of want lodged in my throat. "Of course."

* * *

I didn't bring up the elephant sitting in a corner of Dax's deck until after we'd washed down our hot dogs with icy cold beer straight from the bottle and devoured an entire bag of marshmallows and chocolate and graham crackers, licking the sticky mess off our fingertips. "Remember when I told you that what you saw—"

"On your phone?"

I nodded. "I said it was just the beginning."

"Only a log on the pyre," he added, parroting my own words back to me.

My mouth formed an echo of a smile. "Yes, that." A barely there smile that died as I tried to put words to my thoughts. "What do you think happens to a girl who discovers that 'no' isn't an acceptable word? At least, not in Hollywood. Not if she has any chance of landing a role she'd been groomed for practically since birth. Singing lessons, dancing lessons, audition after audition after audition." I took a breath. "And now this is *the* audition—one that means the difference between having a job and a paycheck and a family and…having nothing."

Dax was studying me closely over the flames of the firepit, the dancing orange light illuminating the severe bone structure and strong lines of his face. The man reminded me of the gorgeous guitars he hung on his walls. Alluring and mysterious. "My experience being a girl is a little limited, so I think you'll have to explain it to me."

I lifted my bottle in a mock toast. "Well, since the girl we're talking about is me, I can tell you. She learns that sex is a commodity. Something given with the expectation of getting something in return. There's no emotion involved, unless you count a lingering feeling of shame, of worthlessness. At least, until she severs that mind/body connection entirely, for her own sanity. That girl goes on to have partner after partner, knowing she is being used, justifying it by telling herself that she is using them, too. Until the cycle feels so relentless, so meaningless, she doesn't see any point in living at all."

The words flowed from my mouth on autopilot, a spill of sewage that wouldn't turn off. I watched Dax's face as he listened to me, his expression tightening as I lay my toxic waste at his feet. "After that first role, what were you getting out of it?" he asked.

"Escape. Once *The Show* ended, I couldn't get out of L.A. fast enough. I wanted to get away from Jack, from Millie, from my mother. At first I told myself I would get my GED and take classes at NYU, be a college girl for a few years, get my head on straight. But it was so much easier to spend my nights partying and my days sleeping. I didn't have to think about what happened in L.A. What I'd allowed to happen. Life was a merry-go-round of parties and private jets, drinking and drugs and shopping on someone else's dime. Rich guys who were only too eager to pay my way."

"What made you get off the ride?"

I knew the question was coming. My basket. My bread crumbs. I'd led Dax here, to the truth. But I still hesitated. My truth was more of a gash, an untreated wound.

That videotaped audition hadn't even been the beginning of the trail. Where had it started, exactly? The first time I'd sat for a head shot—a six-year-old wearing lip gloss and eyelash extensions? Or with casting directors who thought it was appropriate to tell a twelve-year-old to act *sexy*, to flirt like I wanted to be kissed. Maybe at industry parties where I was just one of a dozen other young teens wearing skimpy bikinis around a pool, letting forty- and fifty-year-old men play with my hair and spread sunscreen on my skin. A pretty prop to boost their egos as they crowed about their latest deal.

Draining what was left of my beer, I stood up. We'd finished the last of the s'mores an hour ago and now my stomach was churning from the salty-sweet mess that had tasted so good going down. "I think I'm going to get my feet wet." Only Dax's watchful eyes followed me. Maybe he realized I needed some distance.

I did. I needed to splay my toes in the sand, feel the bite of the cold ocean water on my skin, the bracing wind against my face. I picked my way down the steep trail that led from Dax's stunning home to the beach, sucking in deep lungfuls of salty air, humidity coating a throat that was parched and sore from all the ugliness I'd forced through it today. My eyes absorbed the sheer, undeniable beauty of the seascape, needing it to counteract the video I'd seen this morning, the memories that had been flashing in my mind ever since.

The unremitting current was a balm to my fraught nerves. The tension in my neck and shoulders gradually easing with each step, each lick of the tide. Calm and gentle one minute, ferocious and lethal the next, the sea was a powerful, affirming force.

I wasn't a scared teenager anymore. I was done being verbally threatened and physically assaulted.

Done expecting the worst of all men because I'd seen the worst in some.

So done.

I couldn't change the past.

But…what about my future? What did I want it to look like? Who did I want to spend it with?

I didn't feel Dax's footsteps on the sand until he was standing directly behind me, the scent of him mingling with the briny ocean breeze. My breath hiccupped in the back of my throat as his long, elegant fingers curved over my shoulders in the lightest of holds. "Okay if I join you?"

My heart squeezed at the consideration implied in his question. I inched backward just enough that my back was flush with his chest, my ass tucked between his solidly planted thighs. My arms lifted of their own accord, my hands sliding over Dax's, our fingers interlacing. "Yes."

We stayed like that for a while, both of us looking out at the sea, absorbing its strength through our pores, our breaths synchronized with the rhythm of the waves. The California coastline was timeless and eternal, a barely there blur of distinction between sea and sand and sky.

Eventually I shivered, and Dax wrapped his arms around me, drawing me closer as his shoulders curved around me, their bulk shielding me from the scrape of the wind. I let out a contented sigh when he rested his chin on the top of my head. This felt so good. So right. A comfort I'd never known possible. Contentment I'd never believed I deserved.

"Tell me something true." I flipped the question on Dax, my voice riding on the crash of the waves, rippling in the breeze.

Wanting to see the moonlight on his face, I turned in his hold. He blinked at me, one corner of his mouth kicking up in an ironic slanted smile. "There's nowhere else I'd rather be than right here with you, tonight."

I exhaled, entwining my fingers at the base of his spine. "Thank you for inviting me over."

"I'm glad you came. And I owe you an apology."

"An apology? What for?"

He glanced over my head for a moment, his chiseled jaw clenching and unclenching as he mulled over his thoughts. "Everything," he finally said, returning his gaze to mine. "For being a dick before I knew anything about you. And for being no better than the others who used you for their own pleasure, took without giving."

I tried to laugh off what he was saying with an easy tease. "Don't sell yourself short. You gave as much as you took, believe me."

The energy between us rose several notches, spiking and swirling like the charged air of an impending storm. Dax's hands traveled along the wings of my shoulder blades, fingertips pushing through my hair at the nape of my neck and holding my skull in his hands. His eyes traveled over my face, studying every plane and curve and hollow like a map. With infinite precision, he tilted my head just slightly, as if the exact angle was important, and then he leaned down. Slowly, so slowly, his lips captured mine in the softest of kisses. Just the barest brush of his lips over mine. A breath, really. The kiss of an angel, dispensed by a man whose dark looks and mysterious smile were pure devil.

Sin had never looked so damn sexy.

Once, twice, three times Dax kissed me. Light and sweet. The passion that lay just under the surface kept firmly in check.

Meanwhile, mine was raging out of control. A moan traveled up my throat, skating through my lips as a raspy whine. My fingers unlocked, sliding up Dax's back and kneading the muscles corded tightly on either side of his spine.

"Verity." My eyes snapped open at the sound of my name. It wasn't a groan or a plea or a tease. It was a *pay attention*. "I took a swipe at your confidence, at your worth, every time I walked away from what you wanted to give. In my mind, I was comparing you—your ambition and drive—to a woman whose name doesn't deserve to be spoken in the same breath as yours." He planted a kiss on my forehead, the softness of his lips lingering there. "I'm so sorry, Verity. I really am."

I had to blink back the tears stinging my eyes at his heartfelt confession. Because that's what it was, a confession as much as an apology.

More than that, it was a gift. As if Dax had sliced himself

open to reveal what was hidden deep inside. A place that had never been exposed to the light, let alone another person.

Dax's anxious expression studied mine as he pulled away. I gave him a soft smile. "You didn't have to say that—" I put a finger over his full lips when Dax looked like he was about to interrupt me. "But it means so much to me that you did."

Chapter Twenty

Dax

I wasn't sure Verity had any idea what she was doing to me. Taking my insides out and turning them upside down. They were completely rearranged, her fingerprints all over them.

Almost as if they didn't belong to me anymore.

She'd left a piece of herself behind, too.

But I wanted more. I wanted all of her.

My skin was hot, feverish. But my mind had never been more clear.

Verity Moore. She was sickness and cure. Risk and safety net. The face of an innocent, the body of a sinner. A past filled with darkness, a future shining bright.

My broken bombshell.

My reckless, resilient rebel.

"You came to the water's edge because I was asking things that made you uncomfortable. You still feel that way?"

Verity turned her face to the side, resting her cheek just below my collarbone. "Uncomfortable is the opposite of how I feel right now."

I gathered her even closer, tightening my hold. She felt so damn right in my arms. How had I not known this from the start? Why had I been fighting her so hard? "Good. Because I have something to tell you. Something I haven't been honest about."

She stiffened in my arms, disquiet carving a ridge between her brows.

"'Bombshell Rebel'—I wrote it."

Her jaw dropped. "You? But...why didn't you say anything?"

"I write a lot, under a pen name. No one except Travis knows."

"Those lyrics. Dax." She pulled away just slightly. "It was like you were inside my head. How...?"

"The first time you came over my place, after New York, you called me out, remember? Said you didn't show up for a booty call, or because you were a Barbie doll for me to play with."

She nodded, a blush rising to her cheeks. "Yeah, I remember. I overreacted—"

"No. No, you didn't. I was a dick. A selfish, self-centered piece of shit. But your reaction...You weren't surprised to be treated like that. You were surprised to be treated like that by *me*. I couldn't stop thinking about you, about my behavior. And I worked through it by writing about it." I didn't bother getting into the minutia of putting it into the wrong folder—clearly my subconscious had been active that day.

She gave a slow shake of her head, red tendrils of hair fluttering around her face. "If I told you to take me to bed right now, what would you say?"

My dick smacked the back of my zipper, silently screaming,

Hell, yes! The fucker wanted to throw a ticker-tape parade. "Guess I'd ask if it was because of the song, or because of me."

"For a guy who's supposed to be the quiet one, you sure ask a lot of questions."

I snorted into the wind. "I don't usually care enough to bother." I planted a light kiss on the top of Verity's head. "Can't say that about you, Verity. I care. A lot."

I felt her deep exhale, that last bit of resistance, of doubt—about me, about us—leaving her body. For a moment there was only the crash of the waves, the squawk of the seagulls.

"Knowing you wrote 'Bombshell Rebel' for me is sexy as hell. And I'm honored. It's only further proof that you see me, Dax. You really see me." Verity's eyes were a clear, bright bottle green, her hair a windswept blaze of fire, her skin luminous in the moonlight. But there was so much more to her than just beauty. "Neither of us have been open books, but I feel safe with you."

Verity was was right on both counts.

She was safe with me. I would drown myself in this ocean before I hurt her.

And there were still things she was hiding from me. I could feel them gathering like rain clouds at the edge of the horizon, impatiently grumbling. I just wasn't sure which one of us she was protecting. "When you're ready to share more of the secrets you've been keeping, I'm ready to bear their burden with you. You don't have to carry their weight alone, Verity."

Those dimples carved into her cheeks as she smiled up at me. "You sure you can handle them?"

Verity wasn't the only one of us keeping secrets. "You sure you can handle mine?" Without waiting for an answer, I grabbed her hand as we made our way up the winding path that had been cut into the cliff leading to my house.

As we got farther, I swept her into my arms, loving that she wrapped her wrists around my neck and nuzzled into me. "How am I doing so far?"

"You carrying me to your bed?"

"If that's where you want to go," I answered, the rasp in my voice having nothing to do with Verity's slight weight in my arms.

"Then I'd say you're doing pretty good."

"Only pretty good?"

"Yep. If you want a stronger endorsement, you'll have to earn it."

I entered through the back door. "Is that a challenge?"

The sweet, lilting notes of Verity's giggle had to be one of the most powerful aphrodisiacs on the planet. "Is it working?" she asked.

"Christ, Verity. There's nothing about you that doesn't work for me. Nothing."

The selfish, impatient part of me wanted to get her naked the second we walked inside. The other part of me wanted to take my time, unwrap her like a gift I'd waited a lifetime to receive.

I settled for somewhere in between, coming to a standstill in the center of my living room, letting her slide down my body until her toes were enveloped by the shag rug at our feet.

With the touch of a button, the fire in the grate roared to life. There wasn't much need for fireplaces in L.A., and this one was for show, not for heat, but I'd always been drawn to them. The idea that something so dangerous, so lethal, could be purposely brought into a home, enjoyed for its beauty despite its capacity to burn down the walls around me was strangely appealing.

"This isn't your bedroom," she said, light from the flames licking at her skin, making my tongue jealous.

"Are you complaining?" I didn't care where we were, really.

She shook her head slowly. "Not even a little bit."

We shared a smile, and I gathered her to my chest again, our mouths meeting on a shared sigh of pleasure. Our kiss was a tender sampling of what was to come. Heated breaths, the intensely erotic slide of tongues, the wet warmth of private places.

I groaned, one hand gathering Verity's hair in my fist as I used the other to grab her by her knees and settle us both on the shag rug at our feet. Before she could lie flat, I broke our hold to lift the hem of her shirt and pull it over her head.

Her hair fluttered every which way, falling around her shoulders in a wild tangle. Crimson brushstrokes on creamy skin. "So fucking beautiful," I breathed, curving my palm over her jawline, my thumb sweeping over her pink lips, pushing between the crease of her mouth. She bit down on it, a not-quite-gentle nibble, whirling her tongue around the tip before sucking it into her mouth.

"Fuuuck." My curse was a hollow husk, all bristle and hot air. If life had a pause button I would have smacked the shit out of it and hired some artsy photographer to take a picture. The kind I'd have blown up in black-and-white. The kind I'd hang in my bedroom.

A bedroom I wanted to share with Verity.

I cursed again, this time at the bone-deep certainty that Verity was a woman I wanted to go to sleep with every night and wake up with every morning. I wanted to share smiles and tears, secrets and stories.

I thought I was in love once, years ago.

I was a moron.

What I felt then was nothing compared to now.

Verity was the real deal.

She was *True*.

Slowly, I dragged my thumb from her mouth, sliding it down her chin, down her throat, pushing it behind the center clasp of her bra. "Convenient," I mumbled, easily disengaging it and pushing the thin straps off her shoulders.

Verity leaned back on her elbows, her thighs splayed over mine, eyes shining as brightly as the fire. "I love watching your face when you undress me. You look at me like you look at a guitar or a piano. Appraising, appreciating."

I swallowed heavily. Verity's body was an instrument I wanted to play; there was no denying that. But she was also a work of art to be treasured. "Anyone who doesn't, doesn't deserve to look."

"Tell that to the stylists who pick me apart inch by inch as if I don't have ears." She dipped her chin, her voice becoming a throaty tease. "Lemme see what you're hiding beneath all that cotton."

"If they ever say another unkind word to you, I might have to go down there, explain the extent of their idiocy," I said, not entirely kidding as I lifted my arms, gathering handfuls of fabric from behind my back and tugging the shirt over my head. I tossed it to the side and looked back at Verity, my attention drawn by the sweep of her tongue between the crease of her lips, then disappearing to tuck her lower lip behind her teeth. I could watch nothing but Verity's mouth for days and never get bored. I swear it had a personality all its own.

"Maybe you should take my place, instead." The burn of her stare swept over every muscle and sinew of my chest and abs. "You'd have them stumped—there's not a single thing to criticize."

I pulled her back upright, sliding my hands along the smoothness of her naked back and the ridge of her spine before gripping her ass to pull her into my lap, her legs straddling me. "Fuck, you feel good."

Verity's dimples flashed as her palms rose up my chest, skating down my arms before moving back up again and settling along the plane of my collarbone, her fingers a caress on my neck.

Beneath the want, the lust, the thickness of the desire hovering in the air between us, there was a peacefulness to this moment, an inevitability. I knew that I was exactly where I was supposed to be. Verity was the music of my soul, and I intended to spend the foreseeable future learning her lyrics.

She rested her forehead against mine. "I wish I had the words to describe how your touch makes me feel."

"Try." I wanted to know.

"Like you're pushing me off a cliff." She took a shuddering breath I felt to my core. "But knowing you'll be there to catch me."

"Always." It was a promise.

We shared a long look, so intense there was no need for more words. Our bodies had picked up the conversation, anyway.

Sweeping her hair aside, I sucked on Verity's neck, licking and biting her sweet skin. Her head tipped back, a red waterfall pouring over the arm I was bracing her with, a moan tripping from her lips as I kissed my way to her breasts.

That moan became a gasp as my lips closed over her pretty pink peaks. Everything about Verity was sweet.

With a last nip, I lowered her to the rug, this time sliding over her, bracing my weight on my knees and forearms, my desperate erection nestled between Verity's thighs. Beyond the familiar scents that clung to her skin, I detected the faint whiff of something headier, a more concentrated sweetness.

Inching downward, my journey was set to a soundtrack of moans and cries and soft, soft sighs as my tongue traced the outline of her rib cage, committing each rise and hollow to memory, and savored the tight little dimple of her belly button.

She was wearing navy pants that clung to her shape like a second skin, though the low waist still had a clasp and a zipper to deal with. A damn belt, too.

There was the slide of leather, the clang of the buckle, the metallic whisper of the clasp, the whine of the zipper.

I folded my fingers over the band, making sure to gather the lace of Verity's thong in my grasp as I pulled the fabric from her legs, her skin like warm satin against my knuckles.

Fully naked, Verity was a sight I wanted to soak into my corneas, imprint on my eyelids. So beautiful my heart ached to look at her.

Lowering my mouth to her skin again, I focused on one square inch at a time. The concave sweep of her belly, the slide of her hip, the plush curve of her thighs, the fragile indent behind her knees. Every inch was a marvel. Every inch leading me toward the sweetest, most delicious part of her.

Verity was bare and glistening, exposed and open.

Mine.

Verity

Light from the fireplace fell across Dax's shoulders in wavering streaks of gold, making his gorgeous skin shimmer. Or maybe it was just the haze dancing around my vision, pure pleasure carving its mark into me with each lick of Dax's tongue, each slide of his fingers. He was relentless, finding hidden parts of my body I didn't know existed, eliciting sensations so delicious I wouldn't have believed them possible.

The magic of his mouth was beyond my ability to comprehend. I knew I would never be able to look at his lips, at his tongue, without recalling, in excruciating detail, exactly what they were capable of, the skills he hid behind each sideways smile. I moaned, feeling my sanity slipping away, bit by bit by bit.

My hips arched upward, my thighs trembling against Dax's roughened jawline as he curved his fingers into me. Pressing, seeking, finding. Jesus, this man was winding me up so tight I could barely draw breath.

I was a quivering jellyfish trapped on a shag rug in the Pacific Palisades. And Dax was sucking all my sting right out of me. My only defense. Not only was he immune to the poison I'd harbored within myself—he was hungry for it.

Defenseless.

That's what I was. Completely, utterly defenseless.

His for the taking.

And the very idea of it thrilled me.

I had come back to California to stand on my own two feet, and I had. But now I was splayed out on Dax's living room floor, completely open and vulnerable and *his*—and I'd never been so happy in my entire life.

This moment was beyond a fantasy. Beyond a fairy tale.

White-hot streaks of pleasure lashed my nerve endings into a frenzy, sending a scream cartwheeling from my shocked gasp, my feet twin arrows pointing up at heaven, my hands curling into fists and grabbing at Dax's hair like he was the only thing keeping me tethered to the world.

My orgasm felt like a death. A moment when my heart stopped, my breath caught, my brain activity so overloaded that it ceased entirely.

The rebirth that followed was the most exquisite emergence into light, into life. My heart broke into a gallop, my lungs swelling, my mind scattering like glitter in the wind.

Dax gave a last, lingering kiss before crawling back over me, sucking my breasts into his mouth. The sensitive peaks sent bolts of electricity shooting through me with each nibble. But impatience was winding its way through me, too. I needed to feel Dax inside me, filling me up. I was desperate for us to be joined in a way that we hadn't been before. "Please. Jesus—I want...I want—"

Maybe Dax felt it, too, because soon his face was over mine, his arms solidly planted on either side of my head. A sexy cage I was only too willing to be trapped within. "I want, too. I want you, Verity. So fucking badly." Dax's eyes blazed as his mouth dropped to mine and I tasted myself on his lips. Unexpectedly erotic.

This kiss was more than an exploration. This kiss—it was a claiming.

Sliding my palms down Dax's rib cage, I fumbled with his button, then the zipper, finally shoving at the waistband of his pants with my hands and feet. I needed Dax to be as naked as I was. As desperately needy as I was.

Kicking free of his jeans, Dax settled his length over me, the thick, hard pulse of his erection pressing on my lower belly like a promise. My hips bucked upward, my calves arching over his back, ankles locking and pulling him even tighter against me. His groan rumbled against my lips, and I matched it, my hands roving from his shoulders to his neck, fingers pushing greedily into his hair. I wanted to touch and taste and feel. Everything. All of him. Now.

Dax shifted his weight, his thighs pushing up just enough

that I felt his cock dragging along my stomach, the thickness falling like a spear between my spread thighs, the fat crown poised at the exact split where I was most vulnerable. Just one lunge of his hips and I would be pierced, full to overflowing.

But instead Dax rocked slightly upward, nudging the swollen bundle of nerves he'd so effectively mastered just minutes ago.

I drew a shocked gasp, blinking wildly. Seeing only stars. "Jesus Christ, Dax. What are you doing to me?" My voice didn't belong to me anymore. It was a choked rasp, a barely audible echo clinging to my heaving breaths.

His eyes found mine in an intense stare. "What do you think I'm doing to you?"

I swallowed. "I think you might be killing me."

His chuckle sent goose bumps skating across my skin, streaking down my spine. "True, I'm just getting started. But killing you is the farthest thing from my mind."

I gave an impatient nudge of my hips. "Oh yeah? Then tell me, what exactly are your intentions?"

He dropped a gentle kiss on the tip on my nose, his hips moving again, his cock sliding back into place. "That's simple, baby. I'm makin' you mine."

I was struck dumb, rendered completely mute. It felt as if I'd breathed my hopes into Dax's mouth and he'd swallowed them down, digesting them in a way that they had become his, too.

I found my voice when Dax's features tightened into something that resembled pain. "What is it?"

"I don't want to get up, but"—he lowered his forehead so it was pressing on my shoulder—"I don't keep condoms in my living room."

Condoms. I hadn't even thought about them. Ridiculous given that I'd filmed a PSA advocating safe sex just a few months ago.

Except that right now I felt safe with Dax. Safe enough not to need a latex barrier between us. Not to need *any* barrier between us. "Are you...um...?"

He picked his head up. "Clean? Yeah."

I shivered. The word had never sounded so dirty. "Me too. And I'm on the pill." Before I came back to L.A., I had been tested for every possible STD, repeating them again recently, just to be sure. I was clean.

Glancing down at the most private part of him, which was pressed up against the most private part of me, I treasured the sight, licking my lips as I took in the fierce beauty of his thick length, the boldness of his swollen crown, the single bead of pre-cum glistening from the tip like a fat tear.

"Please." The word emerged ragged, a breathless sound of appreciation.

What came out of Dax's mouth was a long hiss, sharp and savage. He looked at me, that beautiful brow of his furrowed, skin pushing into an indent just above his nose. "You sure?"

Right then, I'd never been as sure of anything else in my whole life. "Yes," I breathed, my hips already quivering with expectation.

Dax's jaw twitched with tension, his teeth grinding together. He reached a hand between us, his frown smoothing, his eyes darkening with a fresh wave of lust. "Jesus, you're so fucking wet."

Another shiver, this one vibrating up my spine as his fingers swept inside my crease, his thumb flicking my clit. Moaning, I bit down on the hardness of Dax's bicep. I was a feverish collection of bones and muscles and crazed nerve endings, completely at Dax's mercy.

If he didn't fuck me soon, I would die. I was sure of it.

Either Dax took pity on me, or his own desire was just as strong, because he choked out another curse, positioning himself dead center, then slowly, so slowly, began pushing into me.

My eyelids fell closed, my back arching so that my breasts pushed against Dax's chest. God, he felt good. The pressure of him invading my slick heat, burrowing into the deepest part of me. It was dark and dirty and delicious.

And I still wanted more. So. Much. More.

Dax made it only a few inches before pulling out and starting over, this time with my slickness coating him, allowing for an easier entry. I hadn't been with anyone in so long and never with anyone like Dax. He was making sex feel old and new at the same time. Like I'd done this dance before, but only in preparation for this exact moment.

Dax was holding himself back, I could hear it in the ragged edge to his breaths, see it in his muscles that quivered from restraint. He was taking care, going slow. And I loved it.

But I wanted to watch his control shatter. I wanted to be the reason his control shattered.

My hips bucked upward, meeting his latest thrust, and I felt him bottom out deep inside me.

Dax's eyes squeezed shut, his face pinching into a scowl. "You're so fucking tight." He groaned. "I don't want to hurt you."

After what I had told him, Dax was treating me like a porcelain doll. But I was no one's plaything. Not anymore. I could have reassured him, but I was so sick of words. Instead, I wrapped my hands around his back, curling my nails into claws.

And I dragged them from the base of his spine to the blades of his shoulders. Hard.

Dax grunted, his eyes flying open in surprise.

"I hurt you first," I growled.

One corner of his mouth kicked up. "So that's how you want to play this, huh?"

"You're not going to break me, Dax."

His stare burned right through me, and he gave a shallow nod. "You know you can stop this at any time, right?"

With him buried deep inside me, I fought not to roll my eyes. "There's nothing to stop if you don't get started."

A chuckle rolled up his chest. "Oh, Verity. You have no idea what you're in for."

His gaze devoured the whole of my face as one hand snaked its way into my hair, pulling just enough that every nerve ending on my scalp woke up. He splayed his other hand across my throat, my pulse pounding against the pads of his fingertips.

Dax's hips retreated, my body mourning the sudden emptiness. But it didn't last long. His mouth descended on mine at the same time as his hips lunged forward, driving his entire length inside me in one thrust, his balls slapping my ass for just a second before he pulled out again.

I gasped into his mouth, his tongue darting against mine in a powerful kiss. Sensations rolled over me, every inch of my body tingling. In between kisses and thrusts, Dax's throaty whisper filled my ear.

You're so fucking beautiful.

I've wanted to fuck you, exactly like this, hard and raw, for so goddamn long.

I'm going to break you tonight, so fucking bad.

And then I'm going to put you back together, piece by piece.

His words were hot. His cock hotter. In an instant, I was burning up, everywhere.

"Not yet, princess," he warned, flipping me over and arranging me so that my hands were braced on the hearth, my knees spread apart, sinking into the rug. Staring into the flames, I felt Dax's hands run over my ass, studying my shape through his palms. Fingers dipped into my crease, running over the tight pucker, which jumped in surprise. But he only lined himself up with my wet slit, dropping a kiss at the base of my spine. "Another time."

I never even considered doing that with anyone, but it wasn't a question in my mind that I would do it for Dax. Just like I had no doubt that he would make it feel as good as everything else. But my thoughts scattered like confetti when he slid into me again, slowly at first. This time it wasn't out of restraint, but because he knew I was so close to the edge. And I was. My breaths fell fast and shallow. I was making all kinds of noises I'd never heard before, little whines and whimpers, thrusting my ass with absolutely no shame whatsoever. I wanted this. I wanted him. I *wanted*.

It could have been seconds or minutes or hours. I was so tense and tight, just barely hanging on to the smooth, cool marble when his movements changed from slow teasing to well and truly fucking.

That control of his finally obliterated.

Dax's powerful strokes invaded my body, each one deep and delicious. His hands were curled around my hips, his fingertips digging into my flesh. The slap of his skin meeting mine, the grunts dripping from his mouth, the dance of the flames in front of my face. My orgasm came on strong and fierce. I held on to the marble ledge for dear life, screaming Dax's name as my entire world split apart. Behind me, though, Dax was still moving, still pounding into me, his movements drawing out my climax in an impossible assault of ecstasy that went on so long my arms began to tremble.

I was losing my grip on the marble.

I was losing my grip on reality.

Just in time, Dax grabbed me around my waist, pulling me up so that my back was flush with his chest, giving a final roar as he squeezed me tightly within his embrace, the wet pulse of him inside me sending another wave of aftershocks racing across my overwrought nerves.

I trembled, feeling a bone-deep contentedness I'd never known existed. My head lolled back on Dax's shoulder, reveling in his strength, in his stamina, in his infinite, exquisite skill.

"I was wrong," I whispered on a shattered breath. "You broke me. I am ruined."

He chuckled, squeezing me just a little tighter. "That's the point. You are beautifully broken. Ruined for any other man but me."

Chapter Twenty-One

Dax

I'm down here," I called, knowing exactly who had slammed my front door. I was sprawled on the sectional, staring into the fire that had been burning since last night. Not sure if I was in the burning pit of hell or if this was what heaven looked like: a shag rug topped by a tangle of pillows and blankets, the scent of sex in the air.

Travis's shoes slapped the stairs in rapid procession. Tearing my gaze away from the flames, I immediately noted his reddened face, set off by a crisp white shirt and immaculately tailored navy suit. "What the fuck, Dax." It wasn't a question.

Verity had left just a few minutes ago, off to meet Piper for something—the details of which Travis obviously knew, hence his perfect timing.

Travis wasn't glaring at me, looking for an answer. But he sure as hell wanted an explanation.

I didn't have one.

Against all reason and judgment, I'd fallen for Verity Moore. Hard.

I glanced up at him just in time to see his eyes slide to the fire, to the pillows and blankets, to the water and wine and the empty box of graham crackers we'd polished off during the night.

A deep sigh rattled his lungs. "Seriously, Dax. What the fuck are you doing?"

This time he was ready for an answer. If only I had one to give.

An image from last night burrowed its way to the forefront of my consciousness. Verity, her eyelids heavy but her eyes contented and glowing, lit from within. Orange light licking at her creamy skin. Lips swollen and dark from our kisses. Her features soft and sweet and angelic.

An angel who'd been well and truly fucked—and was damn pleased about it.

Glimmers of hope, of possibility, came at me like rain. I was drenched in them, wanting a life filled with nights like the last one. But the clouds above could just as easily mete out daggers of lightning as a gentle mist. Lightning that would leave me treading on scorched earth, seeking shelter inside a house on fire.

Guilt stirred inside the pit of my stomach, pitching and clawing at my intestines. Making me sick. Completely disgusted with myself for wanting something—someone—I didn't deserve to have. Not when I was still legally bound to another.

Travis's eyes drilled holes into my skull, seeing the mess inside. Reading the situation I'd gotten myself into, he rocked back on his heels, his eyebrows arching as he switched tactics. "You and Verity, huh?"

I wanted to deny the truth staring us both in the face, tell a lie that would put an end to this awkward conversation, but even if my tongue could shape the words, my brain was fried. Too panicked by the truth to successfully deceive a poodle, let alone Travis Taggert.

"What about it?"

Travis exhaled a deep sigh and perched on the arm of the sectional, smoothing a nonexistent wrinkle from his pants. "First of all, I was quite clear that I expected all of you to keep your dicks in your pants when it came to Verity. I'd like to get through one tour—just one fucking tour—without the whole damn thing exploding in my face."

He jumped to his feet, walking to the window and staring out at the ocean as he rubbed at the back of his neck. "And second, Verity's the real deal, Dax. As her manager, I don't want her distracted. But as a human being, this girl has been through the ringer. Are you planning on being just another douchebag in the long line of them she's had to step over to get to where she is now, where she wants to be?"

It was the same question I'd been asking myself, practically since I first met her. The same question she'd asked me last night. An old-fashioned one. *What are your intentions?*

The only thing I knew for sure was that I would never hurt her. Never again, anyway. "No."

At the barely audible syllable I managed to push through my lips, Travis spun around, his expression as if I'd dropped a bomb. "No?"

I licked my lips, cleared my throat. "No," I repeated, louder this time. "Not goin' to be just another asshole in her life."

Travis merely stood by the window, his posture expectant.

Damn him.

"I'm serious. I don't want to fuck things up. Not with Verity. Not with the tour. Not with the band."

He shoved his hands into his pockets. "I hope you can juggle as well as you play guitar."

Could I? I'd never been able to before. Not sure I should expect things to be different now.

Except—Verity was different. She wasn't like any woman I'd ever known. Not even Amelia. Especially not Amelia. And I was different, too. Older. Maybe even wiser.

Travis walked back into the living room, reclaiming his seat. "When Delaney became more to Shane than just another woman in a long line of them, I wasn't happy about it—at all. I was downright furious, if you want to know the truth. I thought you four needed to have complete allegiance to each other, and to me, in order to remain at the top of your game."

I angled my body toward Travis, giving him my full attention. To say that he was the least introspective person I'd ever met would be an understatement.

"But I was wrong." The words skated through his mouth on a gritty chuckle. "Shane is as focused on NBT as he's ever been. And he's happy. Meanwhile, Landon nearly destroyed his career with that drunken stunt of his and has been hiding in rehab for the past couple of months. Jett is fucking his way through the entire female population of L.A., and trying to pretend that that's all he wants out of life.

"Dax, if you can find some joy in this crazy life we've all signed up for, you should grab it with both hands and not let go. Apparently being happy isn't a career killer." He tossed a wry smile my way, lifting his shoulders in a shrug. "Who knew?"

Choose happy. I blinked at Travis now, wondering if Shane had shared the advice his brother had given him. "Who are you and what have you done with my shark of an agent?"

"I know. I've gone soft, and it's all Shane's and Delaney's fault." His voice turned almost wistful. "Hard to be around them without wanting a little bit of what they have."

I nodded. Love. Mutual respect. Happiness. I had felt the warmth of their genuine affection coming off them in waves that night in New York, each one hitting me hard. "Yeah."

"Think you and Verity have a slice of that?"

A groundswell of emotions rose in me, and the similarity to what I'd seen between Shane and Delaney was unmistakable. "Yes." My answer was immediate.

"Then maybe you should take the crap you've gone through as warning sign, not a roadblock."

Appreciate the road taken and go where you heart leads you.

Maybe that damn horoscope had been right. Maybe my heart had led me to Verity.

"You playin' matchmaker these days?"

Travis reached over, slapping my knee as he stood up. "Yep. And don't worry, I'll invoice you for my services."

I grunted. Travis was the best at what he did, but he didn't come cheap. "I'm sure you will. And make sure those services include severing all ties to Amelia, once and for all."

"Consider it done." He started for the stairs, turning back to face me when he was about halfway up. "Does Verity know?"

There was so much I still hadn't told Verity, I needed Travis to be more specific. "Know what?"

"That you're in love with her."

Panic clutched at my chest. That four-letter word was terrifying. L-O-V-E. And the most terrifying part about it...it was one hundred percent true.

Travis's mouth twitched once before lifting into a full-fledged grin. "Thought so. You might want to fix that, by the way."

I barely heard the front door close over the roar in my brain.

I *loved* Verity Moore.

It was the ultimate irony.

I'd fallen in love with a pop princess.

That's "disgraced pop princess" to you.

I'd fallen in love with a gorgeous redheaded wiseass. A woman whose powerful voice was exceeded only by her bravery.

My attraction to Verity went beyond skin-deep, burrowing into every corner of her soul. Even the parts she'd exposed to me and the dark places she wasn't quite ready to reveal yet. That was okay... We had time.

Because I wasn't going anywhere.

Last night the connection between us had been obvious, a heat that melted all of our edges just enough to leave us fused together. A connection that had nothing to do with sex and everything to do with... *everything*. Every. Fucking. Thing.

I'd spent half the night just staring at her. Watching her eyes flutter in sleep and wanting to know what was going on inside that pretty little head of hers. Running hot hands over her body, memorizing each curve and hollow, savoring every sweet moan and soft sigh.

We showered together this morning, and even knowing she'd be back in a few hours, it had been painful to watch her walk out my front door.

I finally got up. I couldn't sit around my house and mope all day. I didn't feel like surfing or writing songs, either.

I knew exactly what I wanted to do.

Verity

"You're really going to eat pasta in front of me?" I stared incredulously across the table at Piper after she placed her order. I'd left Dax's house early to tape a segment with one of the morning radio shows, and now we were meeting Delaney for lunch before an afternoon meeting with a designer to begin planning my costumes for the tour. In an hour I would be naked, every inch of my body measured. It was bad enough that I'd eaten hot dogs and s'mores with Dax last night. I could not indulge in pasta today.

Piper leveled an apologetic smile my way as she rubbed her swollen belly. "Sorry. Firefly loves the gnocchi here."

Truthfully, I was in too good of a mood to be annoyed about eating a bowl of lettuce dressed with lemon juice. Last night had been amazing. Better than amazing. I'd had so many orgasms that I was still feeling little zings of pleasure every time my thighs brushed together.

The salad Delaney ordered wasn't quite as boring as mine, but nowhere near Piper's choice. She pointed a finger at me and made a circling motion. "Okay, I want to know what that smile is all about."

"It's been on her face all day," Piper interjected. "I thought she would have burst open and told me everything already, but so far all I've gotten is that smile."

I couldn't help it; my grin only grew wider. Trying to conceal it, I bit down on the straw of my iced tea—unsweetened, unfortunately. "What, I can't be in a good mood?"

Piper and Delaney exchanged a look, then stared back at me. "You were chatting with that radio show DJ like he was your long-lost cousin. The man is probably planning a Verity Moore marathon and setting up a shrine to you right now."

Delaney laughed. "You might want to let him down easy, seeing as you're clearly wrapped up in someone else."

"Fess up," Piper added. "Firefly wants to know."

"What are you going to do when you can't use your pregnancy as a reason for everything?"

Piper shrugged, not a drop of remorse on her flawless face. "I'm thinking lactation might be effective."

I grimaced. "Seriously? *Blech*."

She pointed at me. "See. That's exactly what I'm going for. No one's going to argue with me when I have nipple power."

Delaney shook her head. "Well, we have a few months before you can hold your hard-working mammary glands over us. In the meantime, can we stay focused on Verity's love life?"

"Good idea," Piper agreed, turning the full force of her undivided attention on me. "So, who has you farting rainbows this morning?"

I squirmed in the hard-backed chair of the restaurant. "I'd rather hear about your last sonogram. Any more of those 4D pictures?"

Delaney burst out with a laugh. "So you're really not going to admit what's going on between you and Dax?"

This time both Piper and I gaped at Delaney. Piper recovered first. "Dax? Verity's been hanging out with Dax?"

"Are you kidding? The man is so into Verity he doesn't know what to do."

A frown creased Piper's brow. "I think it's scaring me that you're actually making sense, and I was completely oblivious."

"Well, pregnancy is obviously stealing some of your brain cells, because the chemistry between those two is off the charts.

Did you see them at the party? They could barely take their eyes, or hands, off each other."

Piper glanced down at her belly. "Firefly, you're really letting me down here." Now that she was in her third trimester, Piper's belly was obvious, but so far her appetite hadn't increased anything else. She looked like she had sliced a basketball in half and shoved one part beneath her shirt.

The waiter appeared with our food, placing a steaming bowl of pasta in front of Piper and setting down salads in front of Delaney and me. As Piper watched him grate Parmesan over her meal, she gave her belly a reassuring pat. "I take that back. You're doing fabulous."

I squeezed fresh lemon over my lettuce and forked a bite into my mouth. I'd eat dirt if it meant not having to add to the conversation. But all this talk about Dax had brought memories of last night front and center in my mind. I'd never known sex could be like that. Dax had been completely in control and yet entirely attuned to my responses. He'd given me exactly what I wanted, what I needed, all night long. And somehow I'd managed to please him, too. No matter how often he had reached for me in the middle of the night, or I'd reached for him, we were always ready, as if our bodies had been starved for each other and couldn't get enough.

Realizing I was frozen, my fork hovering midair between my plate and my mouth, I blinked away the steamy memories only to find Piper and Delaney staring at me again. "Girl, you have it bad," Delaney crooned.

Luckily, Piper was prevented from chiming in when the phone she kept beside her plate started buzzing. Shoving a bite of gnocchi in her mouth, she picked it up and began texting furiously. "Well, so much for this afternoon's fitting. Apparently the designer's muse didn't show up for work today, so he's closing up shop and will let us know when he, and his muse, feel like working again."

I wasted no time clearing a space on my plate and stealing some of Piper's starchy deliciousness. "Hey!"

I shoved a gnocchi in my mouth, groaning in pleasure. "My muse is hungry."

Piper sniffed, pulling her plate back. "Well, your muse clearly built up an appetite from all those orgasms last night."

My skin blazed. "I'm pleading the Fifth."

"I'm sure you did plenty of pleading last night, too," Delaney teased, her fork a flash of silver as she stabbed one of Piper's gnocchi.

These two knew exactly what Dax and I had done last night…and yet they had no idea. I wanted to gush about every moment. I wanted to proclaim Dax's penis Master of the Universe—or, at the very least, Master of *My* Universe. But somehow I had a feeling Dax wouldn't appreciate being the subject of an intense gossip session, even if my contribution was to sing his praises like a canary.

Piper glared at Delaney when she stole another gnocchi. "The two of you are taking food from a pregnant woman's mouth. You should be ashamed of yourselves."

"If you would do more eating and less talking, we wouldn't be able to take anything," Delaney shot back.

I loved watching the interplay between Piper and Delaney. Piper had mentioned that they'd been frenemies back in high school, but I couldn't imagine it. They reminded me of sisters that adored each other despite their constant bickering. I felt lucky that they'd included me in their friendship. Besides my grandmother, I'd never had any true friends growing up. I never connected with anyone from school, and in Hollywood, it was hard to make friends with peers I was constantly competing against—for auditions, lines, air time. Even though Piper and Delaney had spent most of our lunch grilling me about Dax, I was savoring every moment.

Delaney turned to me. "Okay, I get that you don't want to share all the down-and-dirty details. But here's what I want to know—does Dax actually talk to you?"

I nearly spit out my iced tea. "Does he *talk* to me?"

"That came off weird, I know. But he's always so quiet."

Dax was definitely the strong, silent type. "I don't know that I'd ever call him a chatterbox, I guess, but he's pretty open one-on-one."

"And how much one-on-one time have you been having?" Piper prodded.

"Enough." I glanced down at my lap, smoothing out my napkin. "Enough to know I want to spend more time with him." A lot more.

I felt their eyes meet over my head. "So you and Dax…you're a thing now. A couple?"

I rushed to shake my head. "No." And then I paused. *Are we?* What we did last night wasn't a one-night stand. Not for me, anyway. "I don't know what we are, except for new. This is all very new."

Somehow that word felt right. New wasn't bad or good, confining or dismissive. It just was. *New.* It fit.

Piper made a small grunt and set down her fork across her empty plate. She leaned back in her chair, crossing her arms over the swell of her belly.

I glanced between the two of them, prickles of discomfort staggering across my skin like spiders' legs. "What? Is it so crazy to believe Dax would be interested in me?"

Delaney was the first to reach across the table, closing her fingers over my hand. "That's not what we meant at all. For god's sake, you could have any man eating out of the palm of your hand."

That was just the facade. A carefully constructed image that had been created by everyone else but me. "So he's only interested in me because of what I look like?"

Delaney's expression didn't change. "Of course not. I don't know you very well yet, but you're not at all what I expected you to be—in a good way. Dax would be a fool not to fall for you."

"Thank you." I squeezed her hand, an appreciative smile tugging at my lips.

I was distracted by a flash of white out of the corner of my eye and looked over to see Piper dabbing at her eyes. She waved a hand in front of her face and blew her nose into the napkin. "Don't mind me. Just over here, pregnant and alone."

I felt a stab of sympathy. Here I was, getting all prickly when Delaney was just trying to say something nice. Piper had real issues to worry about. A baby on the way. Single motherhood. The insecurities that had built up over so many years, becoming a protective mantle I wore like armor, slipped just a bit. "Piper, I'm—"

Her phone started vibrating again, and Piper picked it up, flashing the screen at me with a rueful huff. "Someone's looking for you."

"Dax?" I dug in my purse for my own phone, and sure enough there were several texts asking when I would be through for the day.

And just like that, my armor slipped a little further, my lips twisting back into a smile as joy thrummed within my veins. I glanced back up at Delaney and Piper, trying to school my expression back into nonchalance so Piper wouldn't cry again. Instead she started laughing, and Delaney quickly chimed in.

"Write him back," Piper finally said. "I'll be in touch when the designer, or his muse, is ready to work again."

"Yeah," Delaney added. "And maybe Piper and I will go shop for baby clothes."

"You don't have to hover over me, D. Shane is probably clawing at the walls wondering when you're coming back home."

"Don't be silly. We're going to have a long-overdue girls day. Shane's working on a new song, but he's having a hard time without Landon."

"Speaking of, have you had any news on Landon? Where he is, when he's coming back?"

I had begun typing out a response to Dax, but I looked up at the sound of Piper's voice. Barely more than a whisper, it was threaded with tension, her skin several shades paler than it had been just a few moments ago.

Delaney shook her head, dark strands swooshing over her shoulders. "No, just that he's supposed to be back in L.A. soon."

My publicist swallowed heavily, a faraway look in her eyes as she rubbed her belly. Maybe if Piper and I had the kind of relationship she had with Delaney, I would have pressed her on it. But looking between the two women, it was clear that there was an entire backstory that Piper wasn't ready to share with me. Deciding to give them their space, I scooted my chair back and dropped my napkin onto my plate. "I'm going to head out."

"Don't do anything I wouldn't do," Piper advised, forcing cheer into her voice.

"What is that, exactly?"

She blinked. "Give your heart to someone who doesn't deserve it."

For a moment there was silence, and I felt the full weight of Piper's sadness like a kick to the ribs. I reached for my chair. Dax could wait.

But Delaney shooed me away. "Don't you dare—there are no more invitations to this pity party. Go. Have fun with Dax. And not that you should take unsolicited advice from anyone, but ignore Piper over here. Don't be afraid of taking chances—life's too short to play it safe."

Chapter Twenty-Two

Dax

The look of happy surprise on Verity's face made pulling the stalker move of tracking her down worth it. I lowered my window as she crossed the curb. "Hop in."

She threw a last look at the photographers that had erupted into a frenzy the second she walked out the door, ducking into my front seat with a grin like she was playing hooky from school. "I only wrote you back a minute ago. How'd you get here so fast?"

I made a right at the next corner, checking my rearview mirror for a tail, but no one had followed us. I exhaled, my hands loosening on the wheel. "How else? Someone tweeted a picture of you in there. And because the social media bots seem to read my mind, I got an alert on my phone."

Verity groaned. "I hope they didn't catch me stealing pasta off Piper's plate, or there will be a story about me battling an eating disorder by tomorrow."

I glanced sideways at her, sitting in the front seat of my car like it was her rightful place and I'd been too stupid to realize it until now. "Does it ever bother you?"

"What?"

"Celebrity. Fame. Never knowing what someone's motives are for getting to know you."

"Sometimes, I guess. I was pushed into the spotlight before I knew how bright the lights were, or that even the tiniest flaws had no chance of remaining hidden." She checked that the door was locked before leaning her back against it, angling her body toward me. "But I'm probably not the best person to ask about getting to know people."

"No?" My interest was piqued. "Why not?"

She shrugged, red hair bouncing on her shoulders. "I can't remember the last person I met who didn't pursue a relationship with me because of who I was." That laugh of hers trickled out, tap-dancing into my eardrums. "Not you though. I think it's fair to say we're hanging out in spite of who I am, not because of it."

I wrapped my hand around her knee, lightly squeezing it as my laughter mingled with hers. "You don't mind me dragging you away from your girlfriends?"

"Nope. Where are you dragging me to?"

"Ah." I flashed her a wink. "It's a surprise."

She groaned. "I hate surprises."

"I think you're going to like this one. And we're almost there."

A few minutes later I pulled into a nondescript industrial park, loving the confused little frown pulling at Verity's brows as she took in the car repair shops, office buildings, and warehouses lining the street. Shutting off the ignition, I came around to Verity's side to help her out.

"Where are we?"

Throwing one arm around Verity's narrow shoulders, I led her across the parking lot and pointed at the easy-to-miss sign. "A brewery."

"Oh." I felt her earlier excitement deflate a little. "Is this where you buy your beer?"

Pulling open the door, I ushered her into the industrial-looking space. "No. Their specialty is cider."

Verity's eyes widened, understanding creeping into her expression. "You found a place that makes apple cider?"

My grin stretched further. "The sparkling kind."

But that wasn't all. Waving at the burly man hunched over a barrel in the yawning space, I led Verity into a small room just a few feet from where we were standing. The brewery wasn't open to the public today, but the owner was apparently a big Nothing but Trouble fan, which made the plan I'd formulated over the course of the morning that much easier to put into place.

"I thought we'd have a cider tasting."

We had just sat down at the long trestle table when the door opened and Sam, the owner who had been fussing with one of the barrels in the back earlier, came in. "Hey there."

But Verity's eyes weren't on Sam. They were on what he was holding.

"Oh my god." Verity clapped a hand over her mouth, her blazing green gaze barely contained by a set of thick lashes. As Sam set the champagne flutes on the table between us, she dropped her hand, revealing cheeks the sweetest shade of pink. "Amber glass and hollow stems…just like my grandmother's."

Sam started to explain about the brewing process, but Verity cut in. "Excuse me. I'm sorry. But those glasses…Is there any chance I can buy them from you?"

Sam glanced from her to me and back again, looking unsure

whether he would be saying too much if he told Verity I'd brought them myself. "Uh, I'm not really sure—"

I saved him the trouble. "They're yours."

Verity blinked at me, confusion and hope radiating from her expression.

"I found them, Verity. I bought them for you."

One minute she was sitting opposite me and the next she'd flung herself into my lap. Sam took that as his cue to leave. "I've looked so many times, so many places. How—where?"

"I hit a few flea markets."

"You? I brought you to the nicest one in L.A. and you were not a fan."

"I made an exception this morning." When it came to Verity, I was making all kinds of exceptions. The damn girl was worth every single one.

"So you found them at a flea market? Which one?"

"Not exactly. I struck out three times. But then I started talking to one of the vendors and described your grandmother's glasses to him. He remembered hearing about a garage sale up in Glendale where the woman collected crystal."

"So…you went to three flea markets, then to a garage sale in Glendale?" Her expression was incredulous. "For me?"

Incredulous. And heartbreaking. Verity Moore—teen star, fallen pop princess, a huge talent on the verge of a major comeback—was looking at me like an abused puppy being offered a treat. Almost as if she didn't believe me. That I might be faking it. Pulling a stunt to get her within kicking range.

I shrugged, heat rising up the back of my neck at Verity's scrutiny. "It's no big deal."

"No big deal," she repeated, her eyes shimmering as she blinked up at me. "It the nicest thing anyone has ever done for me." Her voice trembled, a single tear shaking free and sliding down her cheek like a liquid diamond.

I couldn't take my eyes off it. That lone droplet charting a path across her flawless skin. Leaving a streak that twisted up my insides and squeezed out every last remaining doubt about her, about us.

I lifted one hand to curve around her face, swiping at the tear with my thumb until it was nothing but a dewy shimmer cresting the rise of her cheekbone.

And then I reached for the two glasses, handing one to Verity. "Cheers, True. You made me believe chances are there for the taking. That risks have rewards, even for me."

She smiled and clinked her rim against mine.

As the sweet cider fizzed against my tongue, I wrapped my arm more tightly around Verity's waist, the indent between her hip and rib cage the perfect hand rest.

Verity Moore made me *believe*.

And this *choose happy* theory…It was brilliant.

Verity

My mother was proving to be more intractable than Travis had given her credit for. Not that I was surprised. The woman was a complete mule when it came to getting what she wanted. And what she wanted was *me*.

Not as a daughter, of course. She hadn't made a single attempt to speak with me directly. Her only interest in me was as a client. Her very own golden goose.

Travis had offered to let me stay in a house he owned nearby, and I'd considered renting a place of my own, but every time I brought up either option, Dax told me not to bother, that we'd be on tour in another few months.

So in the meantime, we were living together.

Yeah.

Color me shocked.

Truthfully, Dax's home felt more comfortable to me than the ostentatious Beverly Hills house. My mother was still there, giving interviews to whatever gossip outlets were willing to print her ridiculous sob stories about me—her unappreciative daughter.

Both Travis and Piper wanted me to sit down for a primetime interview, like Shane did after news of his business relationship with Delaney leaked. So far I'd refused, reminding them that Shane's interview had led to his arrest not long after. If I gave them nothing but pithy press releases and carefully crafted statements, the story would blow over soon.

I hoped.

Of course, the real reason I didn't want to give an interview were all those questions about "Bombshell Rebel" being a thinly veiled jab at Jack Lester. Travis had put out a statement saying that it was impossible, given that I didn't write the song myself. But I wasn't sure that I wouldn't give something away just from my reaction to his name.

I hated myself for taking the coward's way out, for not sharing my story, my shame. But I wasn't ready. Not yet.

Tonight the Hughes Quintet was playing at Walt Disney Concert Hall. Dax had asked me to go with him last week at the brewery and I'd nearly choked on my apple cider. I wasn't expecting it—at all. Then again, nothing about my relationship with Dax had been expected, certainly not by me.

I was feeling very Audrey Hepburn in my sleek, off-the-shoulder black sheath, my hair pulled back in a French twist that was just messy enough to feel modern. I was even wearing pearls at my neck.

Pearls.

The faint strains of Dax's perfectly tuned piano slipped beneath the closed bedroom door as I refreshed my lipstick. Holding my black stilettos in my hands, I followed the haunting notes to find him bent over the keys, dressed in what appeared to be the same suit he'd worn the day we first met in New York. At least playing the piano prevented him from tugging at his collar.

I stood a few feet away, not wanting to interrupt. But Dax's nose twitched, as if he smelled my perfume. The second he looked up, his hands stilled. His expression softening from one of intense concentration to undeniable appreciation.

The bench whined as Dax stood, pushing it back over the floor, my chin tipping up as he strode toward me, the difference in our heights more pronounced when I was barefoot. A shiver of awareness trembled within my bones. With each step he took I realized how deeply I'd fallen for this man.

How much I wanted him in my life.

With my whole heart and mind. With my body and soul.

When it came to Dax Hughes, I was full to the brim, overflowing with want.

Intoxicated by it.

"You look beautiful," he whispered, his breath a minty whisper.

"So do you." The response rolled off my tongue.

Dax laughed. "Beautiful? Now, there's something I haven't been called before."

The sound was so rich and decadent, delicious really, I swear it filled up parts of my soul I didn't know were empty. And the way he looked at me—really looked at me—made me feel like all my chips and cracks were precisely planned, just to let the light shine on his face.

I felt lighter these days, too. That protective mantle I'd wrapped around myself, so thick and battered I could have been a hundred-year-old turtle, was lying on the side of the road somewhere. I didn't know where, only that I didn't need it anymore.

Dax made me want to be open, vulnerable. Even if it meant taking the risk of being hurt.

He was worth the risk.

"No?" I reached for his hand. A rush of sparks erupted at the simple contact, and I led him toward the mirror hanging from the opposite wall. Positioning Dax so that he was in the center and I was to his side, I nodded at our reflections. "See? Beautiful—inside and out."

His eyes were on my face when he gave a solemn nod in return. "Yeah. I see." Dax's voice, normally as smooth and textured as velvet, was a husk of itself, a gritted rasp.

I jerked away from the intensity of his stare. There was a burning grind of emotions inside, all directed at me.

But once I wasn't held captive to Dax's brooding, burning gaze…I was free to take in our reflection. Not just me. Not just him. *Us.*

Holy shit.

Us.

My breath caught for an instant, somewhere between my lungs and my throat, a knotted air embolism that was lost, stuck. My heart raced, erratic and fast. The breathless moment felt like a warning. A reminder that life was fragile. Temporary.

And damn it, I was going to make mine count.

"Do we have time...?" I stuttered, knowing I didn't care how long I'd spent getting my hair and makeup done just right, or that the zipper on this dress had stuck earlier and I was afraid if I took it off I might not be able to get it back on. Or even that I would meet Dax's family for the first time with the taste of him in my mouth, his slick wetness between my thighs, and a damp patch on my lace panties.

Dax grinned, wearing his dark good looks like a weapon as he unclasped the hook and eye closure at my back and tugged at the zipper. It cooperated for him, and the roughened pads of his fingertips traced a devastating path down my spine. My dress fell in a puddle of black satin at my feet, my stilettos dropping, one by one, from my tingling fingers. I watched Dax's large hands curve around my shoulders, then slide down my arms. Entwining his fingers with mine, he brought them up to cup my breasts.

I exhaled a trembling breath, completely captivated by our reflection. His tanned skin so striking against my fair coloring. His body so much larger than mine. All that brute strength, and yet Dax was the most gentle man I'd ever known. Even when he was rough, he took infinite care of me. And he made me want to take care of him, too—in endless ways.

One of his hands slid down my belly as I stared into the mirror, long fingers probing between my thighs. I shivered, moaning Dax's name as pleasure wound hard and fast inside me. "Have I told you how much I like watching you come for me, Verity?"

I shook my head, unable to speak.

He lowered his head, kissing the side of my neck as his hands worked all kinds of magic. "Bought this place because of the view, but all I want to look at is you."

In the mirror, our eyes met.

Everything hit me at once. The look of love on Dax's face, the thrill of his touch, the tempest in my core. The fire he'd been building suddenly raging out of control. I cried out, closing my eyes from the intensity of it all. Until I was nothing but a shattered stack of ash.

And then I dropped to my knees. Clinging to Dax, I took him in my mouth and sucked hungrily. I might never get enough of this gorgeous man.

But I would try.

Chapter Twenty-Three

Dax

For once I was in a great mood heading to one of my family's concerts. A state of mind entirely due to the woman beside me. Verity Moore.

True.

We were running late, but I didn't give a shit. Let them start without me. Let them look over to my assigned seat and see it empty.

It would remain empty for the entire show anyway.

Rather than tell my parents I was bringing someone, I had bought two tickets through the box office.

I wanted to focus on Verity's reaction to the music, not my family's reaction to Verity.

Most musicians regarded their audience with an air of benign negligence. *I play for myself; be grateful you are allowed to observe my talent.* My parents were no different, and yet somehow I always felt their eyes drifting in my direction during their performances. It wasn't noticeable; there was never any eye contact. But today I was happy to stay wrapped up in my own world with Verity.

We made it inside the theater just as the lights began to flash, the curtain parting seconds after we were escorted to our seats. Verity squeezed my hand. "Thank you for inviting me."

I leaned over, my lips a breath away from the fleshy lobe I loved to bite. "My pleasure." She blushed at the blatant innuendo behind my words, goose bumps prickling the satiny skin of her neck.

Music had been the one constant in my life. All kinds. Every kind. Despite my issues with my family, during their shows, everything fell away but the music. It lifted my spirits, affirmed my soul, sustained my sanity. But today it was merely a soundtrack to the beautiful performance unfolding in the seat to my left. Verity's first exposure to classical music.

She sat forward in her chair, mouth slightly open. Appreciation shined from her eyes, excitement vibrating from her body. Verity wasn't just listening to the music; she was experiencing it, *absorbing* it. Her expression vacillating between ruin and rapture, envy and intrigue.

Through Verity, I was hit by a double dose of excitement, a double dose of awe. Compositions I'd heard hundreds, maybe even thousands of times before, felt new to me. Resonant.

Verity was the first to shoot up out of her chair at the end, the final notes still vibrating in the air. I rose to my feet more slowly, along with the rest of the audience. I noticed my parents surprise when they looked our way, though they quickly covered it by giving their traditional bow to the audience.

My brothers walked off the stage, followed by my sister and

then my parents. Rather than rush for the exit, Verity instead slumped back into her seat, regarding me with awe written all over her face. "I had no idea classical music could be so intense, so passionate. Sure, when you play the piano for me, I feel every note to the depths of my soul, but I chalked it up to the intimacy of being an audience of one." She tilted her head to the side, lowering her voice. "That and the fact that you're the sexiest piano player I've ever seen."

I smirked. "So, you liked it?" Few people actually appreciated classical music, including other musicians. I loved that Verity had, and I knew exactly what she meant.

"It was incredible. I had no idea I would enjoy it so much. Words—lyrics—were completely unnecessary." She looked back at the stage and sighed. "I just wish I could have seen you up there with them."

Every time I came to a performance, I was reminded how much I missed it. Even after so much time had passed, it still felt as if a piece of me had not only been lost, but stolen.

We took our time leaving the theater, waiting for everyone else to file out of their seats and through the doors. Although there would be a small reception backstage, mostly for donors and patrons, I had reserved the private room of a restaurant not far from the concert hall. The menu was written in French, the service was atrocious, the food overpriced and undercooked. My parents would love it.

I hadn't told them that I was bringing Verity, but since I was footing the bill, I'd bring whomever I damn well pleased.

It was a short drive to the restaurant, and rather than head directly to our table, we took a seat at the bar.

The good thing about places that practically required a Black Card with your reservation was that there was no "scene." The bar was small and dark, with just one other person nursing a highball glass at one end, his eyes glued to his phone.

"Champagne?" I asked, but Verity shook her head.

"It would be a letdown without hollow stems. Maybe just a white wine spritzer? I don't want to be tipsy when I meet your folks for the first time."

I gave her order to the bartender, deciding to have an aged bourbon myself. Unlike Verity, time with my family called for high-proof alcohol.

Forty minutes later, my parents texted that they were on their way. "I'm nervous," Verity whispered, squeezing my hand as we left our empty glasses on the bar and headed to the private room.

"Nervous? Why?" Verity Moore was the most fearless woman I'd ever known.

"Are you kidding?" Her eyes rounded. "These are your parents. I want them to like me."

I chuckled. "I'm sure they'll like you more than they do me—although that's not saying much."

Verity's brows pulled into a frown, but Julian and Sebastian burst into the room before she could say anything else.

They skidded to a stop in front of us, staring at Verity. "Told you. It's *her*," Seb said in an awestruck voice. Julian just nodded.

Aria followed. I could tell she was just as impressed to be meeting Verity Moore as my brothers, although she did a much better job at covering it.

Despite her claim of being nervous, Verity took it all in stride. Drawing each of them into an excited hug.

When my parents came in, she shook their hands, already gushing about their performance as we all took our seats. "I was so moved. I didn't realize classical music could be so passionate, so powerful."

My father grinned. "Yes, well. When you play the master composers, you don't need sound effects and pyrotechnics to engage your audience."

I let the not-so-subtle dig slide off my shoulders, but Verity apparently picked up on it. "I'm sure you're right," she said, her tone light. "Although engaging an audience of thousands requires a slightly different approach than hundreds, wouldn't you agree?"

"How many people were at your last concert, Dax?" Julian asked.

I shrugged. "In L.A., I think it was about twenty thousand at the Staples Center."

Verity nudged my shoulder. "And how long did it take to sell out?"

I knew what she was doing. It was incredibly sweet, but unnecessary. "An hour and a half, give or take."

She looked back at my parents. "You must be so proud of him."

"Of course we are," they answered, fussing with their napkins.

"So, is it true?" Aria asked. "You're touring together?"

Verity's broad grin mirrored my own. "We are."

"I think we're playing both the Barclays Center and Madison Square Garden in New York. Do you like to be down on the floor, or do you prefer watching from a box?"

I hadn't told Verity that my family had never seen me play, and it was interesting to watch my parents squirm in their seats at her question.

But then my mom flashed Verity an embarrassed smile, offering a very unexpected answer. "Maybe you can convince Dax to invite us one of these days."

"Yeah, Dax. We want to see you play," Sebastian said.

I glanced around the table. "I've asked if you wanted to come to my shows."

Aria pouted. "No, you haven't."

"Really?" I glanced back at my father. "Are you sure?"

He sipped from his water glass. "Dax, I might not understand your music, but I would love to see you perform."

"Me too," my mother added.

"Me three," Aria said.

"Okay. I'll arrange tickets."

My brothers high-fived. "Nothing but Trouble tickets—level achieved!"

Verity

Dim morning light filtered in through the shades Dax had drawn last night. Had he been alone, I knew he wouldn't have bothered, using the encroaching dawn like a visual alarm. Heading outside with his wetsuit and board, surfing until the sun was high in the sky and the best waves had been taken.

But since we made love until the sun began to creep over the horizon, he'd promised today would be a lazy morning.

My naked body lay draped over Dax's naked body, my cheek pressed to his chest, his heartbeat a soothing rhythm. Outside, waves clawed at the sand, crashing and receding relentlessly. The two rhythms—Dax's heartbeat and the tide—should have been a jarring contrast, but instead they were the perfect counterpoint to each other.

Lying here, it was impossible to believe that a more perfect morning existed. Dax and I, tangled up together, our bodies sated, our hearts full.

I hadn't moved, but Dax must have heard the change in my breathing as my mind transitioned to consciousness. His hand swept along my back, fingers combing through my hair cascading across his chest. "Morning," he crooned, his voice still heavy with sleep.

"Don't you mean *good* morning?"

"Yeah? What's so good about it?" Half tease, half groan.

I gave a contented sigh, unable to contain the swell of happiness filling me from head to toe. "Everything," I answered.

"True." He was feeling it, too. Content. Happy.

Everything.

"This is real, right?" The question had been floating around my mind for days, but today it escaped.

Dax gave my shoulder a gentle nudge and I pushed up slightly, so we could be face to face. His eyes narrowed at me, tiny little lines appearing at their corners. "Are you asking because you aren't sure?"

I pulled my lower lip behind my teeth, knowing the answer, just slightly afraid of admitting it. As if saying it out loud would change things somehow. Strip some of the magic away.

But Dax wasn't looking away. His stare burrowed into me, and I searched for evidence that my fears were unfounded. "I have a bad track record when it comes to taking people at face value. My instincts are completely unreliable."

"You mean Jack?"

"Yeah. And his assistant, too. I trusted her when I shouldn't have." I settled back down on Dax's chest, needing an escape from his probing gaze. "But it's not just them. There was this guy, in New York." I felt Dax's muscles twitch, then tense beneath me.

My life had been a merry-go-round of auditions and commercials since I understood what to do when someone said, "Smile pretty for the camera." And once *The Show* went into production, I'd barely had a second to breathe. Three years later, when it was canceled, I'd thought I'd earned some time off.

When I realized the state of my financial affairs, that all of my paychecks had gone straight to my mother, I'd rebelled. Leaving L.A. Drifting through a series of rich boyfriends, as calculating as any trophy wife. I drank champagne like it was water, treated sex like it was a currency, and did whatever drugs would keep me from realizing how low I'd sunk.

Marko was different. He was from Montenegro and had the most charming accent. The kind of guy that sucked up all the energy in the room. He didn't treat me like a Hollywood starlet. In our relationship, *he* was the star.

I thought I loved him.

"We'd been seeing each other for a few months. Marko had a friend staying with him and we were all partying together at a club. When we left, it was the three of us."

"What happened?" Dax's voice was a low growl.

I cleared my throat, blinking against the growing light making its way into the room. "Back at Marko's apartment, his friend kissed me—in front of Marko. I pushed him away, furious. Expecting Marko to be furious, too."

"But he wasn't. He was into it. I started to cry and Marko got mad. He said that if I loved him, I would want the same things he wanted. Marko's friend kissed me again, and I didn't push him away. When he took my dress off, I let him." A shiver of revulsion trembled through me. "The whole thing felt like just another audition. A scene I had to perform to earn the role I wanted—Marko's girlfriend."

Dax cursed, his hand rubbing my neck.

But I wasn't through. "A few weeks later, Marko and I flew to Saint Bart's for a cruise on someone's yacht." I swallowed. "I partied a lot—but these people took it to a whole new level. There was a crew to attend to every need, champagne corks popping all hours of the day and night, cocaine and pills in mirrored trays and crystal bowls all over the place."

I sensed Dax's unease, felt the protection he instinctively offered in the way his arms curved around my back, tenderly stroking my skin. "Every day we'd stop at a different island. People would get on or off; it was hard to keep track. But on the third day a beautiful woman came on the ship, and she and Marko seemed very close. They had grown up together and would speak in their own language even when I was around."

"I didn't want to seem like a clingy American. But eventually, after one too many glasses of champagne, I got upset. I told Marko he was being rude and that he needed to quit ignoring me or I was leaving. The woman, who spoke perfect English by the way, looked at me and said, 'I am his wife and you are nothing, no one. Go.'" My stomach turned as I remembered the toxic mix of anger and mortification that had drenched my veins. "Turns out, there was some odd inheritance rule or something, and they married as teenagers. But for the time being, they had an open marriage. I felt duped, you know. Like I was just a placeholder. Nothing, like she said."

Until *The Show*, I'd spent nearly every day of my life trying to be *someone*. Trying to prove to my mother, to my classmates, to casting directors and producers and anyone with a clipboard in their hand that I was *someone*.

The Show turned me into someone, all right. Someone I didn't even recognize. Someone who didn't know what to say without a script in her hand. Someone who didn't know what to wear unless it came from wardrobe. Someone who was less a person than a Hollywood creation.

And when *The Show* ended, I'd gone to New York, thinking I could be someone else. Someone different. Someone who jet-setted around Europe and the Caribbean with people I barely knew, who barely knew me. Thinking I was finally free, finally able to be myself. Until a virtual stranger looked at me, looked *through* me, and pronounced that I was nothing, no one.

In a way, she was right. What did I matter to her? What did I matter to the guy I'd been seeing—her husband? What did I matter to any of them?

I got off at the next island, and no one bothered to ask why I was carrying a suitcase instead of a beach bag.

It took nearly two days to get from Curacao to L.A. If I wasn't going to matter, I might as well be in a place where nothing mattered. Back in Hollywood. Except I wasn't going to read from a script anymore. My life needed to change.

I thought my life would change once I was signed by Travis Taggert. And it did. But a career shift isn't the same thing as a mental shift. My life truly started to change for the better when I found the right people to trust. When Piper become more of a friend than an employee. Travis more of a mentor than a manager. And Dax…well, when he became just *more*.

Now Dax rose onto his elbow, gently reversing our positions so that I was lying flat, looking up at him. There was a flash of something in his eyes—guilt or sadness maybe. "Verity, how can you be nothing when you're everything to me?" His mouth claimed mine with the merest brush across my lips. "You're fucking everything."

I'd waited my whole life to hear those words. Waited my whole life to find a man like Dax who said them with such conviction, such assurance, it was impossible not to believe him. And I wanted to—so, so badly. Blinking away the tears that threatened, I swallowed down the knot of past hurts. "I love you, Dax. More than I ever imagined possible."

He cupped my face in his hands, the tips of his fingers threading through the hair at my temples. "Fuck, Verity. I never planned on falling in love with you, or anyone else, ever again. But you made that impossible. I love you."

When he lowered his head, his kiss was soft and sweet, leisurely. Why shouldn't it be? We had all the time in the world. "True." He groaned against my lips. "Remind me later to tell you…"

When he didn't finish his thought, I giggled, the sound just barely escaping our mouths. I pushed against his shoulders. "Tell me what?"

Dax buried his face in my neck, kissing and nipping at the sensitive skin behind my ear. "Something I sure as fuck don't want to talk about now."

I was curious, but there were more pressing things on my mind. Like how soon I could feel Dax pushing into me, taking me to a place where words didn't matter.

The air between us crackled with the charge from our sexual chemistry. I sucked in a breath, letting it fill my lungs, make my head spin.

Dax was holding me so tight, right where I belonged.

With him.

Chapter Twenty-Four

Verity

Dax had gone for a run along the beach and I was sitting on his deck, sipping an iced coffee.

I probably should have just poured it down the drain. I didn't need the caffeine, not when I was already feeling impatient, keyed up. Outside, the endless blue sky of an hour ago had turned sullen and moody, bloated with dark clouds that clung to the horizon in thick, brooding folds.

The double ring of Dax's home phone shattered the stillness of the afternoon, and I jumped up to answer the call from the gatehouse. Piper had texted a few minutes ago to say she was bringing over some new branding mock-ups for me to approve. "Send her in," I said breezily, not waiting for the guard to announce Piper's name.

I ran up to unlock the door, leaving it slightly ajar. Knowing

Piper, she would race inside, heading immediately for the nearest bathroom. I returned to the deck, spotting Dax walking across the sand. My hunky rock star was shirtless and broadshouldered, the sexiest thing I'd ever seen. The only thing that could make my view any better would be if the sky opened up right now, rain drenching Dax's rippling muscles and already slick skin.

I was beaming down at him as he jogged up the steps, knowing I was seconds away from being enveloped in a sweaty hug and breathless with the anticipation of it. All thoughts of Piper's imminent arrival had faded, and my focus was entirely on the man I loved with my whole heart.

So I was a captive audience for the moment his grin sheared off, replaced first by shock, then an unsettling mix of hostility and disgust. A tremor of fear rippled down my spine. Like I was in a horror film, seconds away from a brutal, messy death.

Death, messy or otherwise, would have been kinder.

Because when I turned, the woman standing just in the middle of the doorway, her slender shape framed by the rectangular molding, was the very same one who had once wielded a blade, each interaction slicing at my soul. Millie.

Why is she here?

I staggered back, allowing more than enough room for Dax to leap over the final step. But once he was firmly planted on the deck, he made no effort to move any closer. His beautiful hazel eyes had gone dark, entirely devoid of the mossy green and gold that could devour me one minute and burn me up the next. His jaw appeared carved from granite, and his chest was heaving, as if he was fighting to draw air into his lungs.

"What the fuck are you doing here, Amelia?" Her name resounded like a gunshot, the kind that exploded on impact. I swear I felt it invading my flesh, metallic shards tearing thought bone and muscle and sinew. Ruining. Destroying.

Amelia?

Dax

At first I thought I was seeing things. That I'd run too many miles on too little sleep and too much sex.

Was such a thing even possible—too much sex?

No. Not with Verity, anyway.

But somehow I had to be hallucinating. That was the only possible explanation for what I was seeing.

Verity.

Amelia.

Both women, at my house.

It was a nightmare.

I'd fantasized about Amelia showing up here for a long time, even after our initial confrontation years before. But since that fateful elevator ride in New York, all of my fantasies had revolved around Verity. I wanted her. I loved her.

Every bit of that woman drove me wild, in the very best way.

That riot of red hair cascading over creamy shoulders. Ombre eyelashes that went from cinnamon at the tips to ochre when they hit her lids. The perfect frame for the emerald jewels staring at me.

Except that right now Verity's eyes weren't the clear burning luster of emeralds. They were cloudy and troubled, those of a leprechaun who had arrived at the end of the rainbow to discover his pot of gold had been stolen.

Me. I was the thief.

And I was about to suffer the consequences.

Amelia's mouth formed a pout. "Is that any kind of welcome home for your wife?" She said it with an air of triumph. But this wasn't her home, and I sure as fuck wasn't happy to see her.

Wife.

The word had turned Verity's face ashen, her jaw sagging for the briefest of moments before snapping shut. Blinking rapidly as she looked from Amelia to me, waiting for me to say something, do something. To *fix it.*

But I couldn't. I couldn't.

And I was so fucking ashamed.

The click of Amelia's heel as she stepped down onto the deck was the horn at a starting gate. Verity surged forward, away from me. She was a blur of movement, her hair a fiery torch blazing in the dark breeze.

Darting across the deck and inside my house, pausing only to grab the purse she'd made a habit of leaving at the head of the dining table.

Shock and shame weren't mixing well inside my lungs. I was unstable, volatile.

Verity Moore was *it* for me. She was the woman I wanted to spend the rest of my life with. Whatever that meant, wherever that took us.

I wanted to chase after her. But how could I? Not when it was so obvious I didn't deserve her. I should have told Verity everything. I'd meant to, several times. Just this morning, even.

But I hadn't.

I looked back at Amelia. "You gave up the right to call yourself that the day you left me." Bitterness coated my tongue.

"So then why did I only just receive papers this morning?" She tilted her head to the side, regarding me through lashes that were soot black and obviously extensions. Spider legs clinging to her lids, flapping at me.

I could have kicked myself for not signing the papers she'd served me with back in New York years ago. Instead I had tossed the documents in the garbage, packed a bag, and taken the first flight to Los Angeles.

I'd found Amelia after a few weeks in L.A. But she was determined to make it in Hollywood, and by then I was doing the same on the rock scene. I had more success than she did, but Amelia said she'd fallen for another guy.

I stopped wanting Amelia to want me back years ago, and I should have told Travis then to file on my behalf. But it never felt like the right time, given our intense touring and recording schedule. And when Shane and Delaney, and therefore Nothing but Trouble, had been front-page tabloid news for most of last year, Amelia had been the farthest thing from my mind.

Any time would have been better than this one.

I forced my tense shoulders into a shrug. "You haven't been a priority in my life for years, Amelia."

"I don't believe that." She took another step toward me, her hands outstretched.

I inched back as far as I could go without plunging down the stairs. It would almost be worth it to get away from her. "I don't give a fuck what you believe. Not anymore."

She stopped just short of touching me. "I was wrong. Wrong to leave you in New York. Wrong to avoid you here in L.A. Wrong to think we weren't meant to be together."

"The only thing wrong here is you showing up at my house, thinking those papers were an invitation." There was no give to the timbre of my voice. It was hard, cold. A reflection of my soul.

With Verity gone, the light in my life had been extinguished. I just prayed she wasn't gone for good.

Amelia's face pinched, frustration that I wasn't making things easy for her showing in every crease and line. She was a year younger than me, but she didn't look it. "Why, because you're shacking up with Verity?"

"You know Verity?" The name sounded strange coming from Amelia's mouth. Formal. An accusation. My mind struggled to process how Amelia would know Verity, but then I realized—who didn't know Verity Moore? She was famous, her face more recognizable than mine. But still, something about the way Amelia spoke was off, almost as if she knew Verity personally. I squinted down at her.

She hesitated, looking over my shoulder as if the answer were written on the horizon. "I know who she is, Dax. Everyone does. She's not right for you."

I hated the patronizing tone of her voice, as if Verity were somehow beneath her. The truth was exactly opposite. "You don't know shit. Not about Verity and not about me."

"How can you say that? We practically grew up together. I know you better than anyone."

Thunder rumbled from somewhere far in the distance, low and sonorous, an echo of the seething tide. "You knew the naïve kid I used to be. I've grown up, Amelia, and I've sure as fuck moved on. There's no room for you in my life anymore."

"But don't you see—that's why I left New York. Why I left you. I was young and naïve, too. Getting pregnant…" Her throat worked as she swallowed back tears. "I was still a kid myself. I was terrified, and after the miscarriage—*after we lost our baby*—I felt like I needed to start over. Start fresh."

Damn her for bringing that up.

Images came flashing back at me. Red blood on white sheets. My frantic 911 call. The flashing blue and white lights of the ambulance. Shiny speckled gray floors, doctors in white coats. The smell of Windex and ammonia. Amelia's screams when she woke up. The look of devastation on her face.

I had married Amelia when we found out she was pregnant. The day I found her in bed, in a pool of blood, had been the scariest night of my life. Afterward she'd been so sad, so fragile. I told Amelia the miscarriage didn't matter to me, that I would have married her whether she was pregnant or not. And it was the truth. I loved her.

But it didn't matter. She left a few months later.

I shook my head, blinking away the memories. When I faced Amelia again, my throat was tight but my tone had softened. "We were both kids, and now we're not. We're nothing anymore." I felt the first raindrop splatter on my cheek, and I sidestepped her to head inside. She could get to the driveway using the stairs that ran along the perimeter of my house. "Go home, Amelia. Have your attorney call mine and let's sever ties."

"You're making a mistake, Dax. I'll go after you for half of everything you've earned." I closed and locked the door behind me, her threat rolling off my shoulders.

We'd never lived as a married couple in California, so she had no claim on anything I'd earned here, although I was perfectly willing to give her some kind of settlement just to make her go away.

But my most valuable asset, the one *I* should have protected, the *woman* I should have protected, had just walked out the door.

I had to get her back.

Because I couldn't live without her.

Chapter Twenty-Five

Verity

I sat in Dax's driveway for a few minutes, trying to calm my racing thoughts.

Jack Lester's assistant, Millie.

Dax's ex, Amelia.

Correction: Dax's *wife*, Amelia.

Amelia and Millie…were the same person.

Amelia/Millie was Dax's wife.

Dax was *married*.

Oh my god.

Pain screamed from every nerve ending.

How was this happening to me?

This was an entirely different level of deception than that night in the Caribbean, and I didn't have nearly enough scar tissue to lessen the stabbing pain of Dax's betrayal. I'd been gutted by a single word. The hurt compounded a thousand times over by Dax's complicity.

Millie. Amelia. Wife. Married.

My brain was shredded, trying to make sense of it all.

Knowing it made no sense at all.

Why hadn't Dax told me about her? Was I just an affair for him? Someone to play with while he and Millie—Amelia—were on the outs?

But no, that didn't make sense. I'd never heard anything about Dax being married, not even a whisper. I'd never noticed a ring on Millie's finger, or picked up on a single sign that she was devoted to anyone other than Jack Lester. And there was no way Dax had seen her while we were living together. When would he have had the time?

Wiping the tears from my face with shaking hands, I backed out of Dax's driveway onto the street, slowing down to go through the gate. Just as I nosed beneath the rising metal bar, Piper's bright blue Mini pulled up on the other side. Keeping my sunglasses firmly covering my eyes, I lowered my window.

She waved at me. "Hey, you got my message, right? I said I was coming."

I could feel my chin trembling and knew I would burst into tears if I attempted even a single word. I saw Piper's lips tighten, a frown pushing between her brows. "Follow me," she said, before reversing and pulling out in front of me.

I drove on autopilot, following her to a midsize apartment complex and parking in the lot a few spots down from her. For a pregnant woman, Piper still moved fast and was pulling at my door before I'd turned off my ignition. "Come on. I just have to pee, and then you're going to tell me what the dickhead did."

My first instinct was to defend him, but in the next moment

I realized that yes, Dax was a dickhead. Hearing Piper call him that, and repeating it silently inside my head, made me feel just the tiniest bit better.

"Hey there, Shania. Bet you didn't expect me home so soon," Piper crooned as she pushed open her door.

"I didn't know you had a dog." I sniffled, offering my hand for scrutiny.

Piper dropped her purse on the floor and headed straight for a small hallway just beyond her living room. "Yes, the only other good thing to come out of my last relationship, actually." Shania trotted back to me when Piper closed the bathroom door, and I walked over to the couch. As if the dog knew I needed comforting, she sat at my feet, putting her head on my knees. "Maybe if Dax had gotten me a puppy I wouldn't be so angry about his wife," I whispered, gurgling a laugh through my tears.

God, could my life get any more ridiculous?

When Piper came out of the bathroom, she went directly into the kitchen and returned with two pints of Ben and Jerry's. "Cookie dough or pistachio?"

"Cookie dough, definitely."

She handed me the ice cream, along with a spoon. "Good, because otherwise I was going to have to tell you that Firefly prefers pistachio."

Another laugh trickled out as I pried the cover off and used my spoon to dig out a chunk of dough. "Firefly is very particular."

"You're telling me," she acknowledged. "So, what happened?"

I shoved a bite in my mouth and decided to come right out with it. "Did you know Dax was married?"

"What?" The blatant surprise flashing across Piper's face convinced me she'd had absolutely no idea. "You're kidding, right?"

I pushed my spoon back into the container. "I wish I were."

"Where did you hear that? It could be a fake story, planted by—"

"The woman who showed up at Dax's house was very real." I wasn't ready to admit that I knew her yet.

Piper was quiet for a moment, scooping an enormous bite of green ice cream onto her spoon. "And there's no way it was just a big misunderstanding?"

"I don't see how. Dax didn't deny it."

"Well, did he look happy to see her?"

I shook my head. "No. He looked nearly as surprised as I was. And then angry."

"Angry." Piper rolled the word around in her mouth like it was one of the nuts in her ice cream. Her eyes snapped back to me. "Then what?"

"Then I left. I wasn't going to stick around and witness their happy little reunion."

A chirping sounded from inside Piper's bag. She set her ice cream on a coaster, then retrieved her purse. "It doesn't sound very happy."

I groaned an acknowledgment as Piper checked her screen.

"I have about thirteen texts from Travis and Dax. They want to know if you're with me."

Remembering that my phone was charging on my nightstand—no, Dax's nightstand—I was hit by a wave of sadness. I would never again spend a night in his bed, wrapped up in his arms, my body thrumming with desire, a cocoon of happiness enveloping us both.

Because Dax was married.

Because Dax was a liar.

Because he'd treated me like I was nothing, no one.

Piper thumbed out a text on her phone as I shoveled more ice cream into my mouth. "Well, I guess there's no need to worry about getting fitted for costumes. Even if I still wanted to go on tour, there's no way Dax would—" I stopped abruptly. "You know, who cares what he wants. I don't want to go on tour with him. There."

I was feeling pretty proud of myself until I noticed Piper staring at me with one eyebrow raised like an impatient teacher.

"What?"

"That's the hurt talking."

"Exactly. Because I'm hurting."

She put her phone aside. "But you're also a professional. There are contracts and monetary penalties if you don't hold up your end of the bargain."

I put down the tub and resettled myself on her couch, tucking my bare feet beneath my thighs. "Travis can figure something out."

"Travis is just going to say he told you so for getting involved with Dax in the first place. You know that, right?"

My stomach was churning, taking all that creamy deliciousness I'd just ingested and converting it into spoiled milk. "What would you have me do, then?"

Piper grunted. "I'd have you put your big-girl panties on and pretend like it's his loss." She patted her belly. "Look at the bright side—if you still want nothing to do with Dax after the tour, you can walk away from him free and clear."

The dose of reality put things in perspective. Piper was right. After our tour I would never have to see Dax again. Meanwhile, she would be tied to her ex forever.

There was a white flash of lightning outside the window, and then we both jumped as a deafening *boom* shook the air. Moments later rain lashed the glass. I stood up, crossing the room to peer out at the parking lot. The rain was coming down so heavily, it splashed off the asphalt.

Piper came up beside me and ran a reassuring hand over my back. "Everything will get sorted out somehow. I'm sure of it."

That made one of us.

I was still standing by the window, peering at the rain, when I saw a familiar car streak through the parking lot. I didn't wait for it to jerk to a stop before spinning around and glaring incredulously at Piper. "You told him I was here."

Piper at least had the decency to look slightly guilty. "Travis is my boss, Verity. And in case you haven't noticed, I kind of need this job."

I had begun to think of Piper as a friend, and maybe she was…but her loyalty was to Travis first.

The truth stung. Salt on fresh wounds.

She gathered up the ice cream and spoons, Shania her four-legged shadow. "I'll leave you to it."

The soft *click* of her bedroom door was covered by the pounding on her front door.

"Verity!" My belly clenched just imagining Dax standing there in the pouring rain. His hair wet. Clothes clinging to his skin.

"Verity!" The second time my name left his throat, I weakened. And by the third, I broke. I wanted answers, and I wasn't going to get them staring at the back of Piper's front door.

When I opened it, the reality was a thousand times better than my imagination.

Dax didn't attempt to enter Piper's apartment, and I didn't step aside to let him in. There was an awning over her door, so the rain wasn't directly over his head, but Dax was soaked just from walking across the parking lot. His wet shirt clinging to every ridge and ripple of his sculpted arms and torso.

The sight of him was enough to steal the oxygen from my body. If I wasn't careful, he would no doubt steal my willpower, too.

"True," he whispered.

I recoiled as if he slapped me. The fresh blast of anger was exactly what I needed. It cleared my mind, opened my lungs. "Don't you dare call me that anymore. You lost that right."

Dax exhaled, roughing those long fingers through his wet hair, clawing at his scalp as if he wanted to peel back his skin and expose the thoughts crowding his mind. "I don't know what to say," he finally managed, his throat so tight each word emerged flat, almost strangled.

"That makes two of us, but apparently you're the only one who can explain what just happened. Because it's pretty obvious you've left me completely in the dark."

"I didn't mean to. I just..." He looked around, finally realizing he was still standing outside. "Can I come in, or can we go somewhere?"

"Where, back to your house? Or mine?" A laugh shuddered from my throat. "No. Come in. Piper said we could talk here."

I retreated to the couch, but Dax only came far enough to close the door behind him, leaning against it like it was the only thing keeping him upright.

"Why didn't you tell me?" The question broke free, a desperate whine. I hated the sound of it.

"Fuck, Verity." Dax closed his eyes, pinching the bridge of his nose. When he opened them again, they shined with regret. "I should have. I know I should have. But Amelia hasn't felt like much besides a bad memory in..." He trailed off, sighing heavily.

"She's not a bad memory. She's your wife."

"Only on paper."

"So, what? What does that mean? It's on paper. A legal, binding document. A fact. Does what it's written on makes it less true?"

"No. Damn it. That's not what I meant."

"Then explain it to me. Because I'm having hard time understanding why you didn't tell me that you're married."

Staring at him now, I remembered all the intimate moments we shared, swapping stories from our past, making light of the bad times. It had felt mutual, a give-and-take. And it had felt good. Really, really good. But this grenade of truth had blown those memories to bits.

"Were you…? Were you waiting for her?"

"No!" It was practically a shout. Dax crossed the room in three strides, dropping onto the couch and pulling me into his lap. I didn't bother struggling. I felt about as strong as the tissues crumpled inside my fist. "No," he repeated, his tone subdued. "I gave up on her a long time ago. I swear."

"I just…I just don't understand. Why *her*?" The woman was awful. What had Dax ever seen in her?

He was looking at me curiously. "You know Amelia?"

Shit. No, I was not going there. If I admitted my connection to her, this conversation would become about me. And I didn't want that. This was about Dax and his deceit.

"I know that she's the reason you didn't want to get involved with me. The reason you've refused to date anyone in the music industry." I took a breath. "She's the reason you thought we could only be a fling. But you never told me that she was more than just an ex-girlfriend who broke your heart. You never told me you married her. You never told me you were *still* married to her."

I didn't look at Dax, and he didn't say anything. Just wrapped his arms around me and pressed his lips to my temple. Letting the silence speak for him. It wasn't enough. "Not telling the truth is as bad as lying." Now we were both guilty of that.

"I know." He gave a somber nod. "I haven't seen Amelia in years. And yes, I followed her to L.A, but she isn't why I stayed. Not by a long shot. Did I hope that someday we'd get back together—for a long while, yes. But by the time we met, Amelia was just a bad memory."

"Verity, I told Travis to file on my behalf the morning after we spent the night together on the rug in front of the fire. That's why Amelia showed up today—because she was served with divorce papers. And, honestly, I don't know how the fuck she got past the gatehouse. She's not on my list, and I sure as hell wouldn't have told the guard to let her in."

I cleared my throat. "It was me. I—I answered your phone. I thought she was Piper."

Dax exhaled. "I meant to tell you about her. This morning, that reminder I told you to give me—it was about Amelia. I just didn't want to talk about her while we were in bed, naked. You have to believe me."

His defense rang true to me. I did believe him. But…Could I *forgive* him? Maybe. But not right now. Not unless he actually followed through with divorcing Amelia. And that was an ultimatum I wasn't willing to issue. If Dax really meant what he said, he would take that step on his own. Maybe then I could forgive him. Maybe then I would forgive him. But right now, I needed to get my own life sorted out. "Dax, I need you to leave. I need you to leave right now."

The muscles beneath his damp clothes became bars of steel. "You don't mean that, Verity. Tell me you don't mean that."

"I do," I whispered. "That's exactly what I need from you right now. I need you to leave me alone."

His hands came around my face, holding me as if I were fragile china, looking into my eyes like they would reveal something different than what had come from my mouth. It was painful, but I met Dax's stare. The intensity between us crackling with all that remained unspoken. And when he bent low to press a kiss on my lips, I kissed him back with desperation, with hunger, with want. With every emotion filling me up and ripping me apart.

I got lost in our kiss. Lost in the moment. And it felt damned good. Our lips bound, our breaths shared, our hearts pressed chest to chest, their rhythms synching. Two bodies connecting. I could pretend my heart wasn't hurting from lies. I could pretend my head wasn't aching from betrayal.

But I couldn't pretend forever.

When Dax pulled back—slowly, regretfully—I knew he felt it, too. Rather than let go, I kept my arms around his neck and leaned toward him, tilting my head forward so that our foreheads touched. Tears spilled onto my cheeks, snaking their way down my skin until they hit Dax's chest.

I wanted him to feel the weight of my sadness. I wanted him to drown in my tears.

Outside the wind raged. Lightning and thunder ripping apart the skies. For once, the weather mirrored exactly how I felt inside. Racked with pain. Heavy and dark and vengeful. Like I wanted to lash out at anyone and everyone in my path.

A few minutes passed before I could bear to move. I crawled to the other end of the couch. Pressing my back into the pillow, I wrapped my arms around my legs and hugged them into my chest. "Please leave, Dax. You're not mine. And I'm not yours. You need to go."

He groaned, rubbing his hands on his thighs before pushing unsteadily to his feet. He stood there for a moment, like a tree that had been hacked at its base and hadn't quite decided which way to fall. "I can fix this, Verity." He pivoted, taking slow steps toward the door. "I can, and I will." His voice grew stronger with each word, and I envied him that. Strength that came from intention.

My mistake had been thinking that he could fix me. Only I could do that. And it was about time I did.

Dax

I knew I wasn't alone the moment I stepped inside my front door. There was a lingering scent of perfume in the air that didn't belong. But no woman had been inside my home since Amelia showed up and chased Verity away nearly two weeks ago.

Jesus Christ—was Amelia back? Had she broken in this time?

I wouldn't put it past her, that was for sure.

Goddamn it. I thought I'd been perfectly clear, straight to her face. Our relationship ended years ago, and I'd moved on. We both had. It was time to make it official and get a divorce.

I had told Travis just to give her whatever was necessary to go away, but he was refusing to give Amelia a cent more than she deserved—which was basically nothing.

Slamming the door behind me, tension pulled at the muscles lining my spine, clawing at my shoulders. Heading downstairs, I noticed that the door to the deck was open.

The woman standing with her back to me, staring out at the Pacific, wasn't Amelia.

I jogged down the remaining steps and went outside. "Aria, what are you doing here?" My family wasn't flying back to New York until tomorrow, but I hadn't expected to see them again this trip.

My sister spun around, throwing herself into my arms. "Don't sound so thrilled to see me." Her words were muffled against my chest, and I exhaled a deep breath, realizing that my surprise had come off as irritation.

"I'm always glad to see you; you know that." The last time she was here on a school break, I'd given her a key and left her name with the guardhouse as a permanently acceptable visitor. Now I curved my hands around Aria's shoulders and pushed her away just enough to look into her face. "Do Mom and Dad know you're here?"

The way she pressed her lips together, her eyes sliding away from mine, answered my question more effectively than words. I groaned. "Do you want to call them, or should I?"

Aria's eyes blazed with anger as she shrugged out of my hold, stepping away from me. "I'm not a kid anymore, Dax. And I'm really tired of being treated like one."

As far as I was concerned, seventeen was still a kid. And Aria looked younger than that. She was a tiny little slip of a thing, with waist-length brown hair and deep brown eyes. Her skin tone was the same as mine, although you would never know it. After so many years in California, I had a perpetual tan, while Aria was pale with olive undertones. I towered over her.

"Let me guess—you told Mom and Dad about your plan to move to L.A."

Her posture deflated a bit. "After meeting Verity, I thought they would understand. Did you know that she got cast in *The*

Show when she wasn't much older than me? And look at her now."

I would have loved to be looking at Verity right now. "Yes. I know all about her experience with *The Show*." More that I wanted to discuss with my sister. "And I'm not saying you have to leave. Just that I have too much shit going on to be fielding phone calls from Mom and Dad wondering where you are."

Aria was eager to change the subject. "Do you mean Verity? Or should I say Daxity?"

I groaned, roughing hands through my hair and striding to one of the deck chairs. I slumped into it, stretching my legs out. "We're not talking about her, or me, right now. Let's get back to—"

"Oh, come on. I was with you two, remember? I've never seen you so goggle-eyed over anyone. Not even Amelia."

"First of all, I've never been goggle-eyed in my life. I don't even know what that means." My sister started to speak, and I raised my hand. "I don't want to know, either. And second, don't talk to me about Amelia. In fact, don't even mention her name. Ever."

I practically spat the words, and didn't miss the rise of Aria's eyebrows as she moved away from the railing and sat in the chair beside me, tucking her feet beneath her and perching her elbows on the arms. "Um... What's going on? Have you seen—"

"Don't," I warned.

For a moment there was only the crash of the waves and the squall of the gulls. Looking down at the beach below, I imagined Verity as she'd been the other night. Standing at the water's edge, her bare feet sinking into the sand, froth swirling around her ankles, salt water licking at her calves. Her arms had been wrapped around her chest, as if she was trying to hold herself together and only barely succeeding. I left her alone as long as I could bear it, knowing she needed space to deal with all the emotions that had risen up in her, as relentless as the tide.

But I hadn't been able to wait for very long, an inexplicable force pulling me to Verity, to her pain and strength and vulnerability. Wanting to share the burden, shelter her from its impact.

"Dax?" My sister's voice, quiet and tentative, blared at me.

I blinked, and the image was gone.

Scrubbing my hands over my face, I pressed my palms against my eyes for a moment before dropping them into my lap. "Yeah?"

"I'll text Mom and Dad if you tell me what's going on between you and Verity."

A wry smile twisted my lips as I let my head fall back against the cushion of my chair, feeling the sun warm my skin. "I don't work on a barter system."

"Fine. There are two sides to every story. If you only want me to hear hers—"

I twisted my neck to face left. "Verity gave you her number?"

"Mmm-hmm. When we went to the ladies' room, I told her I wanted to get into acting. And she said if I was serious, I could call her to talk about it."

Like me, Aria was a musical prodigy. And even though I was her brother, I knew she was beautiful. The thought of her getting wrapped up the world Verity had described was terrifying. It might not be a bad idea if Verity shared even a fraction of what she'd been through. Maybe then Aria wouldn't be in such a rush to leave home.

And then something else occurred to me. "Your interest in Hollywood is pretty sudden…Has anyone approached you?"

"Sudden? I've wanted to move to L.A. for months."

I squinted at her. "Who? Who suggested it?"

"No one. Don't be ridiculous." Her denial was too fast, accompanied by bright pink patches on her cheeks.

"What the fuck, Aria?" I exploded. "Do you know how many assholes are out there who would say anything just to get in your pants?"

"I'm not an idiot! I—I know someone."

"Who?"

"I can't say."

Gripping the arms of the chair, I bolted upright. "Yeah, you can. And you will."

Aria jumped to her feet, her hair lifted by the wind and trailing behind her like ribbons as she scurried back into my house. "You wouldn't want to hear it, anyway."

Chasing after Aria, I grabbed her by the arm before she could get to the stairs. "Are you talking about Amelia?"

"What if I am?" The flash of guilt that raced across her features before transitioning into rebellion was like a punch to the gut.

"She's just using you to get to me. You know that, right?"

She wrenched her arm from my hold. "Not everything is about you, Dax. We live in a big world, and I'm sick of being overshadowed by our parents, by you, by everybody. Amelia understands that, and she wants to help me."

"Help you how?" Whatever deadbeat had promised Amelia he'd make her a star clearly hadn't followed through. Was she getting Aria's hopes up for nothing?

"Are you kidding me? Amelia works for the producer of *The Show*. She said she could get me an audition with him. They're casting for something new right now."

And as my jaw dropped, muscles weighted down by a devastating combination of horror and regret, all I could do was watch Aria run up the stairs and straight out my front door.

Jack Lester's assistant. Verity had said her name. What the fuck was it?

Not Amelia. I would have noticed that.

There was a woman. Millie. She was the producer's assistant. She coordinated his auditions—the ones he oversaw personally.

The memory roared into my brain like a migraine.

Was my Amelia the same person as Verity's Millie?

It was too awful to contemplate.

And then I remembered the look on Verity's face—*before* Amelia had called herself my wife.

Her sculpted features had pinched together in a mask of horrified recognition.

Recognition.

Chapter Twenty-Six

Verity

You shouldn't be carrying that." I rushed to swipe the cardboard box from Piper's hands. She looked ready to tip over from the weight of her belly protruding from her otherwise still thin frame. The last thing she should be doing was carrying a heavy box filled with my stuff.

After much back-and-forth negotiation, Travis had finally arranged, through my mother's lawyer, for me to have two hours in the Beverly Hills house for me to pack my things.

"Don't worry. It's empty."

She relinquished it into my grasp, and I realized she was right. It was empty.

"Where's the—"

"Bathroom's down that way, on your left." Piper flashed a grateful smile as she walked away. She'd finally stopped wearing heels, and her Tory Burch flip-flops slapped the marble floor.

I brought the empty box up to my bedroom. Truthfully, there wasn't much I wanted, but I did have a memory box I'd filled with letters from my grandparents and some trinket jewelry and photographs they had given me over the years. My passport, vintage T-shirts I couldn't replace, comfy pajamas. Not a lot, but nothing I wanted my mother digging through either.

"Hey, Verity?"

I stepped back out onto the landing. "You don't have to come up." Piper had been running around a lot for me today, and she was making me nervous.

I'd signed the lease on a new apartment this morning. Well, technically, Travis had signed it. I was quickly learning that just about everything had to be done through shell companies to keep my name off things like home addresses, phone numbers, and bank accounts. Information was a currency these days, and celebrity information was more valuable than gold.

He'd insisted on sending Piper to pick up the keys and meet me at my mother's house even though I'd told him it wouldn't be a secret for long since I had no plans to enter and leave the building wearing an opaque veil.

"Why don't you find a place to sit and rest. I'll be right down."

She leaned an elbow on the banister. "Where's your mom's office?"

"It's right there," I said, pointing at the closed set of French doors off the foyer. "But I don't think I've ever been in there."

There was a mischievous gleam to Piper's eyes as she grinned up at me. "First time for everything."

I went back into my bedroom and retrieved the box, then carried it down the stairs. Piper was already in my mother's office, sitting in her chair, the drawers of her desk open. "Anything in particular we're looking for?"

"Technically, anything with your name on it is fair game."

I rolled my eyes. "Not sure that you'll find too much of that."

I set the box down on the floor and went to stand beside Piper. My mother's desk was one of those large executive monstrosities, with a set of file drawers on either side. Piper's manicured fingernails quickly flipped through the tabbed folders. "Ah," she said, pulling one out. "Birth certificate."

"Yes, a very exciting discovery," I teased. "Thank you."

"Wait. There's something else." She pulled out a few sheets of letter-sized paper stapled together. "Oh, I never even thought to ask, but I guess Verity isn't your given name."

"I was born Victoria, but I guess Vicky was a pretty popular name when I was a kid. My mom changed it to Verity when I was in kindergarten, or maybe first grade. She said an unusual name would make me stand out at auditions." I shrugged, leaning back against a bookcase.

Piper set both documents on the desk. "And before I forget," she opened her purse, "I have the keys to your new place and your phone."

The phone I'd left at Dax's house. Keys to a new apartment because I wouldn't be going back to Dax's house. Ever.

"Thanks." I hid the quiver in my chin by turning away and tossing them with the rest of my things.

I pivoted back at the sound of Piper's groan. "I might not be able to get out of this chair. If you have to hire a crane, make sure you put it on Travis's credit card. This is a work expense. After I take a nap first."

I looked over at her rounded belly. "What's going on in there?" I asked, as it seemed to twitch.

"Ugh." Piper smoothed a hand over the fabric of her shirt. "Baby has the hiccups. She had them all last night, too, which is why I'm so exhausted." A naughty smile pulled at her lips. "Well, that and I read that sex was a way to get them to stop. Something about female orgasms soothing—"

I clapped my hands over my ears. Her baby shower had been last week, and the craziest part was when Landon showed up—mostly because Piper had been more surprised to see him than anyone else there. "Please stop. Major TMI, Piper. If you can't get up from a chair without help, I don't even want to think about you having sex."

She laughed. "Fine, but just you wait. I'm storing up all my advice for when you need it."

"I don't think I'll be needing it anytime soon, and even then, I'm not sure I'll want to hear it."

"Well, never say never." She nodded at my box. "Is that all you're taking?"

"Yeah."

"Okay, then. Add these…" Her voice trailed off as she peered at the other papers arranged on the surface of the desk. "Uh, Verity. You might want to take a look. Your name's not the only thing that was changed."

Dax

My parents' worried faces filled the screen of my phone. "Is Aria with you?" my mom asked. "She said she wanted to do a little shopping before we leave tomorrow, but it's been hours and she's not answering our calls."

"Yeah, she was here."

They immediately appeared relieved. "Oh good…Wait. What? Did you say she *was* there? Or she *is* there?"

"Was." I felt too guilty to bluff my way through their interrogation. "We had an argument. She stormed off. I'm leaving right now. I'll find her."

I hated the worry that crept back onto their faces. Especially knowing they had every reason for it. "Did you know Aria was in touch with Amelia?"

"No." My father's reply was immediate.

My mother's reply was nonexistent.

A fact my dad and I realized at the same time. I watched as he looked her way. "Aria was talking to Amelia? You knew...and you didn't say anything?"

"It wasn't a big deal. And it was months ago. Aria and I were shopping, and we bumped into Amelia in Saks. She said she was in New York for work. We went out to lunch together, caught up. It was nice."

Nice?

As if she heard me, my mom looked back into the camera lens, directly at me. "Amelia was like a daughter to me, to us. When she left, it was as if we lost a child. Again. And then you left and..." Her voice trailed off as she reached for the necklace at her throat and began twisting it. "I was just heartbroken. That's why I didn't push for you to come back to New York, even to finish Juilliard. I knew you were hurting and I didn't want you to know that I was, too."

My father's hand curved over her shoulder. "It was a tough time for your mother, Dax. A tough time for us all."

There was something I was missing, something they weren't telling me. "I don't—"

Her chin trembled. "I...I had a bit of a breakdown. Just like after your sister."

Just like after my sister. And then I remembered. "That place upstate—the apple orchard."

"Yes. I was there that fall. Your father would bring you up on weekends. The Center was on a farm. We would have fresh apple cider and sometimes we would make sugar cookies. Do you remember?"

Vanilla and cloves. "I remember."

On-screen, my mother turned to my father. "That's why I didn't tell you about running into Amelia. I didn't want you to worry about me."

He kissed her forehead. "I want to worry about you. It comes with the job description."

"Seeing Amelia, it was like old times—just for the afternoon. Kind of like how we go to the farm at least once every fall and come back with gallons of fresh cider. Sometimes a little sadness makes you appreciate the sweet."

It felt as if I was meeting my mother—both of my parents, actually—for the first time. I'd never looked at my situation from her point of view, and to do so now was jarring. But there was a more pressing problem I needed to resolve, and I wanted to do it without worrying my mother unnecessarily. I swallowed heavily. "So that's—you haven't seen or talked to Amelia since then?"

"Well, I think she and Aria may have texted occasionally. I'm not really sure. I didn't want to pry. Amelia was like an older sister to Aria."

The older sister she'd never had. "Okay, I'm going to track down Aria. I'll call as soon as I find her."

"Please hurry. This isn't like her."

It wasn't. This was all Amelia's bad influence. "I'll do my best."

I hung up before either of us could voice the unspoken thought that buzzed between us.

What if my best isn't good enough?

Chapter Twenty-Seven

Verity

I pushed off the bookcase and looked over Piper's shoulder. She extended a fingernail, pointing at the different years given for my birth date. According to my birth certificate, I was twenty-three. But my name-change document said I was twenty-four.

I checked my passport. It said I was twenty-four.

"So..." I stared at Piper in confusion. "Which is it?"

Piper already had her phone out of her bag, quickly snapping pictures and e-mailing them to Travis. "There's got to be some sort of explanation. I'm sure he'll have a paralegal track it down in no time."

While she was doing that, I ran out to my car and grabbed the purse I'd left on my front seat. Flipping open my wallet, I confirmed what I already knew. My driver's license had me as twenty-four, too.

Whatever the explanation was, I knew it wasn't an accident.

I returned to my mother's office to find Piper staring intently at the name-change document. "Do you remember anything that was going on around the time you went from Vicky to Verity?"

I threw myself into the small settee across from the desk. "Not really," I said. "I was auditioning a lot, but I wasn't getting anything except an occasional commercial. My mom really wanted me to book a TV show. I almost did…" I ran my fingertips over my lips, remembering.

"You almost…" Piper prodded.

"Yes. There was this show I auditioned for at least a dozen times—sort of like *The Sound of Music*, but set in present-day American suburbia."

"I remember that show. I loved it."

"Me too. Anyway, I got to the very last round of casting. But they went with someone else, and I remember my mom being really angry. She told me I didn't get the part because I was too young."

Piper frowned at me, then began pecking at her phone again. "California labor laws regulate the number of hour minors can work. The older you are, the more you can work."

"I wonder how old the girl that—"

"She's your age—well, the same age you are on everything but your actual birth certificate," Piper announced, showing me her phone with the Wikipedia entry for the actress who'd landed the role I auditioned for. "I don't even know how it's possible to alter the age of someone on a legal document, but for argument's sake let's say it can be done. Would your mother make you older so you would have a better chance of being cast in the future?"

The call from the studio had come while I was home. I'd been coloring in one of those dime-store coloring books my grandmother had bought for me. I remembered looking up from the page to see my mother's face turning bright red, her eyes brimming with hate as she glared at me. One minute the phone had been in her hand, and the next, it was flying through the air. It slammed into my arm, the one holding the yellow crayon, and I'd had a bruise for weeks.

"Absolutely," I said, my vocal chords tight. "She would have done anything."

Piper shot me an empathetic glance. I couldn't look away fast enough. Clearing my throat, I powered on the phone Piper had returned to me. "I'm just going to check…something." Had the device been a swimming pool, I would've dived right in, hiding beneath the water until my lungs felt like they were about to explode. Until my heart was aching from lack of oxygen.

Until a nearly twenty-year-old memory wasn't as painfully vivid as if had happened yesterday.

I stared at the screen, using it as a diversion until I managed to blink the words into focus. I scrolled through the social media notifications, Google Alerts, missed calls, and texts…until one in particular caught my attention. I read it once, twice, a third time. Hoping I was reading it wrong. That the horrifying collection of letters didn't spell what I thought it did.

But I wasn't.

And it did.

The blood that had been running so hot just a moment ago turned to ice in my veins. My thoughts focused on only one thing. One incredible girl who was about to walk into a terrible situation.

I couldn't erase my past, but I'd be damned if anyone else had to repeat it.

"I have to go. Now."

Dax

Most Manhattan residents don't bother getting their driver's license, and my sister was no exception. The last time she came to visit, I'd set her up with an Uber account so she wasn't completely dependent on me to take her places. Hoping Aria hadn't thought to establish one of her own, I pulled up the app and breathed a sigh of relief when the details of *my* most recent ride appeared on my screen. A ride that originated at my house and ended in Beverly Hills.

I zoomed in on the map. The intersection of Wilshire and Santa Monica Boulevard.

The Peninsula Hotel.

Stuffy and pretentious, it was where my parents often stayed when they were in town. Was Aria cooling her heels in the lobby? But no, I remembered that my parents had decided to stay at the Beverly Wilshire this time around.

She coordinated his auditions—the ones he oversaw personally.

My blood turned to ice in my veins.

What if Amelia had arranged an audition for Aria?

I tried calling Verity, but it went straight to voice mail. I left a disjointed message about what I knew, what I thought I knew, and where I was headed.

Tossing my keys to a valet half an hour later, I strode over to the reception desk and put my phone with a picture of my sister four inches from the clerk's face. "Have you seen this girl?"

The woman stepped back. "I'm sorry, sir. We can't give out personal information on our guests."

"She's not a guest. An Uber dropped her off about twenty minutes ago."

"I'm truly sorry, sir. I can't—"

I took off my sunglasses and leaned over the desk. "Aria Hughes. My sister. My seventeen-year-old sister. I need to know if she's here."

A flush rose up her cheeks as she made a hiccupping sound in her throat. "I think I need to get my manager," she said, scurrying off before I could stop her.

Something about this didn't feel right. And when I turned around, I knew why.

Because in the bar, just across the lobby from the front desk, was a familiar face.

"What the fuck," I growled, my angry stride covering the ground between us in seconds. "Where is Aria?"

Amelia concealed the twinge of guilt that pulled at her features with a surprised huff. "Dax? If you wanted to get together for a drink, you should have called first. I'm meeting someone."

"My sister?"

"What? No, of course not." Her nervous gaze darted to the open entrance, and mine followed.

Landing on the woman walking through it.

Verity pulled up short, looking between Amelia and me, green eyes huge in her face, red hair dancing across her shoulders. "Dax." My name skated through her lips on a gasp.

Amelia stood up, gathering her purse. "I don't need to be here for your little reunion."

Verity's stare hardened. "Actually, you do. Aria texted me. She said she was on her way to meet you. She wanted advice for her audition with Jack Lester." Her eyes bounced to me, guilt and fear swirling inside them. "I'm so sorry. I—"

Just then a man wearing a suit with the same color scheme as the receptionist appeared behind Verity. "Ah, I see you've found each other." He looked from me to Amelia. "I'm sure she'll re-unite you with your sister."

I fucking knew it.

There was a red haze clouding my vision as I spun on her. "If anything happened to Aria…"

Amelia swallowed, trying to edge past Verity and me. "I—I'll go upstairs and get her."

"We're coming with you—and so help me god, if that bastard laid a hand on her…"

The hotel manager cleared his throat nervously. "We don't want any trouble here."

I wrapped my fingers around Amelia's arm at the same time as I reached for Verity's hand, propelling our unhappy threesome toward the elevators. "Then you had better come with us."

The ride up to the presidential suite was the longest of my life.

The video I'd seen of Verity was playing in a relentless loop inside my mind, except that her tear-stained face had been replaced with my sister's. It was punctuated at random intervals by images of Jack Lester's face.

There were no tears coming from his eyes, though. They were wide open, bugging out of their sockets, and filled with fear. Because my hands were wrapped around his neck.

Chapter Twenty-Eight

Verity

If Jack Lester hurt Aria—in any way—I would never forgive myself.

I hadn't told Dax that his Amelia was my Millie because I didn't want his dishonesty to be linked with my mistreatment. Sure, he said he was going through with the divorce, but...

I was sick of broken promises.

And so I let my stubbornness get the best of me.

Now Dax was learning the truth in the absolute worst way possible. Because Aria was in Lester's crosshairs.

Fury radiated from Dax's skin, so thick and potent inside the confines of the elevator, it was suffocating. By the time the doors opened, my head was spinning.

Dax grabbed the key card from Millie's hand as we walked down the hall, waving it in front of the sensor at the far end of the corridor. The second the lock disengaged, Dax slammed the door open so hard it bounced off the wall on the opposite side.

"Dax?"

I recognized Aria's voice at the same time as Lester's angrier, "What the fuck?"

Peering around Dax's shoulder, I was relieved to see that Aria was still fully dressed.

Lester was sprawled on the couch, his white dress shirt open to expose a bloated belly matted with salt-and-pepper hair.

"Did he touch you?" Dax's hands were fisted at his sides, his jaw clenched, the vein at his temple throbbing.

Aria glanced at him, pink patches of outrage appearing on her cheeks as she lifted the sheaf of paper in her hands. "What? Of course not! We were discussing a script." Her eyes swept over the group of us now crowding into the foyer before landing back on Lester. "I'm so sorry. Please ignore my brother—"

"Fuck that." Dax wrapped his arm around his sister's shoulders and pulled her to his side. "You ever contact her again and you're going to regret it. You, too." The last sentence was directed at Millie as he speared her with a withering glare.

The hotel manager's obsequious apologies were cut off once the door closed behind us. Aria shrugged off Dax's hold, her anger a match to her brother's. "I can't believe you're ruining this for me, Dax! You're not the only one in our family who should get to make it in Hollywood."

"Aria." Her name was a gritted rebuke as he jabbed at the call button for the elevator.

"Don't 'Aria' me, Dax. You're not my parent, and frankly, you've been a shitty brother." She folded her arms over her chest, looking every inch the surly teen she was.

I edged toward the stairwell, not wanting to intrude on what was a very private family moment. And I knew Dax had an uphill battle on his hands. Aria was a smart, angry teenager who wasn't afraid of her brother in the slightest. When the elevator door opened, I cleared my throat. "Why don't I leave you guys to—"

Dax reached out for my hand. "Please, come with us."

The question in his eyes burned into me. *Will you tell her what he did to you?*

The only reason he hadn't spoken it aloud was to protect my privacy. The situation Aria had been led into was obvious to everyone but her. Lester was grooming her. But even if I shared my own experiences with Aria, even if I showed her the video—she might not believe me. Or, more likely, she wouldn't believe that what happened to me could happen to her.

But I had to take that chance.

Dax

I loved my sister. I really did.

But today Aria was making it very hard to like her.

She had thrown herself into the backseat of my car as soon as the valet arrived, squeezing into the smallest possible corner and scowling out the window as if she wanted to be anywhere else.

Standing beneath the covered entrance of the hotel, Verity glanced toward my car. "I think Aria needs some time, Dax. I don't think she's in the right mind-set to hear what I have to say."

I sighed, squeezing the back of my neck as I rolled my shoulders. "You're probably right."

She put a palm on my chest, right over my heart. "Why don't you drop her off with your parents, and I'll meet you at your place. I think we have a lot to talk about, too."

For the first time since watching Verity run away from me, I took a deep breath. My gaze found hers, and what I saw sent a rush of hope washing over me. I covered her hand with mine, then stepped forward so that we were toe to toe. My other hand curved around the back of her skull, my fingers pushing into the riot of red. I dipped my chin, pressing a kiss on her smooth forehead. "I'd like that."

It was only a few blocks to the Beverly Wilshire. Aria could have walked, but I was glad she didn't realize how close the two hotels were. I called my parents before merging into daytime traffic, and they were waiting downstairs by the time I pulled out front.

They had no idea what had actually happened—nothing, thank god—but watching the way they clutched Aria to their chests, pressing fierce kisses onto the top of her head, I saw the weight of their shared fears for their daughter. And when they turned to me, relief and love written all over their faces, I finally felt like a part of the family again. Being a parent couldn't be easy, and maybe I needed to grow up and stop thinking the worst of them at every turn.

The city passed by in a blur as I drove home. Now that Aria was safe, all I could think about was Verity coming over. She was coming *home*.

Because that's what my house was when Verity was with me.

A refuge. A *home*.

And it has nothing to do with floors and doors, walls and windows. It's the way our heartbeats synched when she was in my arms. The way our hands instinctively entwined when we walked side by side. The way we could read each other's expressions as easily as the dictionary.

Beach house. Tour bus. Chartered jet. Fucking cardboard box.

Verity was my refuge.

And I will be hers.

Chapter Twenty-Nine

Verity

My phone buzzed just as I pulled into Dax's driveway. I didn't want to look at it, wanted to dive within the warm bubble of Dax's affection. I had gone without it for too long. But what if it was Aria—maybe she had realized how close she'd come to danger and needed to talk?

It wasn't Aria.

Piper: There's someone you should meet—a journalist writing an exposé about Jack Lester. Apparently there have been rumors about him for years. You aren't alone.

I stared at Piper's text for a long time, at the last sentence of her text. You aren't alone.

You aren't alone.

It shouldn't have surprised me, especially after seeing Aria in

Lester's hotel suite with my own eyes. And Lester himself, with his unbuttoned shirt gaping open over his dress slacks. Easy access, he'd once joked to me. Bile rose up my throat at the mental image I'd give anything to permanently erase.

Nothing had happened between Lester and Aria…But if we hadn't walked in on them when we did, it would have. Maybe not then, maybe not even next week or next month. But eventually, it would have.

I slipped my phone into my purse as I walked up the front steps of Dax's house. Just this morning, I never would have imagined that I'd be back here so soon…if at all.

I knocked lightly on his door and let myself in. I could see Dax sitting in the deck, a guitar over his thighs. For a moment I just watched him, thinking about Piper's text.

She had sent me the contact information of the journalist. Quinn Campbell. *What does she know? What did she hear? What has she seen?*

Those questions were uncomfortably familiar. I'd wondered the same about Travis. Fearing what the answers might be, what they would mean for my future.

Today I had an entirely different set of fears.

How many girls had Jack Lester hurt? Had my silence back then, and for all these years, allowed him to abuse the women—girls—entrusted into his care? How many lives had he tainted with his particular brand of brutality?

These were the questions I needed answers to. Plus one more, my own.

What would it take to stop him?

Ready or not, whatever the risk, I needed to try.

Whether Dax wanted to be by my side was a decision only he could make.

Dax

"You want me to move in with you?" The frown creasing Verity's forehead didn't look anything like the elated grin I was hoping for.

"We were living together before. It would be the same."

"But…it was only temporary. I just rented a place." Her mouth opened and closed several times as she processed the new information. "And you're *still* married."

"A technicality."

Her frown morphed into a glare. "We've had this discussion already. You're married. End of story."

"Now look who is seeing only black-and-white. I think this is one of those mixed-bag situations."

"Okay, I will grant that in your case, maybe things aren't quite so clear cut. But, Dax. If there's anything I've learned through all this mess with my mother and Lester, it's that I've spent way too much of my life ceding control to other people."

I gritted my teeth at the sound of that man's name. "That's bullshit. Don't lump me in with him—"

Verity put a steadying hand on my arm. "Please, hear me out."

I gave a shallow nod, squinting against the late-afternoon sun.

"I trusted a lot of people I shouldn't have. But the person I never learned to trust was me. I'm trying to do that now, and if you really love me, you'll understand that I need to take things slow."

I stepped closer to Verity, wrapping my hand around the soft curve of her cheek, the silky slide of her hair covering my fingers, my wrist, my forearm. My other hand went beneath her ass, lifting her up so that she was sitting on the railing of the deck, her knees on either side of my hips, ankles interlocking behind my legs. Our faces were barely an inch apart, the green of her eyes not quite tranquil, but not a roiling sea. "True, I want to take care of you. Don't you know that?"

Her smile was slow, her dimples deep. "I know you do. And I know your intentions are the very best. If I were a damsel in distress, I'd be grateful. But I'm not. If I want your help, I promise I'll ask for it."

My aggravated groan was carried away on the breeze. "And what if I'm the one in need of rescuing?"

"I'd better be your first call," she responded, no hesitation at all.

A ribbon of steel was woven through her words, and I pulled back further to take in the whole of Verity's face, the straight set to her shoulders, the determination shining from her stare. "You did, you know. Rescue me. The first time I met you in that elevator in New York. You saved me without even knowing it."

Verity wiped a tear away at that admission and then cleared her throat. "Can we talk about today for a minute? About Lester."

My head fell so that it rested against Verity's shoulder, her collarbone a narrow bar pressing against my forehead. "Do we have to?"

"Piper heard that there are other girls—like me, like your sister."

She might as well have reached a hand into my gut and twisted my intestines into a knot. "I wish I could say that I'm surprised."

"If I had come forward years ago, maybe there wouldn't be."

I lifted my head, already shaking it. "You don't know that."

"I do. In my heart, I do. I can't stay silent anymore." She took a quick breath. "I'm going to tell my story. My career is not nearly as important as making sure Jack Lester never hurts any-one else. And if he goes down, Millie—*Amelia*—will too."

Verity was studying my face for my reaction. As if she ex-pected me to be bothered by what she'd just said. Like I had some kind of connection to Amelia worth protecting.

The only emotion I felt for Amelia was fury. Sizzling, seething fury that set my veins on fire. "Good," I said to Verity now. "And after you bury her, I want to be the first to dance on her grave."

Verity

Knowing I had Dax's support meant everything to me. He made another batch of spiked cider and we spoke late into the night, pulling up her recent articles and taking turns reading them to each other. The next day I contacted Quinn Campbell and set up a meeting.

On the phone, she said she would come to me, but I wanted to get a sense of Quinn Campbell, beyond her byline, so I'd asked where she was right then.

As it turned out…Quinn Campbell was a hustler.

That was my first thought as I walked into the downtown pool hall. The place wasn't far from my apartment, and I didn't want to wait for any doubts to seep in and chip away at my re-solve.

I had my hair in a ponytail and not a speck of makeup on my face, although I was glad for the deep shadows that divided the pool tables, each lit by a hanging fixture centered above it. There were at least a dozen in the loft-like space, and a long bar that took up an entire wall.

I'd looked Quinn up online, and I recognized her immediately. But in her head shot she'd been wearing a stiff white shirt and a serious expression. Tonight her face still had that same look of intense focus, but she was wearing skintight black leather pants and a crimson draped top, wielding a pool cue with expert authority as she cleared the table. The man watching her had his arms folded, looking resigned to the fact that he'd already lost.

I walked to one of the bistro tables set up near the back of the room and took a seat. Quinn acknowledged me with a brief nod, joining me after she'd pocketed her final shot. I was surprised to realize she was so tiny. Five four at most, with a figure that was the reason size zeros were invented.

"I wasn't sure that you'd show." As introductions went, it was another mark in her favor. Straightforward honesty delivered directly.

I returned the favor. "I wasn't sure I'd want to talk to you."

She quirked a smile. "How about I grab us a couple of beers?"

"Beat ya to it." The man she'd been playing slid two Coronas onto our table.

Quinn accepted them with a sigh. "Thank you. And if you go away, I might give you a chance to win your money back."

The man grumbled, slinking off with a forlorn look at Quinn. She turned back to me. "You can drink it. My brother owns this place and I've known Chris," she inclined her head toward the man who had brought us the beers, "since we were kids."

I wiped at the thin film of condensation coating the glass with a fingertip, unsure what to make of her. "Are you a reporter or a pool shark?"

Her wide mouth opened, releasing a husky laugh. "Neither, actually."

A ripple of apprehension skimmed over my nerves. I expected a denial of the first occupation, not the second.

My mind immediately thought the worst. Had Quinn Campbell been hired by Jack Lester? It made sense—he preferred to hire others to do his dirty work.

Before I could ask the question, or bolt entirely, Quinn spoke again. "I'm a journalist, not a reporter."

I blinked at her, confused. "What's the difference?"

"In your world, it's reading a script versus acting it out. Anyone can read words on a page. Reporting is just putting them there—presenting information to an audience. Journalists are actors in their own way, digging for the stories, exploiting nuance and examining competing narratives to uncover the facts of what actually happened. We shape our stories with the truth, while also recognizing that the lies and cover-ups are an essential part of the story and should be told, too." Quinn's expression brightened as she spoke, exposing a passion I felt when I got behind a microphone.

"I should also say that I write about power imbalance and misogyny. About people who project an image to the world that is completely antithetical to the person they are to others. I use my stories to shine light in dark places and my words to expose darker souls."

I leaned forward. "You don't get much darker than Jack Lester."

"Grab a flashlight and tell me all about it."

"Where should I start?"

She put her phone on the table, tapping the green button to record our conversation. "Where else? At the beginning."

Epilogue

Dax

A few weeks after walking in on my sister in Jack Lester's hotel room, Verity and I flew to New York to talk to Aria. While the twins were at an after-school activity, Verity shared her experiences at the hands of Jack Lester, including Amelia's involvement.

I offered to stay with them, but I'd been quickly shooed from the room.

It was just as well, since every time I heard what Verity had to deal with, I thought my head would explode.

Instead, I went over to Shane's place and decided to tell some truths of my own, revealing that I'd been writing songs for years, including the one Verity and I would be performing on our tour. Shane didn't quite understand why I'd kept it a secret all these years, but he didn't bust my balls. Too much.

And we'd gone onto his terrace, cracked a few beers, and decided to write one of our own. "Truth."

It was accurate for both of us. For Verity and Landon, too.

The jury was still out on Jett.

"Truth" was the first single we released in more than a year, and it struck a nerve, rocketing to the top of the charts immediately.

We were kicking off the tour tonight, with "Truth" as our opener.

I hadn't thought anything would compare to walking back onstage with Shane after the charges against him were dropped.

I was wrong.

Tonight had barely begun and it was already better.

Not just because our sales numbers were completely insane. Or because Shane was looking happier than ever with Delaney by his side. Or because Landon was hitting his drums even harder than before. Or because Jett was, well, Jett.

For me, this tour was as much about Verity Moore as it was about Nothing but Trouble. Verity wasn't just opening for my band—she'd opened my heart. Split it wide open and dove inside. Made a place for herself before sealing it back up tight. I felt her in every beat.

And I fucking loved it.

I fucking loved her.

Normally I'd be hanging out backstage with the guys before our set, but tonight we were all clustered to the side of the stage, waiting for Verity to kill it out there. Usually, our fans were still streaming in as our opening act was starting, impatiently waiting for us to take over. But not many people in the world weren't fans of Verity Moore these days.

When Verity decided to work with the police and Quinn to

share her story of abuse at the hands of one of the most powerful producers in Hollywood, I was worried. Despite backing her completely, I hadn't been sure how or if Verity should go public. It had seemed like a hell of a big risk. Jack Lester wouldn't capitulate easily, and her reputation was far from squeaky clean.

It could have been career suicide.

But thank fuck Verity was braver than I was.

She hadn't just won the PR battle.

She'd triumphed—personally, professionally—in every way that mattered.

Her previous title—disgraced pop princess—was gone and buried.

Verity Moore had joined the ranks of the #metoo movement as a leader. A rebel with a goddamn cause.

She'd used her voice to rise above victimization. Her name was a battle cry.

#WeDeserveMoore

My *True*.

I still wasn't sure that I deserved her...but I did my best to prove it a little more every day.

Out of the corner of my eye, I noticed Quinn mouthing instructions to the photographer who was capturing the tour from Verity's perspective. After a series of front-page articles had led to Lester's arrest and a plea deal for Amelia, Verity and Quinn had signed a seven-figure book deal. HBO was producing a documentary on Verity's career comeback and her emergence as a voice for the silent survivors.

Who would have ever thought I'd find truth when I had surrounded myself with so many lies? Not me.

But I had.

And now the truth was—I was head over fucking balls in love

with Verity Moore. Jesus. Our band was falling like dominoes. First Shane, then Landon and me. Jett might even be teetering, too. He'd been following Quinn around like a lost puppy, but so far she had barely looked his way. And from what I could see, it only made him want her more. I almost felt sorry for him. Almost.

I'd come to terms with a whole lot of truth since meeting Verity. Before her, I thought I needed to avoid relationships with musicians, or anyone in our fake, fucked-up industry. The truth was, I just needed to avoid fake, fucked-up people.

Before Verity, I had stayed away from my family because I thought I'd disappointed them. The truth was, I'd avoided them because I wasn't willing to own up to my own insecurities.

Whoever said "The truth shall set you free" was a goddamn genius.

Lights swept over the crowd in long beams of color, highlighting raised arms and shaking signs, white letters on dark clothing, smiling faces just waiting for the show to begin. The energy in the arena was a visible, simmering thing. I felt it with each indrawn breath, pinpricks of electricity penetrating my body at a cellular level.

Verity appeared from above, on a zip line that was the kind of expensive special effect unheard of for opening acts.

But Verity Moore wasn't just any opening act. She was special, in every way.

The fans erupted into applause that went on and on, well after Verity finally descended to the stage in a jumpsuit that was the sexiest goddamn thing I'd ever seen. Lace the same color as her skin, sparkles in all the right places. I knew she'd had to be sewn into it before the show, but damn if I didn't want to rip it off her.

I was so entranced by her performance, I almost missed my

cue to go on. Almost, but Landon was keeping time again, and he didn't hesitate to jab me in the back with one of his drumsticks. Not that I minded at all. I was just grateful he could hold the damn things again.

And when I turned around, it was impossible not to burst into laughter. Landon Cox, legendary bad boy onstage and off, had his three-month-old daughter strapped to his chest. Wearing an enormous pair of headphones to protect her ears, Luci's eyes were round as saucers, following the lights streaking inside the arena.

I gave her tiny socked foot a gentle squeeze, mumbled a goodbye to Travis and the guys, then pretended to ignore the grins of Delaney and Piper, and even Quinn.

The same person who had come up with the zip line idea had tried to convince me to use some kind of stunt to get me onstage, but I'd shot him down. My two legs had carried me this far, and they knew exactly which direction to head in when it came to Verity.

Only my years of training kept my fingers on the guitar when Verity smiled at me from behind her microphone. The damn girl could light up the night with her smile. And her voice...I had no words for the magic that came from her mouth.

And she was singing my words.

Words I'd written just for her.

My bombshell rebel.

Verity was everything I'd ever wanted, wrapped up in a sexy-as-fuck package. But it was what was inside her that really did me in. Her resilient spirit. Her relentless drive. The way the sight of her made me feel so fucking alive.

Tonight might be the start of our tour, but most importantly, it was one more day in a long line of tomorrows.

Verity

I've been dreaming of this night for as long as I could remember. Center stage. Thousands of fans singing along to my songs. A hit album. My name rising up the charts. Control over my career. A name that wasn't immediately followed by "disgraced."

That word wasn't my burden to bear any longer.

Millie and Jack Lester were not just disgraced—they were guilty. Once it came out that I was really seventeen in that video, not eighteen, the charges had gotten even worse. They were both in jail, where they belonged. Where they couldn't hurt anyone else.

Tonight was the first show of the Nothing but Trouble/Verity Moore tour, and I was happier than I'd ever been.

Lights. Music. Love.

The first two were a given. But the third…

I'd had no idea how good it felt to love. How good it felt to be loved.

Loving Dax. Being loved by Dax. It was magic.

And I don't mean supernatural, although I couldn't help but feel that somehow, in some way, my grandmother had a hand in our romance. The definition of magic that rang most true to me was, "A mysterious quality of enchantment." There was definitely a mysterious quality to Dax Hughes. And I was completely enchanted by him.

Tonight, despite our days of rehearsals and sound check just a few hours ago, when Dax strutted onto the stage, his guitar slung over his shoulders and a smile that shone from his eyes…I was completely under his spell.

From the roar that swept through the arena, so was everyone else.

There were a few people in the audience tonight that were

attending their very first Nothing but Trouble show. Dax's parents, his sister, and his brothers. They were in the front row. His parents looked a little shell-shocked, but Aria and the boys were clearly loving it.

I had sent my mother a VIP pass, along with a note saying that she was always welcome to my shows and back into my life if and when she was willing to speak with me openly and honestly about the past. I was willing to hear her out if she would give me that same respect, too. I had it delivered by messenger to her house in Florida, where she had retreated after Quinn published her first article recounting my experience with Lester.

So far, there had been only silence. But if things changed, I was going to err on the side of forgiveness.

And that first article…I hadn't thought seeing my story in print would affect me. After all, I'd already lived it. But reading the actual words in black-and-white, especially the stories recounting experiences similar to mine, was absolutely devastating. I got through it with Dax's help. We spent several days hunkered down in his house, our phones powered off, Wi-Fi disconnected, televisions unplugged. He ordered in food, and we drank cider out of the champagne flutes he had bought for me.

Since then, there had been more days—most good, some bad—all of them made better with the *clink* of crystal and the press of Dax's mouth on mine. And now we were here, sharing a stage, sharing our lives. Together.

My throat was almost impossibly tight as I stared into Dax's eyes, but each lyric managed to escape on time and in tune, words that lingered in the air around us, breathy shards of glimmering possibilities.

Anything was possible.

Everything was possible.

And when the song ended and the lights went dark, I melted into Dax's embrace. "I fucking love you," he growled.

We were still mic'd.

The crowd went wild.

Cocooned within Dax's arms, I felt a peace I'd never known.

* * *

Six Months Later

Dax

"I was wrong." Verity pushed a cardboard box into my hands.

"Oh yeah? About what?" Flicking an eye at her Audi, I tried not to get my hopes up at the assortment of bags and boxes spilling from the backseat. Our tour finally ended last week, and Verity and I had spent most of it in bed. My bed.

Except that I wanted it to be *our* bed.

We'd been practically inseparable for the past six months while we were on tour, but this morning she had finally left, saying that she needed to get back to "her place." I hated the way that sounded, hated the way my house felt without Verity in it.

Because I wanted it to be our home.

She took another box from her car and closed the door by bumping her ass against it, then looked at me with a sheepish smile on her face. "About the apartment. You were right. I don't need my own place to be my own person."

I bit down on the grin threatening to swallow my face. "I to—"

"Uh-huh." She jerked a chin at the front door, bright bits of gold gleaming from her eyes. "How about a little less *I told you so* and a little more *getting naked*?"

I took the steps two at a time. "Done."

Verity

Dax bit down on my shoulder, the graze of his teeth punctuated by the swipe of his tongue. "We need to get up."

I nestled deeper into the curve of his body. "Mmmm. Just a few more minutes."

His low chuckle caressed the sensitive skin behind my ear, sending a wave of goose bumps down my spine. "The caterers are going to be here any minute."

"Really?" I squinted at the clock on the nightstand. Offering to host Shane and Delaney's post-wedding brunch had seemed like a great idea—but I hadn't factored in partying until two a.m. at their wedding, or that the caterers would want to begin setting up at the crack of dawn. "How about we change it to a lunch? Do you think anyone would mind?"

"Hmmm." Dax lowered the sheet, kissing the wing of my shoulder blade, the curve of my hip bone. "Well, Shane and Delaney might have an issue with that, seeing as their flight is this afternoon. And you know how Piper is with Luci's naptime."

I groaned. Piper was an absolutely incredible mother, but she was as regimented about her daughter's nap schedule as a four-star general planning for war. I rolled over in Dax's arms, knowing he did a much better job of waking me up than any amount of caffeine. "You win. I'm up."

The corners of his lips lifted as he kissed the tip of my nose. "Yeah. Me too."

The double ring of the landline came just as Dax rolled over me, his forearms bracing most of his weight. "Damn it." His head dropped, his hair tickling my neck for a moment before he grabbed for the phone, telling the guard to send the caterers through. "I'll let them in and meet you in the shower."

He threw on track pants and a T-shirt, disappearing behind the door as I stretched beneath the sheet. Finally agreeing to move in with Dax was the best decision I'd ever made. There was nowhere else I'd rather be, no one else I'd rather be with.

I thought about the day I came back to L.A., not knowing if I would ever get another chance in this town. Not knowing if I had a single friend or ally.

Everything about my life was different now, in the best of ways.

Dax joined me in the bathroom a few minutes later. A round of hot, steamy shower sex made up for what we didn't have in bed earlier.

The rest of the morning passed quickly. I spent most of it upstairs, unpacking the boxes I had brought over from my apartment last week. Piper arrived early, with Landon and Luci. I swiped the gorgeous nine-month-old from her father's arms, pressing a kiss into her shock of white-blond hair. "Oooh, I've missed you, Luci girl," I cooed.

She giggled, clapping her chubby hands on either side of my face and smiling up at me.

"Well, hello to you, too, Verity." Landon's rich baritone was filled with teasing as he stepped inside.

"Sorry," I said, lightly kissing his cheek. "Your gorgeous baby is very distracting."

"Where did—"

"Right here," Piper called from farther inside the house. I spun around, not even realizing she'd walked past me.

She was already downstairs, hanging up a sign reading: Con-
gratulations, Mr. & Mrs. Hawthorne! There was an
enormous canvas bag next to her, too, no doubt more decora-
tions. Piper hadn't missed a beat since having Luci. She was even
more organized than ever…and blissfully in love with her husband and daughter. From the sappy expression on Landon's face,
the feeling was entirely mutual.

Jett and Quinn were the next to arrive. They had had a tumul-
tuous relationship while we were on tour, but things had seemed
to even out for them. Dax said he'd never seen Jett in better spirits. I let Quinn steal Luci from me, but only because I realized
that I'd forgotten to unpack the champagne flutes I wanted to
use for our first toast to the newly married couple.

The glasses Dax had found at the estate sale in Glendale. I had
never had a reason to unpack the rest of the set, until today.

Keeping out of the way of the caterers, I retrieved the white box
from the bottom of the buffet that ran along the wall between the
kitchen and the door to the deck. It was only after I unrolled each
individual champagne flute from its wad of Bubble Wrap that I
noticed the white envelope taped to the bottom of the box.

Curious, I ran a fingernail underneath the piece of Scotch
tape, freeing it enough to open the flap. *Oh my god.* Tears welled
up, overflowing my eyelashes as I stared at a photograph of my
grandmother and me, each holding a glass and smiling at each
other as we clinked rims. My grandfather must have taken the
shot, I realized.

It didn't seem possible that these glasses could actually be my
grandmother's…and yet it did. My mother had called an estate sale company to deal with the contents of my grandparents'
house. She'd probably just given them a key and cashed their
check. If they were bought by a collector, as Dax had said, it was

possible they were stored in their original box, maybe never even used.

I heard the doorbell ring again, then a raucous greeting for the newlyweds. Wiping my eyes, I went to put the picture back in the envelope and noticed a familiar scrawl on the back. *My sweetest gift.*

A shuddering exhale ripped from my lungs as I looked out the window to the endless blue sky stretching along the horizon. Knowing I'd just been given a gift from beyond the grave.

Dax appeared at my side, his hand curving around my waist as he pressed a kiss to my neck. "You okay?"

Wordlessly, I passed the picture to him.

"This…this is you?"

I nodded. "Dax—"

"So these glasses, they don't just look like your grandmother's—they *are* your grandmother's?"

"Yeah. Pretty crazy, right?" I didn't know what to make of it actually. Because it felt like more than just a coincidence. It felt like a message.

Serendipity.

Dax gave a slow blink, looking from me to the glasses and the picture of me and my grandmother. And then he sank down to one knee. "I've been carrying around this ring for the past few days, feeling like I would know the perfect moment to ask you to be my wife."

Dax

Verity's eyes bounced from my face to the ring I was now holding and back again. Her mouth opening in a perfect O, features conveying a mix of shock and adoration.

I bought the ring last week. My entire family had flown out to see our final performance, and Verity and I met them the next day for lunch. Afterward, Verity and my sister, who had grown close, had gone off shopping while my father took the twins to see a former instructor of theirs who was now teaching at UCLA. On our way back to their hotel, my mother and I passed a jewelry store. The display of diamonds caught my eye, and I couldn't keep walking.

My divorce from Amelia was final, not that we'd ever truly had a marriage.

Verity and I had been inseparable for the last six months. And my fears about getting involved with someone in the industry had been completely unfounded. What mattered was finding the right *person*. Verity wasn't perfect and neither was I. No one was.

But we were perfect for each other. And my passion for music ran so deep, it made my love for Verity even richer, all-encompassing.

"Oh shit." Jett's voice boomed from the other side of the room. "Man down, man down."

I looked over my shoulder to see my Nothing but Trouble family gathering around us in a semicircle.

"Zip it," Shane responded, his arm around Delaney. "Dude's finally coming to his senses."

"Yeah, besides, a man can do some of his best work from down there."

"Landon," Piper screeched, her cheeks flaming as she elbowed him in the side.

"Don't you worry, Pippa. My considerable skills are for your pleasure only—"

"Jesus Christ, would you let the man propose already?" Travis was standing at the top of the stairs, looking at us all incredulously.

Verity giggled, and I turned back to her, a wave of the most potent love I'd ever known slamming into me. "I never knew what was *true* until I met you. And despite the craziness that comes with our lives, I hope you will do me the greatest honor of wearing my ring, becoming my wife…because you're already my everything."

A lone tear tracked down her cheek, but I couldn't even think of wiping it, or better yet, kissing it away, until Verity answered me. She lowered herself to her knees in one graceful movement. "I didn't think there were men as good as you. My mother gave me a name that meant truth, but you've taught me how to live it, embrace it. I love you, Dax, and nothing would give me greater joy than sharing forever with you."

I didn't hear the comments from the peanut gallery assembled behind me, or their applause. My entire world was in front of me. My light, my love, my truth.

And soon, my wife.

Author's Note

I began plotting this book just as the #metoo movement was picking up steam. Also around that time, I watched an episode of *Law & Order SVU* about a child star who was sexually assaulted. Not only did no one believe her, but she herself accepted it as a part of the culture. When I woke up the next morning, Verity Moore was as real to me as my childhood best friend. I hope I've done her justice.

Romance novels often feature controlling, abusive men as sexy alpha heroes. Frankly, I love a brooding alpha. But whether on the page or in real life, I cannot stand when men treat women as if we are somehow *less than* simply because we don't own a penis. The choice to share our bodies, our minds, our everything—is ours and ours alone.

I hope no one reading this has ever had that choice taken from her...but we all know it happens way too often, even in this post #metoo time. So, I have a second hope—that everyone who needs a champion will find her very own Olivia Benson.

Did you miss Shane and Delaney's story?

Keep reading for an excerpt of *Rock King*, available now!

Chapter One

Shane

Fucking Malibu.

The last traces of sleep evaporated as I stared out at the sea from the terrace off my bedroom, my right hand running through the hair on my head as my left idly plowed a destination farther south. I was naked, but the waist-high plants along the perimeter would block the view of any intrepid paparazzo. Inhaling air thick with salt and fog, I closed my eyes and listened to the rush of the waves crash along the beach.

Normally the rhythm of the tides soothed me.

But not today.

My eyes snapped open, scowling at the relentless surf. The sun was just cresting the horizon, the ocean a quivering mass of gray and blue, littered with bruised shards of purple and orange. It wasn't the view that was pissing me off. I'd been on edge before I got out of bed. Before I went to sleep. Hell, I'd been a bundle of nerves since we finished the album.

One more week until the latest Nothing but Trouble tour kicked off.

One more week and, for two hours out of every twenty-four, my view would be stadiums packed with thousands of fans screaming my name.

The rest would be filled with impersonal hotel rooms, private planes, tour buses, and way too many people I didn't want to look at—let alone talk to—fighting for my attention. Autographs. Selfies. Groupies with glossy lips whispering invitations for everything from blow jobs to backdoor action. Easy sex with an STD chaser.

No thanks.

My last counterfeit companion walked out a month ago, when I'd been spending every available second in the studio tweaking the last couple of songs, which had taken forever to get right. She'd already found someone else to sink her claws into, an up-and-coming actor who made sure he was photographed in public, the more compromising the situation the better, to cover up the fact that, behind closed doors, he was about as interested in tits as a kid with a milk allergy.

Not that I missed her. It was time, and we both knew it. She had gotten what she'd wanted out of being Shane Hawthorne's "girlfriend": name recognition, a place on the Best Dressed lists, even a small part in a big-budget movie. It was time for someone new. Past time, actually. Someone who engendered more than apathy.

Except I hadn't met her yet. Maybe she didn't exist.

Of course, if she did, I sure as hell didn't deserve her.

My gut twisted, forming a gnarled, ugly clump leaching anxiety and tension into my bloodstream. The truth was, no one deserved me. I was a jagged knife, the tip of my blade edged with poison. Brutal. Messy. Lethal.

The wind was strong this morning, stronger than usual, and each salty gust chafed at my skin. I welcomed the abrasion, wishing I could be swept up. Swept away. Days like these were too long, littered with too many opportunities to get lost in my own mind. That was a dangerous place for me. Dangerous for everyone around me.

Being on the road sucked. But staying in one place, trapped with my memories, with my guilt…well, not even a beach house in Malibu could make that bearable.

From the half-open door, I heard my phone. Recognizing the ringtone, I headed back inside to take my agent's call. "Hey, Travis." He slept even less than I did, and that was saying something.

"I'm just confirming. You're coming tonight, right?" Travis only had one setting: steamroll.

My disgruntled sigh fogged up the screen. "Let me guess. There's someone you want me to meet."

"Of course. Several actually. You'll have your pick."

Agent. Lawyer. Matchmaker. Travis was a one-stop shop for me. He'd been on the hunt for my next girlfriend for a while now, and I was still single. Neither of us was happy about it. Left to my own devices, trouble was always too close for comfort. "Fine. I'll be there."

Disconnecting the call, I took my first deep breath all day. Travis and I had a deal. He found candidates worthy of being "Shane Hawthorne's girlfriend," but I had ultimate approval. I don't mean prostitutes, either. Hell, I practically had to beat chicks back with a stick. Everywhere I went, there were girls begging me to fuck them against the nearest wall, or dropping to their knees on the dirty floor of a public restroom. Three hundred and sixty-five days a year was my only constraint when it came to sex.

But life on the road was different, and the first few weeks of a tour were especially nerve-racking. So many new people, so many moving parts. It wasn't easy to get back into the groove of things. Waking up in a new city every day, surrounded by a sea of new faces—I needed the people in my inner circle to stay the same. My agent, bandmates, tour manager…and my girlfriend.

I know how it sounds. Sleazy with a capital *S*. But sex isn't part of the deal.

Not that it didn't happen, of course, just that it wasn't what I was paying them for.

Being the girlfriend of a rock star shouldn't be a hard position to fill, but it was. Sexy, beautiful, reasonably intelligent—those were basic requirements for someone I'd be spending months in close quarters with. And she needed to be drama-free, someone who liked my music but wasn't a super-fan, stalker chick. My "girlfriends" were a thin veil of armor against the hordes of groupies that clawed their way toward me, offering anything I could ever want. And too much I didn't need.

Truthfully, I didn't mind the groupies. At my core I'm a hustler, too. Been hauling around a five-pound sack filled with ten pounds of problems since the day I was born. But I've made it, busted my way to the top of the fucking heap. Lead singer of Nothing but Trouble. A list of hit songs so long a tattooist couldn't fit it on my arm if he tried. More money than I knew what to do with. A dozen Grammys at last count, and even an Oscar for best original song last year, the only golden statue awarded to an otherwise unremarkable movie.

I hired Travis years ago to build up my career, and now we

were in protection mode, just trying not to crash and burn. *Shane Hawthorne* was a brand now, one worth millions. And yet, losing everything we had worked for would be so easy. Just one offer of things I couldn't resist: an asshole named Jack Daniel and that gorgeous white powder that made my brain feel like a shaken snow globe, cloudy with glitter.

So, maybe tonight I would meet my next girlfriend. Someone contractually obligated to be by my side at every show and party, every press junket and photo op. Someone with me day and night, pretty enough I wouldn't mind the view. Someone with a fun-loving personality, who knew better than to actually fall in love with me.

I've done a lot of stupid things in my life, but that was a line I had yet to cross. A line so far in the distance it wasn't even a smudge on the horizon. And I wasn't heading it its direction anytime soon. Preferably never.

Love was the one luxury I couldn't afford.

Assuming I felt a spark of connection with one of the women at Travis's house tonight, he would lock her into a nondisclosure so tight the press would never find out that she was just an employee, a prop. That our relationship was fake.

What she wouldn't know, what no one except Travis knew, was that we would have something in common.

Because *everything* about me is fake.

Shane Hawthorne, resident King of Rock 'n' Roll and the cause of dripping panties everywhere, from shrieking tweens to bored housewives, is a sham. More myth than man.

Shane Hawthorne doesn't exist. He's the stage name I used for the first time at sixteen, expecting to be hauled off by a pair of cops if I so much as breathed my real name.

Sometimes I've wondered what my fans would think if they

knew the truth. Would I still be hailed as *People* magazine's Sexiest Man Alive if anyone knew who I really was?

Who am I? I don't even know anymore.

Fraud.

Runaway.

Addict.

Murderer.

Not so sexy now, am I?

Delaney

"Delaney? Delaney Fraser, is that you?"

I froze as the familiar notes of a voice I hadn't heard in years practically stomped up my spine, leaving angry hives in its wake. The voice, and the person belonging to it, were from a life I'd left behind several years ago.

Bronxville, the insulated Manhattan suburb where I'd been raised, was not merely three thousand miles from Los Angeles; it was in an entirely different galaxy. And yet, this particular meteor had dropped into the upscale steakhouse where I worked without disturbing anything but my peace of mind.

My pivot was purposefully slow, needing a minute to firmly affix a smile onto my face and every ounce of concentration I could muster to remain standing. "Piper. Wow, small world. I didn't recognize you."

"Me?" Piper Hastings, former queen bee of the Bronxville School, took a step back and looked me up and down as if I were a mannequin wearing an outfit she was considering. "I almost didn't recognize *you*."

I managed a small shrug. "We've all changed since graduation,

I guess." Although, I've probably changed more than most. The last time I saw Piper, I'd been solidly on the chubby side of average, sporting braces and barely tamed hair. The excess weight was gone now, along with the braces, and I kept my hair under control via daily altercations with a salon-strength straightener, a life-changing invention I'd only recently discovered.

Piper wasn't buying my brush-off. "You've more than changed—you're practically a new person. Or at least half of the one you used to be, anyway. What did you do?" She'd always been irritatingly tenacious, a dog with a bone.

How exactly to answer Piper's invasive questions? Heat rose up my neck, probably depositing telltale patches on my cheeks, too. Gee, Piper, after the Accident, food just didn't hold much appeal anymore. "Nothing really, just a hormone imbalance." These days, lies came easy.

But Piper only nodded enthusiastically, her perfect blond hair swinging. "I'm so jealous. I have to practically live at the yoga studio just to fit into my jeans!" Her face was expectant, as if waiting for a round of applause. I gave none, and she continued her rapid-fire questions. "So, what are you doing in California? Did you transfer?"

My eyes narrowed. Could she really not know? After my father was held responsible for my mother's death, life as I knew it came to a screeching halt. "Something like that." I proffered a question to stem the tide coming from Piper. "How about you?"

Piper flaunted a Colgate-bright smile. "I graduated from UCLA two years ago and now I'm working in public relations for a Hollywood agent. Super-agent, really. Wild horses couldn't drag me back to Bronxville."

I returned the grin, although mine was only half-hearted. "Same here." Because no one, wild horse or otherwise, would be doing the dragging. My father was in jail, my mother was buried six feet under, and keeping in touch with friends from my former life hurt too much.

I wanted what they still had. Family. Security. A belief that life would magically work out for the best.

I knew better now.

Piper made a sweeping arc with her hands. "So, you work here?"

Eager to extricate myself from Piper's well-manicured claws, I slipped back into waitress mode, pen hovering above my order pad. "Yep. What can I get for you?"

"A glass of sauvignon blanc, if you have it."

"Sure. Be right back." I had to force myself not to run to the bar. Despite knowing Piper Hastings for most of my life, that was probably the longest conversation we'd ever shared.

By the time I returned with her drink, an older man had seated himself opposite her. Medium height with a build that was solid without being stocky, he had an attractively shaved head. A starched white button-down shirt set off his tan, and gold cuff links flashed at his wrists. Setting down Piper's wineglass with only the slightest wobble, I turned to him. "What can I get for you, sir?"

Piper spoke up before he could answer. "Delaney, this is my boss, Travis Taggert. Travis, Delaney's an old friend from back home."

Old friend? Talk about an exaggeration. I would have laughed, but Travis's dark, appraising eyes didn't inspire levity. "Nice to meet you, Delaney." His voice was gruff but polite.

"Likewise. So…" I cleared my throat, itching to get away again. "Something from the bar?"

Another nod. "Grey Goose, rocks, three olives."

Travis's hooded gaze followed me as I crossed the restaurant to fetch his cocktail. "Delaney," he said on my return, "I'm having a party tonight. You should come. I'll bet Piper would love to spend more time with one of her friends from back home."

The glare Piper gave Travis from across the table belied his assessment. "I don't get off until late tonight," I said, not exactly jumping at the chance to hang out with her either.

Travis responded with a short shake of his head, the restaurant's recessed spotlights glinting off his bald scalp. "Not a problem. My parties don't get good until late, anyway."

I flicked a tongue over suddenly dry lips. "Well, I'm not exactly dressed appropriately, and I don't have a change of clothes here," I said, looking down at my standard waitress attire of white shirt and black pants.

"Oh, Delaney, that's too bad. I guess we'll just have to do it another time," Piper chirped, the obvious snub bringing back memories that filled my mind like a swarm of angry bees, buzzing and stinging at will.

Oh, Delaney, you don't really want to try out for cheerleading, do you? I mean, being out in front of the stands, representing our school, it's just such a huge responsibility. And, of course, the uniforms aren't exactly forgiving.

Oh, Delaney, this party's not really for the whole school. Just a few friends, and friends of friends. You understand, right?

Oh, Delaney, I'm jealous you have so much free time to study. Between cheer practice, football games, hanging out with my squad and all the players, and of course, chairing the prom committee, I barely have time to crack a book.

How many "Oh, Delaney's" had I heard from Piper and her friends over the years? Too many. And her caustic tone was just as abrasive now as it was then.

Travis rolled his shoulders, eyes narrowing as he looked back and forth between us. "You two are just about the same size, and I've never seen you in the same thing twice, Piper. I'm sure you have something for Delaney to wear."

My breath caught in my throat. Was I really the same size as Piper Hastings? I cast a discreet glance her way. Not quite, but not too far off either. Grief was a pretty effective diet. "That's really generous, but I just don't think—"

Piper let loose a high-pitched chortle. "After being on her feet all day, you can't blame Delaney for not wanting to put on a dress and heels." I gnashed my teeth at the latest comment from the peanut gallery. Piper didn't want me at Travis's party; I got the hint, loud and clear.

Travis, not so much. He flicked an exasperated glance at Piper. "Last time I checked, I had plenty of seating. Besides, no one turns down an invitation to one of my parties, Delaney."

A tingle of curiosity pricked at my skin. I wasn't in high school anymore. Why was I letting Piper exclude me from all the fun?

Fun. Did I even know what fun was anymore?

Maybe it was because I hadn't been to a party in three years. Maybe it was because I was enjoying the irritation smeared across Piper's face a little too much. Maybe it was because Travis didn't seem like he was going to take no for an answer. Maybe it was all three, because when I opened my mouth, not a single one of the dozen excuses I had at the tip of my tongue emerged. "Well, I guess I wouldn't want to spoil your perfect track record."

"Great." Travis slapped the table with a resounding *thwack*. "What time does your shift end? Piper will pick you up here."

"Around eleven, sometimes a little after," I answered, my brief flare of rebellion already fading. Partying with Hollywood A-listers? Not exactly my crowd, any more than Piper's cheerleading squad and the jocks they hung out with had been in high school. "But there's no need for that. If you give me your address, I'll call an Uber." *Yeah, right.* Another lie. Without a doubt, I'd be in my pajamas by midnight. As usual.

My hesitation must have been obvious, and Travis was clearly no fool. "Absolutely not. Piper will be happy to pick you up after your shift ends, with something suitable to wear. Isn't that right, Piper?"

I winced at the little daggers of outrage glinting from her wide-set eyes. "Sure thing, boss."

"Good. It's settled, then," Travis pronounced.

Settled? Crap. *What have I done?* "Are you sure, Piper? I don't want to put you out of your way," I sputtered, silently begging her to get me out of the mess I'd created.

An overly bright smile twisting her perfectly lined and glossed lips, Piper's voice was honey with a saccharine chaser. Nauseatingly sweet with an artificial aftertaste. "Don't mention it. Coming back to pick you up, bringing an outfit, it's no trouble at all. I'm just thrilled you don't already have plans."

I hadn't made *plans* in three years. Why bother when life stole your lemonade and pelted you with rotten lemons instead? If I wasn't working, I was usually home with my nose buried in a book or binge-watching shows from my Netflix queue. Living through fictional characters whose lives were so much better than mine. "Well, okay then." I pushed the words out of my mouth, wishing I could swallow them whole instead. "I guess I'll see you later."

Travis set down his cocktail. "Going to be a good crowd tonight. Trust me, you won't regret it."

Too late. I already did.

But what the hell, just add it to the list. I'd accumulated a lot of regrets in my twenty-four years. What was one more?

About the Author

TARA LEIGH attended Washington University in St. Louis and Columbia Business School in New York, and worked on Wall Street and Main Street before "retiring" to become a wife and mother. When the people in her head became just as real as the people in her life, she decided to put their stories on paper. Tara currently lives in Fairfield County, Connecticut, with her husband, children, and fur-baby, Pixie. She is represented by Jessica Alvarez of BookEnds.

Learn more at:

www.taraleighbooks.com
Twitter @TaraLeighBooks
Facebook.com/TaraLeighAuthor

You Might Also Like…

And, right now, the last thing Rowan needs is true-crime novelist Evie Fleming nosing around the most notorious deaths in Los Angeles—including the ones that haunt his own family.

To make things worse, he's torn between wanting the wickedly smart writer out of his city...and just plain *wanting* her.

While researching her latest book, Evie suspects that a dangerous new killer is prowling the City of Angels. Now she just has to convince the devastatingly handsome cop that she's *right*. Soon Evie and Rowan are working together to try to find the killer, even as their attraction ignites.

But when the killer homes in on Evie, she and Rowan realize they'll have to solve this case fast if they want to stay alive.

It's all a matter of timing

Griffin Sullivan is handling the ultimate balancing act. Between being a single dad to an active six-year-old and the crazy demands of his job as a hockey coach, finding love is not in the cards. But when the team's goalie is rushed to the ER, he's immediately captivated by the gorgeous, sassy nurse on duty...who just happens to be the sister of one of his players.

Sadie Braddock has always had a big, open heart and a bit of a wild side. But since her dad got sick, she's closed herself off to life and love. Relationships are way too complicated—and so is Griffin. He's also funny and tender and sexy as hell. How can something that feels so right come at the worst time ever? Then again, someone to lean on may be exactly what they each need—if they're only brave enough to take the risk.

DIANA GARDIN

LAWSON

A Delta Squad Novel

When a fake relationship turns real, this Navy SEAL learns that love can be deadly in this thrilling, fast-paced novel that proves "no one does romantic suspense like Diana Gardin" (Susan Stoker, *New York Times* bestselling author).

I'm a natural protector, whether I'm guarding political big shots or celebrity VIPs. It's true that I failed—once. When I was a SEAL, when it mattered most. But that's *never* going to happen again. Especially not during my first op with Night Eagle Security. So if there's one thing my new partner, Indigo Stone, should know, it's that she's safe in my hands...

Not that she wants my help. With amber eyes full of intelligence and a body covered in ink, Indigo is one of the toughest people I've ever met. But this job has us deep undercover, playing car thieves and lovers, and we'll have to become pros at faking it. But when feelings turn real, I'm reminded that emotions are dangerous...especially when one wrong move can be deadly.